The Tallystick

❧ AND OTHER STORIES ❧

The Tallystick

❧ AND OTHER STORIES ❧

Bryan MacMahon

POOLBEG

Published in 1994 by
Poolbeg,
A division of Poolbeg Enterprises Ltd,
Knocksedan House,
123 Baldoyle Industrial Estate,
Dublin 13, Ireland

A catalogue record for this book is available from the British Library.

ISBN 1 85371 338 4

Portrait of Bryan MacMahon by Derek Speirs
Background cover photograph by Mike O'Toole
Cover design by Poolbeg Group Services Ltd
Set by Poolbeg Group Services Ltd in Garamond 10.5/15
Printed by Colour Books Ltd, Baldoyle Industrial Estate, Baldoyle, Dublin 13

The Publishers gratefully acknowledge the support of

The Arts Council / An Chomhairle Ealaíon.

AUTHOR'S NOTE.

Some of these stories have not yet appeared in print: others have had varied careers. "The Cloak of Fire" and "The Time of the Whitethorn" have been published in magazines in the US.

"Apples for Sale" was published first in Irish and I have translated it for this collection. "The Telescope" was one of a series of short stories first broadcast by the BBC, and later published elsewhere in Ireland. "The Gentry Bell", "The Time of the Whitethorn" and "Jack Furey" lead separate existences as one-act plays of which the last two have won national drama competitions in Ireland. "The Tallystick" first appeared in the pages of "The Irish Press".

2 February 1994

❧ PRAISE FOR BRYAN MACMAHON ❧

"The Sound of Hooves" – Bryan MacMahon is manipulating the craft of storytelling in surprising and risk-taking ways: fantasy, rage, humour, all have their place. It makes for exhilarating reading."

Irish Press

"MacMahon strikes a blow for all who choose to live apart from the Modern Machine."

Sunday Telegraph

"The joy of living runs through his stories like a shout in the blood."

Time

"A collection that is cause for celebration."

The Irish Times

"Definitely recommended."

Books and Bookmen

"A radiant celebration of sex, I find it at the least as convincing as DH Lawrence. From beginning to end, the book grips, thrills and fascinates. It is a crowning achievement."

Sunday Independent

"Traditionally Irish excellence you could call it."

Guardian

"Bryan MacMahon has a skilful mastery of atmosphere and a rich store of imagery."

New Statesman

"There is not one story in the collection that I did not admire and enjoy."

Spectator

"Language is a large supple animal tamed to MacMahon's disposal ... always lending full support to the conveyance and rarely if ever distracting attention to itself.

The lasting impression is one of memorable and vivid images of human situations carefully presented."

Irish Independent

"Here is a writer who possesses the sensitivity of a poet and the rich, hearty humour of a peasant, a compassion for his fellowmen plus a rollicking remembrance of things past, a dramatist's understanding of conflict, a knowledge of the human heart, and a style as economical and exact as a theorem in geometry."

New York Herald Tribune

"You have done something that very few other writers of fiction have done—AE Coppard? Occasionally VS Pritchett? Alain-Fournier?—You have written short stories based on common life in the mood of a prose-poet ... the wonder of it to pedestrian prose-writers like me ... is that you have created as a result, an extra art-dimension."

Extract of a letter from Seán Ó Faoláin
to Bryan MacMahon, 27 June 1985

To the memory
of
Seán Ó Faoláin

CONTENTS

❧ A LESSON IN LOVE ❧

The night air is hot in the bedroom where, on the double bed, their backs turned to each other, the young butcher and his teacher wife lie.

From the shuttered shop far below the tang of meat seeps upwards.

Neither the man nor the woman is asleep. His body makes a mound in the bed; she lies in a foetal crouch. Somehow the woman's posture conveys a sense of waiting - and planning.

This impression is strengthened by the way her eyeballs glint in the wan light of the window.

The townspeople spoke respectfully of Young Jim's authority in the weekly mart. There was his ability to weigh a beast with his eye; added to which was his courage in bidding and his mental ability with figures. Yet, walking through the shop after a tiring day in school, Eleanor, his wife, had often noted how subdued he had become on her entrance. The woman customer too recognised the change in the husband's manner and smiled knowingly.

To the wife, this recurrent incident had steeled her to penetrate a maze of pretence and evasion on the part of her husband. Lying there, her body still and her mind alert, she reviewed the problem.

Her eyes betrayed her awareness that he knew what was going on in her mind. His father, Old Jimbo, who had dropped dead at a street fair some time before the marriage, had had the same secret fault as his son. The young wife feared that her children-to-be would inherit the word-blindness. She knew that her mother-in-law, Old Jimbo's widow, now living on the edge of town with her married daughter, was watching her every move.

Eleanor sighed secretly; she well knew that if she had formed plans to attack, she also needed plans to defend.

The faint ticking of the alarm clock was heard in the quiet room.

Young Jimbo made the first move. Rolling onto his back he clasped his fingers about his poll. His wife could not help recalling what a bitter old man had once told her: "A man gets to resemble the animal he has most dealings with." Her husband had the strong body of a bullock and the small eyes of a pig. She had been wryly consoled by the old fellow's later comment: "But, of course, a pig is a most intelligent animal. Did you ever hear of a pig being killed by a motor-car?"

He slept without a pyjama top. His powerful body was like a storage heater. His heat was welcome in winter, their first together. But here and now when the warmth of the summer day had penetrated the slated roof above their heads, the proximity of his body was overpowering.

Almost audibly the woman sighed. Time now for her to lure him to make his next move. She rehearsed every step of the way ahead. Even from her limited experience of teaching she was convinced that what was called dyslexia did not exist: it was a word used by lazy educationalists. Why, if a child could identify a single key in a bunch of keys, that same child could identify a word out of a page of words. And thus be taught to read. To her, the child unable to recognise different words was a locked safe. The true teacher was a safecracker.

Her back was still turned to him. No concave and convex bodies tonight. Was it her turn to make a move?

With a sigh she now rolled partly onto her back. Faking irritation she threw back the light covers from the upper part of her body. Her second sigh faked drowsiness tinged with exasperation. Her husband still lay flat on his back, his eyes wide open, his fingers firmly clasped behind his head. She waited. The Jimboes were stubborn. After a time, with a murmured equivocal "Mmhh" she stretched her catlegs so that her feet now lay on the cooler part of the bed. On their way downwards she ensured that her toes grazed his ankle. She also allowed her hip barely to touch his hip. Still no move on Young Jimbo's part. Belatedly she regretted that she had not turned fully: had she done so she could have verified that he was not falling asleep.

Does he sense the benign trap? she asked herself. The bait on the plate is my hot body. It needs only the animal touch to release its spring and cause its teeth to snap. But I must be patient: the instant he sees the primer in my hand he is off like a redshanks. The hero of shop, fairgreen or mart is transformed into a retarded child.

Clearly his public bravado signified the over-compensation of his hidden incompetence. His suffering was so unnecessary. Consider the roundabouts I have had to go to so as to coax a stammered confession out of him. This because the protocol of our relationship had to be observed. And what harm but it seemed that everyone in town was aware of his secret.

The town! The instant she, a stranger, was seen in his company for the third time, hints came like a shower of darts. The sly sniggers of middle-aged matrons making common cause by means of oblique comments. Wasn't it well for Young Jimbo that the girl was a teacher? But wasn't it odd that an educated young woman could waste her time and perhaps her life on such a man? But if Eleanor read false pity in the women's eyes, she also read jealousy. Their daughters had been passed over. And the Jimbo family was well off, with "old money" in the bank. "Mark my words," the more bitter among them said, "that girl is making a hard bed for herself - and let her lie in it!"

The more vicious among the women mock-gently questioned a shop account. "Is it as much as that, Young Jim?" or, "Would you ever look it up in the book?" This though the enquirer well knew that the only ledger the young butcher kept was the ledger of his memory.

After their marriage matters tended to come to a head. The old widow in her time had made some attempt to keep the shop accounts in order. But prior to her son's wedding, Eleanor had quietly stipulated that the shop and its accounts would not be her concern. So Young Jim had to rely on his mental agility alone. Rumour spread that Houlihans in the Main Street kept better meat. Andy Houlihan kept accurate accounts. And that one could see the weighing scale or the price marked clearly on the sections of meat already cut. Customers began to move away from Jimbo's.

The young wife sighed deeply. How was it that her man, using only his eyes and fingertips, could tell the weight of a live beast almost to the pound and also predict almost to the penny the profit it would yield when the same beast was slaughtered, skinned, hung up, cut down and sliced ready for the cooking - while that same man could become utterly dull when it came to interpreting a series of squiggles on paper, a task a child could master in a month.

The room grew hotter. Eleanor felt womanly. To herself she confessed that she needed to be needed physically. The warmth of the night was certainly a factor as also was the sense of suffused light as the moon rode higher above the houses on the opposite side of the narrow street.

Earlier that evening she had tried out a new way of fixing her hair. The furniture of the living-room hadn't seemed right: after school she had shifted it about. She had had a shower. Had used a new brand of talcum powder. Was it all gone to waste? Was Young Jimbo unable to decipher simple womanly signals? And yet, she realised that if she were to reach her goal, this desire that so naturally filled her, had this night above all nights to be used - but controlled.

You are now guilty of emotional blackmail, her conscience accused her. A phrase from the marriage service, when it occurred to her, she set aside with a grimace. She pleaded the equivocation and volatility of woman's nature, the shuttling of the female mind from the boudoir to the sanctuary. "He can't go on like this," she said almost aloud, as if rebutting a charge of failure to keep the terms of the marriage bond. "I cannot bear to see my husband become the butt of small-town ridicule."

Remorselessly the clock ticked on. It was as if it were counting down to the moment of explosion.

Eleanor allows her raised knee to touch his thigh. The heat of his body becomes still more palpable. She is conscious that her leg now forms an isosceles triangle of sorts between her body and that of her husband. She relishes the sensation of finding the hem of her nightdress sliding down her thighs to bunch about her middle. "Progress," she whispers to herself, as the man grunts. Mock weariness masks her allowing her knee to fall fully sidelong across his thigh. Through the narrow slits of her eyes she tries to gauge his reaction. Her knee now registers the breathing rhythm of his body. He fails to respond.

A quiver of surrender on her part is banished as she recalls the sneers of the townspeople. They have forgotten that she is a teacher. As yet, marital duty in its widest implications must take precedence over marital desire.

Ah! A deep-throated growl indicates that Young Jimbo is about to make a move. His powerful hand curls to something like a bear paw. The finger claws move to grasp the flat of her inner thigh. As the fingers unclasp prior to a deeper clasping she shrugs a rejection. The man growls animal-deep.

Eleanor identifies her husband as the giant of legend seated at the table and herself as Jack-in-the-Oven. Presently his blazing hand tries again - it moves confidently in crude caress to where it lies half on flesh and half on lace. The woman smiles - my mountain of mutton is about to swing around eager to overwhelm me. With scant respect for my feelings. The fingers spread to stiffness so that the love clutch will tighten more surely than before. Here it comes! The time is now.

Her bare buttocks bounce on the bed. On the rebound she pivots sideways and swings outward until the balls of her feet thump on the floor. She is aware that bounce and thump have both conveyed the desirability of that which he seeks. She stands at the window. The panelled shutter to her right is moonlit. Standing in the parting of the lace curtains she experiences a needle prick of remorse. Has her response been premature? Over-gestured? Would a subtle response have been better? Perhaps she should have physically rehearsed that last movement. She hopes that the window light will enable him to see through her almost see-through nightdress.

Wait. Think. Behind her on the bed is what she hopes is a befuddled male animal.

Eleanor assures herself that she is in command. But a twinge of uncertainty remains. This weakness of hers must be overborne by the will. Surely it is only in certain respects that the man is dull. The surgical accuracy of his hands in the shop, the authority of his public voice, his almost imperial gaze when in the company of men, all these indications, though impressive, have not as yet been fully probed and interpreted by her. Was it true as local legend had it? That the Jimboes, father and son, drank enamel mugs of hot blood gushing from the throat wound of a bullock sprawled and bound to the iron ring set in the floor of the slaughter house? As yet she had seen no evidence of this: the local sting also added that this practice should have added to the virility of father and son, but had failed obviously since Young Jimbo was an only son.

The woman's body is cooling. The new tang on the air of the bedroom she identifies as being that of her own sweat. The sweat of fear? Or desire? Or simple woman heat? And now, since she had taken part in small-town dramatics, on the pretence of observing something on the narrow pavement far below, Eleanor moves a step forward into the spotlight of the moon.

From the bed comes a slurred sound. Good! It indicates that the machinery of his brain is creaking. With luck, anger bubbles beneath his perplexity. The woman's body temperature falls from coolness to coldness. She has scarcely to alter her stance to pick up a bed-jacket from the back of a nearby chair and whisk it across her shoulders. The slight turn of her head allows her to catch the glow of a white angry eye. A mere shiver passes across her body. She vaguely hopes that the trembling of her buttocks will lure him to bring matters to a climax. "Now, I am all woman," she tells herself.

Her mind is now on the overdrive of intuition. A scrawl of cloud drifts across the face of the moon. A dog barks in one of the yards of the houses farther up the lane. Entering from the Main Street a night walker has begun to whistle. Eleanor tilts her head to read the time on the phosphorescent hands of the bedside clock. Twenty minutes past two. On the dressing-table a phosphorescent Madonna glows. Eleanor risks a glance at the bed. His torso bare. His belly a hillock. Hands still clasped about his poll.

Feigning impulse she turns and snatches open a side drawer of the dressing-table. Rummaging she releases a smell of perfumed silk. She takes out an infant primer. Slams the drawer shut. Returns to her place at the window. Turns over the pages of the slim reader. She realises that she is exhausting her options.

Should she begin to retreat? Attribute her restlessness to illness? To tension of the month? To classroom irritation? Even hint at pregnancy? She stifles the temptation to yield. Eleanor is taken by a sense of outrage.

Think of it! Newspapers, race-cards, hotel menus, demand notices for rates, political handbills - all convey nothing to him. Abstract ideas are beyond his ken. Metaphors and similes appear to him as broken jigsaw puzzles. Poetry as the lisping of idiots.

What then are his landmarks? The thumbing of live hams, the sad music of a cow close to calving, manure spread on land, the worming of a hound.

His vocabulary? "I bought chape at Carrigaline." "There's a baisht with a roomy dug." "Here's a handy shank o' lamb, Missus." His noblest experience of nature's year? Seeing a cow going into aftergrass for the first time. His nouns? Blood, salt, chops, dung, mince, tripe. His verbs; slung, flung, hung, dung.

Still no response from the bed.

Eleanor pauses for a reappraisal. Perhaps she could have brought about this struggle of wills on another pretext. On the imprint of a soiled boot on a carpet, on a fouled ashplant left in the scullery, to what destination they would drive on a Sunday afternoon? Somehow the issue had clearly demanded the bedroom as the fitting arena of contest. Now he has built a barrier. Of course he realises that this is the time and place of fate.

A question enters the woman's mind. If she wins, what will be the price of victory? She had once looked down on the yard from a high rear window of the house. In a mixture of horror, awe, revelation, revulsion and admiration she had watched her husband prepare to kill a beast. There was something hieratic about the way he stood aside as the helpers pinned the squealing pig on the long wooden table. She fancied she could still hear the grating noise and the flash of the long knife moving backwards and forwards on the sharpening steel. She then recalled the way in which having set his half-smoked cigarette standing on its wet butt on a stone projecting from a stone in the wall, he had slowly advanced on the prone beast. More priestly still his features as the knife parted the almost willing flesh and dug deep in search of arterial blood. The high-pitched screams and the bubbling gurgles issuing from the archaic mouth of the dying animal were followed by the shuddering convulsions of the trotters.

She had backed away from the window to control and indeed to analyse her unexpected reactions to the almost ritual slaughter below.

Then, as now, she experienced the flattening of her belly. Then as now, her nipples became as tense as hazelnuts. Then, as now, there was the fishgasping of her lips, the almost involuntary pointing of her tongue, the unease of her bare arms that sought to be uplifted, the tremor of her body that indicated a primal desire for desire.

Eleanor smiles. To herself she says, "If tonight I should conceive, the infant will be an embodiment of literacy and lawful lust." She glances at the primer still in her hand. She knows the text by heart.

SAM IS IN THE VAN. TARA IS ON THE WALL. GO ON MAMMY. GO ON THE TRICYCLE. DADDY SAYS I WILL GO ON THE TRICYCLE TOO.

The moonlight begins to enter the room. It creeps up along the red coverlet. The moon is a mute question mark. Amused perhaps at the nightly conundrums posed by man and woman.

Eleanor allows a faint snarl-sigh of impatience to escape her lips. She then identifies herself as a bitch in heat, and yet rejecting the advances of an importunate male dog. As if denying or confirming the identification she moves quickly back into bed. She switches on the reading-lamp behind her head. Sitting up she turns over the pages of the primer. Donkeys, circus wagons, motor-cars, blue and red, a farmyard scene, a red ball on a beach, a cross-section of the Zoo - all parade before her in brilliant colours.

On every picture, on every page there is always a boy and a girl, a Mammy and a Daddy, a male and a female.

ANN HAS A PRAM. JACK HAS A CART. JACK WILL MILK THE COW. MARY WILL BRING THE PAIL. WATCH THE BULL, JACK.

Male and female. Always.

The young wife tells her elbow to graze her husband's shoulder. It obeys. No reaction. Turning the pages the woman's eyes continue to smoulder in response to the vivid illustrations in the book. The nouns used are solid: dog, car, book, monkey, ball, cake, jam, bus, horse, ice-cream. The verbs strike home. Play, toss, come, dig, ride, fall, beat, grip. The reiteration of a basic plot.

What exactly is my plan? the wife asks herself. Beside me, my bullock of a man stares up at the ceiling. If only he would ... ah, here it comes again, the heavy lazy paw.

As she shifts her body a bare inch away she feels his body stiffen. She pauses. Why doesn't the fool try again? For a moment she exchanges roles; he is now the teacher; she is willing to be taught. But there is a protocol of approach which he first must learn.

Deliberately, Young Jimbo unclasps his fingers from about his poll. Good! Then almost before she realises it he has swung his heavy body out of the bed. Sitting on the bed edge, he gropes for his slippers. Standing, he snatches his light-weight dressing-gown off the back of a chair. Old boards creak as he moves to the window. It is his turn to part the curtains. To cause amusement to the moon. There is a long pause.

"The priest was a liar so," he growls at last.

"Priests say what suits," Eleanor says equably. When he fails to reply she adds, "You didn't tell him about the other thing."

"I told you before you took with me."

"You told me, yes. Against your will."

"You knew about it already."

(She did know. For her own good, the jealous women said.)

"You can't be always like this," Eleanor says.

"It's done me up to now."

"It's no life for a man."

"It'll do me the rest of my road. With you or without you."

She pauses. As if faced with a rebellious child in school she calmly goes on. "Will you go on signing your scripts with a scribble? Dodging print everywhere? 'I forgot my glasses,'" she adds, miming his voice. Reverting to her own voice, recalling that other girls had treasured love letters she adds: "What use is my writing you a letter if I'm away from home?"

"We have a phone."

"Butchering is your trade: teaching is mine."

"You got your way with the cold room. And the band-saw in the shop."

"One avoids waste. The other halves your work."

"The meat is different out of the room. The band-saw leaves bone dust on the chops. The priest said you've no right to deny me."

The woman's voice softens - "This is our first quarrel, Jim."

The moonlight is on his twisted face. "If you knew how hard readin' leans on me, you wouldn't carry on like this," he blurts. "Everyone laughin' at me at school. Fellas I would now buy up out of my waistcoat pocket. Master Dee, curse o' Christ on him, 'Next', he'd say at the readin' lesson. He never meant me for next. He always passed me over. I could have cut his throat with a knife. This thing is a wall I cannot go through."

A fistful of lace curtain is balled up in his fist.

The wife's resolve quavers. Before she can respond,

"Keep your bloody body," he adds. "I might go elsewhere when I go up country to the marts."

The Tallystick

The woman's heart beats a tattoo. She has not foreseen this defiance. Or has she? Wait, she counsels herself. Now for the first time the public side of his character is being revealed in private. Isn't this what you sought to evoke? she accuses herself.

Young Jim turned from the window. His clenched fist dragged down the lace curtains and the bamboo pole about his head. He tore the encumbrance from him and glared at the bed.

"You'll catch cold, Jim," Eleanor said softly. Purring like a cat she added, "It's warm here beside me. Come on love." She told herself that this was the first time she had used the endearment. "A few letters and a few words - that's not much to ask. It's only that I want to make you the equal of any other man."

"The equal? Ask in the shop! Ask on the hurling field! Ask on the streets of Carrig!"

The wife tried to make amends. "The better, if it pleases you ... they say that only for the one drawback, you're a better man than your father."

"They say!" he shouted. "Who say?"

"People."

"Not to my face."

"By their smiles they say it."

"Let the bastards smile. I know different. They say! Let them say!" The man's voice had climbed to its highest pitch of anger.

The woman accused herself. Taunting and defiance - were these the proper weapons of a wife? Wheedling might have been more effective, even if it went against her grain.

Then, funny how a simple phrase can infuriate a man, she thinks. He is still shouting, "They say" as he paces the floor. Now his fist is pounding on the door. She hears the crack of a splitting panel. As he gropes angrily for the doorknob, she springs out of bed.

She clings to him, her carmine fingernails gripping him wherever they can. Panting, sobbing, clawing she pleads. "Jimbo love, hold our differences here. If you leave the room it will be serious!" Still he continues to shout as his fist smashes another panel. "Give in to me,

Jim," she sobs. "We're one flesh. Pride and shame should have no place between us. Don't go, Jim. I beg of you."

The advocates of her breasts are close against his body. She clings to him in desperation, her hair tangled with the black hair of his bare breast. On a sudden lunge he drags the door open; she flings herself against it and manages to slam it shut.

Close together now. His body relaxed a little. He has begun to breathe brokenly. A pause, then, delicately, ever so slowly, she draws him backwards towards the bed. Inch by precious inch gentling him downwards, implying, "That's it child. Prepare to be trained. Prepare to be loved."

Prone both. Draw one of the covers gently over him. His cropped head is black against the white pillow. Now she lies close against him. Soaking in his weakness. Sensitive to his every movement. Later, later, touch will be all powerful in the delirium of congress. But not yet. Fingertips be patient. Wait. It is because of his incompleteness that I love him. The pair lie without movement.

Presently she steals her hand over the bedcovers. Her fingers find the primer. With its pictures of duck and clown. Ever so slowly she draws herself upward in the bed. She swivels, then squares her buttocks on the bed, places the open primer on the lectern of her drawn-up knees. Flicks on the reading light above the head of the bed.

Classroom scraps now turn over in her mind. "The moon comes every night to peep through the window where I lie." "Roley poley, roley poley, in, in, in; roley poley, roley poley, out, out, out;" "Sing a song of sixpence, listen to the duck."

Aloud, "Jim!"

No response.

"Please - Jim!"

"Uh?"

"Turn, Jim. Just for a moment. Sit up a little. Look at this."

A long silent pause. Alleluia, he's obeying.

"Is your hand sore?" she whispers. "Let me see it."

She lifts the hand. Says, "Iff" at the sight of the blood. Brings the man's hand to her open mouth. Sucks strongly on the source of the blood. "There!" she adds as the blood seems to have ceased flowing. "Don't let it soil the sheet."

She turns over a page or two of the primer. "Jim. These little scrawls are letters. Twenty-six of them make up the alphabet. Each letter is a brick. Put bricks together and they make a wall. Letters put together make a word. See."

He is glancing sidelong. Though still angry, his silence is not the silence of refusal.

"This letter is O. A roundy O. Watch my mouth - O.

Give me your finger. Trace the O on my lips. Please love, say it."

Barely audible; "O."

"This one is standing tall - trace it on my knee - it's I. Say it, Jim."

"I."

"Good. This one is S. Like a drunken man. Like Sam Sheridan of a Saturday. Ess! Your finger. S says suh, suh, suh, steak. Suh, suh, salmon. Suh, suh, sheep. Trace it on my thigh. You've three letters now. Let's go back. This one Jim? Please."

"O."

"Right! This one?"

"Shank."

"Well, it's S for shank. Ess. A simple letter now. Like a crooked cross. X . Say it. Trace it."

"Ex."

"Now we have O, I, S and X. Great! Now I'll put S first, then I, then X. I'm putting three letters together to make a word. And the word is? Ess-eye-ex. It's a number, Jim - what is it?"

"Six."

"You're a dote. Now let me put ... what's wrong?"

"I've an early mart in the morning."

"I know. I was going to say S-E-X ... but we haven't done E yet, so we'll see about that word later. One last thing ..."

"The alarm clock is set for six o'clock."

"S-I-X-6. Good. One more thing. Just to give you an idea how reading goes. Give me your good hand. I'll put your finger under each word as I read.

DAN LIKES NORA. NORA LIKES DAN. DAN HAS A BALL. HE PLAYS WITH NORA. DAN AND NORA HAVE FUN. There! First lesson over. It wasn't hard, was it? But any time you want me like-you-know, you'll have to earn it by reading. I'll be the star on your copybook. You're not going to sleep, are you?"

"For God's sake, woman, will you let me rest."

"I'll let you rest. I'll quench the light. Let me put my hand around my scholar. I feel happy now, Jim, don't you?"

He growls drowsily. Her arm tightens about him. She nestles against his back. The man's body is like a furnace. She hopes there won't be blood on the sheet. Well, if there is, she tells herself, what does it matter?

The moonlight shines fully through the uncurtained window. It silvers the recumbent forms on the bed. The whistler passes on the pavement below. The woman raises her ear off the pillow.

"Jim."

"Jee-sus!"

"Listen."

"Whassit?"

"Young Dannihy. He's whistling. Toselli's serenade."

"Almighty God."

The woman replaces her ear on the pillow. She begins to sing softly.

"Like a golden dream in my heart ever smiling

Lives a vision fair of happy love I knew in days gone by."

She tickles him gently then says with a giggle. "Sing a song of sixpence; listen to the duck."

"Sleep, woman, for Christ's sake."

"You've set my sleep astray." She claws him to silence. Then, "Remember at the races the way I gripped you as the jockey fell. The time we first met. Was that the very first race won by a lady jockey in Ireland?"

"I forget ..."

"Don't sleep. I promised you a reward."

"Mnnh ..."

"Nora likes to play with Dan."

He groans.

"I'll spell a word on your back. With my fingers, Mmm. S - E - but we haven't learned E yet."

Another groan.

"You don't have to go elsewhere, Jim. You didn't mean that, I know. You never said how you liked my short nightdress."

No reply.

He is fast asleep. The bullock is pole-axed. The woman tells herself. Can you beat a stupid man?

To hell with it, let him sleep. In the small hours she could nudge him into claiming his reward. By now she knew her limitations. And had gained a sense of timing. She was making progress in school - and in the home. All she had to do now was to control the insubordinate children of her imagination.

The moon! There it is, right in the centre of the top pane of the window. "But lo from high Hymettus to the plain, the queen of night asserts her silent reign." Hymettus a place of flowers and honey. Of marble too. The old wallpaper of this room must come down. Harbours earwigs. The slaughter in the yard must stop. He must use the town abattoir. Like it or not, I'll get a microwave oven. His Ma and his sister, their eyes watching my waistline. Not yet, not yet. Sol pauses on the hill. If I have a son all will be forgiven and forgotten. How is it that the old lady never taught Old Jimbo to read? Tried but failed? Liked to keep him in subjection? I'll win, for I am trained - and possessed. My plan is marked for daily, monthly and yearly progress. Other goals in my yearly plan - a spacious house on the little height in the Fattening Field, half a mile outside the town. A split-level house facing the south. The S of a driveway to the door. Arches and urns. A magnolia tree. Cordylines are vulgar plumes. Maybe a copper beech or two. The Fattening Field is sacred soil to the Jimboes. They will be coaxed by a muscular smile and an infant-to-be.

Closer still to her husband. As old Nora had it, "Every woman is the boss but it's a fool lets her husband know it."

The moon. Floodlighting Young Jim's bare shoulder. Evoking the sparkle as of jewellery from the tawdry appointments of the room. Bringing the red coverlet of the bed to the glow of a fire. The moonface objective and aloof. If she moved her head just a little Eleanor could see it clearly. Over the centuries the moon had watched Mary and Joseph, Iseult and Tristan, Dervorgilla and Dermot, Kitty and Charles Stuart - even Dan and Nora of the lesson. Now the moon watches Eleanor and Young Jimbo.

Quarrels and reconciliations come lick alike to the moon. A faithful keeper of secrets too. "Comes every night to peep at folks asleep, and she never makes a sound." The sun is of day and man: the moon is of night, woman and love. The moon determines the ebbing and flowing of a woman's blood, notes her snarling when she wishes to be left alone, her later yearning to surround and exhaust. To spurn and welcome. To surrender and conquer. To know abandon and exaltation. The systole and diastole implicit in the words Eva and Ave.

Eleanor is faintly conscious that she is yielding to sleep - should we ... waste the golden hours of youth far apart? Down, down, down. A faraway giggle, a womanly snuggle, then with the faintest breath of her mind, "Sing a song ... of sixpence ... listen ... to the ... duck."

JACK FUREY

The old woman stops praying. Her head turns to address the younger woman. The words tremble as they leave the thin lips.

"Was it to the crossroads inspection that Dáibhí took the bull?"

The younger woman pauses in her ironing. With a quick look through the kitchen window at the as yet distant struggle between returning man and beast, she draws fully on her cigarette. "Aye, that's where he took the bull."

"A lovely bold beast," Old Grace says, "he should throw good calves."

Underbreath from Josie, the daughter-in-law, "What your son won't throw, good nor bad."

"We always kept a good bull. Even before my poor husband Tom Flanagan married in here."

"Aye!" with a touch of sarcasm.

The old woman in the rocking-chair holds up her long rosary beads. Rising slowly to her feet, she peers out the window. Her open mouth fails to indicate that she sees her son and the bull struggling down the hill road leading to the farmhouse.

Unsurely she turns. Glances up at the red votive lamp beneath a picture of the Sacred Heart. Casts an eye on a white enamel gallon on a cup-hook at one end of the dresser. Drags open a drawer of the dresser and begins to rummage in it.

"What are you looking for?" Josie asks.

"My mother-of-pearl prayer book. Tom Flanagan's mortuary card. They're gone."

"Gone where?"

"Stolen."

Josie thumps the iron upright on the end of the ironing-board.

"The letters from Sister Josephine in Vancouver," the old woman whines. "My child of Mary medal. Gone."

Turning, "The Christmas dues are to be entered in my name. My poor husband's name is to be crossed out in the book. I'll give you the money today for the priest."

"It's not Christmas. It's June."

"It's not?"

"It's not."

"Oh," in bewilderment. Advancing, then pausing. "And who are you my girl?"

"Jesus, Mary and Joseph!" barely audible. Aloud, "I'm Josie, your son Dáibhí's wife."

An interval of puzzlement. Then: "You think I'm losing my wits?"

In a stage whisper, "Damn sure you are." Aloud, "Not at all."

An angry bellow is heard. Outside the kitchen window a bluetit is clinging upside down on a branch. A hundred yards beyond the bird, man and bull are erratically approaching. Presently they will be over the little bridge and come through the open gateway. The old woman looks up at the gallon. Plaintively she says, "Wet the tea and I'll be off."

"Off where?"

"To the meadow. My father and the men will be waiting. 'Grace, don't forget the tea,' they said."

"You're sixty years too late."

A single web of spittle links top lip to lower lip in the old agape mouth. Sixty years too late? How can that be? The gallon is hanging where it has always hung. Now, the same as on that terrible wonderful day in the long ago. A day that still exists in the always now.

The lid of the gallon of tea I keep tightly in place by pressing it down on a clean cloth spread across the vessel's mouth. The parcel of hot buttered meal bread is under my arm. It is an errand I like. First the pause at the parapet of the little bridge above the stream. Then the careful climbing of the stile beside the crab tree. The walk along the brambly path by the low river bank. The briars try to hook my dress and the nettles to sting the bare calves of my legs. The coming out on the floor of the wood where the bluebells are dying and the meadowsweet stands bushy, creamy and tall on the thickets. Taller still the foxgloves, their purple thimbles ready for the fingertips of children. My nostrils opening and closing at the onset of the wood smells. The hum of insect life on all sides of me. The babble of the river just below. Inevitably there is the lowing of a single cow.

"I must get the gallon or I'll be late."

"Leave it there! There's no meadow and no men."

"You're a bold lassie!"

"Time for you to have your bread and hot milk. Then off with you to bed."

"I'll go when Dáibhí comes back with the bull. And brings my snuff."

The younger woman spreads, irons and folds a man's grey shirt. The smell of hot iron on damp cloth pervades the kitchen. Now and again she casts an eye on the approaching struggle outside. Her eyes are spaced well apart; she has wide, almost Polynesian features. Her body has thickened with the passing years. Her hair in front is cut straight across in a sturdy fringe. There are traces of sweat on the few dark hairs on her upper lip.

Josie sets the iron standing, takes a shallow dish from the gleaming dresser and goes to the range. She breaks shop bread onto the dish and pours hot milk on it. "Sit and eat!" she tells the old woman.

Grace looks down at the plate. Sniffs. "If my decent husband was alive ... " she begins.

"It's years since you mentioned his name."

"I pray for him every day."

"Tell me the date of his death."

"Tom Flanagan, rest his soul, died of a heart attack," the old woman pauses to grope across the years ... "on a morning exactly twenty-eight years ago last April 26th."

"Right."

"You want to put my head astray?"

Christ give me patience. This old woman has been a load on me for eighteen years. Without chick or child to comfort or divert me. Year in, year out, the farm answers to the turning of the seasons. Bulling time, calving time, seeding time, reaping time. For me it's foddering beasts and scouring vessels. And Grace Flanagan with her single child and her notions of respectability as the leaves fall from the torn calendar of her mind. Time and overtime she was dead and gone.

Sharply, "You're slopping the milk all over the table."

"I was used to proper food."

"That's wholesome bread. And wholesome milk."

"What's this?"

"That's brown sugar."

"Brown ... sugar!" With scorn.

"Brown or white, it's all the bloody same. When your son comes in don't say I starved you. Are you going to eat or not?"

"I'll finish my rosary."

"Patience, Jesus, patience!"

Close to the yard gate, the dark-haired man and the black-hided beast take turns circling each other. The bull's eyes are crazily defiant. The man keeps the strain on the rope which is tied fast to the nose-ring of the beast. The grind of sturdy boots has evoked from the road edge the stench of crushed wild parsley and wild garlic.

Milk dribbles over old mauve-coloured lips. When Grace speaks, as if to herself, her voice is mock-youthful and mock-cultured.

"I had two plaits of hair. He liked to loosen them and run the hair through his fingers."

"Who?" the younger woman stabs. Despite the distraction from outside she is suddenly alert.

Old Grace's eyes shuttle in craftiness. "The chief thing is to save one's soul," she says, looking down on her lap.

"No fear of you!"

"Would you say so?"

"The most devout woman in the parish."

"I might be stopped at the gate."

"What gate?"

"The gate of Heaven."

"You! Pillar of the Church! Faithful wife! Dutiful mother! What'd stop you?"

"A small thing might keep a person out."

"What kind of thing?" When Grace did not answer, Josie blurted, "Finish your food. Dáibhí is at the gate!"

Head bent over the table, Grace is sloshing up her food. Accurate in keeping jabot and blouse unstained. Craft, haste, age and dignity competing in the old woman's eyes.

From outside the window comes the raised voice of the son. The sound causes the mother to spoon faster. On the old-time comb holding her trim poll of hair in place brilliants flash.

From the farmyard comes a roar of "Up, you black bastard!"

Grace wipes her lips with shivering fingers. Taking her dish with her she rises. She moves to the window, one half of which is opened to one side on its hinges. The old lady's eyes are aglint with pride. The wife continues to thump down the iron on the folds of another heavy shirt.

Man and bull are just outside the window.

Tremulously raising her voice, "Did the bull pass, Dáibhí?" Grace asks.

Glancing over his shoulder the son's face is suffused with effort, anger and pride. Reluctantly he growls, "Aye."

The mother makes the sign of the cross in gratitude. Still holding the dish she returns to the table. She looks down at the almost empty vessel in her hands. She moves slowly to the range. She spoons more bread and milk onto the dish. Returned to the table her nose curls as she looks at the brown sugar in its bowl. Covertly watching the older woman's every movement, Josie puts away the ironing things. She pokes the fire and places a saucepan on the main ring of the range.

The shouting and thumping outside is followed by the sound of a stall door slamming shut and the rattle of a bolt shooting home.

Standing for a moment in the open doorway of the back kitchen, Dáibhí, from under heavy black eyebrows, looks from his mother to his wife. He does not speak; he kicks off his heavy boots and draws his shirt over his head. Washing his hands and powerful upper body at the scullery tap he looks out on the yard. Drying himself he stands masterfully surveying the kitchen. The wife has grown meek: she opens a cupboard and lays a clean white shirt on the side-table. She places delph on one end of the kitchen table then moves to tend the saucepan on the range.

"You should be in bed, mother," Dáibhí says. He pulls on the clean shirt.

"I'll go now, son."

"Did you have your supper?"

"I had ... a class of a supper."

Josie flares. "Blast you! That's your second helping!"

"All right!" Dáibhí says sharply. To his mother, "Off with you now, woman."

"Did you get my snuff?"

"I forgot. 'Twill be got tomorrow. Bed now!"

"Forgot my snuff," Grace murmurs on the way to the bedroom. She takes the dish with her. She leaves the room door a little ajar. "Forgot my snuff," she is heard saying remotely.

Josie clatters more delph and cutlery onto the table. She pours out stew for her husband.

The stew is hot. After the first tasteful: "That bull should throw good calves," Dáibhí says.

"What did the inspector say?" his wife asks.

"Walked round the beast a few times. 'That's no speak-easy bull,' I said. 'He's better than your collar-and-tie buggers'."

Josie indicates a grudged interest.

"The bull began to play up," Dáibhí went on. "I gave him rope to show off his temper. When I dragged him up to Jodhpurs he was a mass of froth. The punch was put to his ear then." After a pause, "I'll maybe get a premium. The middlin' farmers around here will now get prime calves out of their perished heifers."

"You forgot her snuff."

"I had a mad day."

"Not half as mad as I had. Tea to the meadow all day long."

"Must be the noise of the mowing machine at Lynch's that set her off."

"She needs nothing to set her off. Every day she's getting worse. I'm telling you now what I told you before."

"I've heard all that!"

"Heard but didn't heed. She won't be put away in time."

"I want no more of it!"

"If her head is roasted on a hot range. Or if she falls into the stream … "

"Let it lie!"

Josie turns away. She snaps on an old radio.

"Turn off that bloody yoke," Dáibhí shouts as the sound blurts out.

"It's newstime."

"Turn it off!" Dáibhí shouts.

The wife obeys. She goes to the bedroom left. Slams the door behind her. The man laughs.

The meal over, Dáibhí sprawls on an armchair. Dusk gathers outside. The sky grows overcast. The Sacred Heart lamp glows. Dáibhí belches. From the stall the young bull bellows. From Lynch's upper field a cow lows in reply. Dáibhí yawns fully, then stretches his legs. Entwines his fingers on his stomach. Closes his eyes. Smiles as he begins to nap.

Time passes. The birds fall silent. In the far west the golden underbelly of the clouds begins to pale. Quivers pass over Dáibhí's features. He wakes scowling. Josie, an old cardigan slung over her nightdress, is standing barefooted with her back to the dresser. She is drawing heavily on a cigarette.

Speaking sidelong Dáibhí says, "I saw Lousy Larry in Hannigan's bar."

The wife does not reply.

"He was talking to Hannigan. He shut up when he saw me. I felt like smashing a glass in his face."

"Let him have the right o' way if he's entitled to it. You can open another passage through Dorney's."

"If he sets foot on that path, he'll drink his own blood."

"Your temper will be your downfall. I don't know where you were got, with the gentle father you had."

"The dam had spunk," Dáibhí says easily.

Wearing a long white nightdress with a black shoulder shawl, his mother comes up out of the room. She has the empty dish in her hands. "Did you get my snuff, Dáibhí?" she asks.

"Jack Sweeney will bring it tomorrow," the son replies.

The old woman turns back to the bedroom. She pauses just inside the open door to listen to her son's voice which suddenly has a black joy in its tone.

"The best of good news in town," he says.

"That so?" In Josie's mouth the cigarette glows.

"Curse o' Connacht is dead."

"Who's that?"

"Old Furey."

"Furey, the schoolmaster?"

"The ex-schoolmaster."

"X or Y - he's stone dead."

"Lord have mercy on him."

"Lord damn him into hell! The world is rid of one tyrannical bastard. Black Jack Furey! Only once I saw my father in a rage."

"When was that?"

Grace is standing just inside the room door. She is listening.

"The day I stood up to Furey in the school gallery. 'Fight him back' my father shouted when he heard about it afterwards."

Lowering his voice Dáibhí adds, "Herself coaxed him out of going to the school."

"Where did he die?"

"In St Gertrude's. Under the knife. A prostate operation. Too miserly to go to Dublin and have it done properly. Bought cheap: paid dear. 'I'll make you a scholar, a soldier or a fool,' he'd shout. Most of the lads'd wet their britches in terror."

"Not you, I suppose?" Tolerantly.

"Not me! Nor ten like him! I should have split his head with a slate before I ran out of the school door. Never spoke to me after that. I was the only scholar that cowarded Furey."

"Lick alike, you and him."

"If I thought we were alike I'd hang myself."

"When is the funeral?"

"Thursday at four o'clock. The scholars will be told to march. Instead of throwing his drunken body into the tide. They'll bury him without me."

"Let the dead rest."

Grace opens wide the room door. She is still carrying the dish. She walks forward with a steady gait. Son and daughter-in-law watch her. "Who's dead?" she asks in an almost normal voice.

"No one that matters," Josie says.

"Back to your bed," from Dáibhí.

"Who's dead? I say. Is it a classmate of mine from the long ago?"

"No one who matters a damn is dead," her son growls.

Grace's fingertips are trembling on the edge of the dish. "The box of life opens: the box of life shuts," she says quietly. "You tell me nothing."

"She'll keep asking this for days," Josie whispers.

"The living and dead are all the same in her mind," Dáibhí says in an undertone.

Josie turns, then blurts, "Old Master Furey is dead."

Grace turns with a slow dignity. Her face drains of the remnants of its colouring. Her eyes have grown large. The dish falls to the floor out of her hands. "Who did you say?" she asks in a steady voice.

"Tck-tck," Josie crouches to pick up the pieces of the plate.

"Furey that was schoolmaster in Foyleconeen! Died in St. Gertrude's this morning," Dáibhí speaks harshly.

"Jack Furey couldn't be dead," Grace's tone is reasonable.

"Do I have to swear it for you?"

"Let her be," Josie says coming to her feet. "It makes no matter whether he's dead or alive."

"It matters to me," Dáibhí says.

"Will I tell you what matters to me," Josie snaps. "Trying to please you and your old … "

"My old what?"

"Your old dotin' bitch of a mother."

"Say that again and I'll drag the throttle out of your barren throat."

"Hush children!" from old Grace. Turning she whine-sings, "Lies and jealousies! Lies and jealousies!"

Her tone of voice is so unwonted that son and wife look up in perplexity. It is as if hitherto they have been able to predict the unpredictable in the old woman's moods. Not now! For one thing her carriage is altered. One who is ultimately old, by some quirk of life or mood, by some lesion or slip of time and awareness, is girlish again.

I am in the woods, the old woman's gestures convey. Insects are humming about me. I feel as a full woman feels. Within the compass of my close-fitting skin I am conscious of my hips and my body-honey. I am newly and naturally aware that I am a lure. Something like a salmon fly in the hatband of an angler. I walk on the pathway above the edge of the swirling river. I pause. He is here.

Aloud she says: "He's not dead. It's all lies and jealousies." A tear pauses on her cheekbone then races down the old features.

"Let her cry," Josie mutters. "It will do her good." To Grace with rough sympathy, "Come on. After a sleep you'll feel better."

"That June day. I was lovely then. Too lovely maybe. Have you my snuff, Dáibhí?"

"I forgot, mother."

Recovered now, Grace Flanagan. A lifetime of practice in the art of recovery. Addressing Josie, "His mind was taken up with the bull."

Suddenly she raises her out-of-tune voice and begins to chant quaveringly.

"By the banks of the Roses, my love and I did stray,
My love took down a German flute to play me a tune,
And in the middle of the tune my love to me did say,
'Molly, lovely Molly, I must leave you.'"

Step by step, Josie directs the old woman into the bedroom. Returned to the kitchen, "I'm going to bed," she says. Dáibhí does not reply. He sits in his chair amid the invading dusk. His white shirt glows. The votive lamp shows a more vivid scarlet. Through the western window the last bar of sunset lies above the horizon.

As she goes to her room Josie looks keenly at her husband. Let him go over the events of the day, she tells herself. He'll maybe continue with his nap. Time for me now to be able to read his brain. He'll curse Lousy Larry over the pathway. And Jack Furey over some real or imagined slight. He'll recall his victory over the Inspector of Bulls. He'll polish the details of today's incidents so as to impress the neighbours in a later re-telling. He'd call this a good day. "Let the heifers come in their season," will be all his cry. "A natural bull stands ready to serve them."

Dáibhí, chin on chest, is asleep. The kitchen is quiet. The amber horizon is quenched. A breeze from the estuary seems to foretell rain. The kitchen clock ticks.

There follows the creaking from an old bedstead. The faint padding of bare feet. As her bedroom door opens, Grace appears. She wears a long white nightdress with a black knitted shawl over her shoulders. Her walk is stately and graceful. Her lips are moving though no sound is heard.

The bee of young womanhood is droning in my head. Beneath my bare footsoles, bluebell leaves turn alternately green and silver. I enter the wood. Crushed camomile releases its oil. The scent of summer is strong and male upon the air. Foxglove flowers still beg for the fingers of children. Briar-hooks clutch at my dress urging me to stay. But I am conscious that my body is in season.

Grace goes to the mirror which hangs on the wall beside the votive lamp. She preens herself before her dim reflection. Dáibhí's eyes come slowly open. His mother giggles as her fingertips prink the edges of her grey hair. Old Grace is now young Grace on a far-off afternoon of summer. Her voice is a mimicry of its hour of prime. As she turns her head this way and that the old woman assumes various roles.

"Cocking your cap at the young schoolmaster, Grace O'Hanlon," she says in a low voice. "Take care! Furey by name and Furey by nature," - a chiding neighbour this. Now as herself, in the always now. "I must look my best. He might be fishing in the pool under Drake's Wood. A lovely dark young man, the new schoolmaster. With the devil's own temper, they say. Jack Furey. Jack Fu-ree! When he looks at me from under his eyebrows I get weak, helpless and open. So weak I could fall. Like at Mass last Sunday. And the Sunday before!" Then, "Have sense Grace O'Hanlon! It's a shame for you. You're promised to Tom Flanagan! How can you do that to a decent man?" Again, "This fine weather is upsetting. I hope he's fishing. I hope he's not. My sleep has gone astray. Why did he have to come here? There's Lynch's cow lowing for our bull! I must be careful not to stumble and spill the tea."

Again the voice alters. The old woman crosses herself and joins her hands. Putting her lips close to the mirror she begins to whisper but not in such a low tone as to be inaudible to her son.

"Bless me, Father, for I have sinned. Yes, Father, I'm promised. I know it's not fair. But I can't put the other man out of my head. No, I've never been close to him - yet. But I feel it in my bones. I'll do my best to forget him. My very best. Thank you, Father."

Dáibhí makes no movement.

Again the old woman blesses herself. Her hands joined under her chin, she begins to hum the air of the parting song of young lovers. The red glow of the little lamp is strong on her sideface and shoulder. She sways a little. The humming fines out into silence. Then tick-tock, tick-tock from the clock. Faraway a cow lows as if to remind the natural world of her needs.

Grace is directly behind the figure of her son. She leans forward to where he is seated in the half darkness. She looks at him in puzzlement for a moment or two. The tone of her whispering is now alien to that used to the priest.

"A lovely day, Mr Furey. Have you caught any fish? Yes, I'm going to the meadow. I'm in a hurry. Well, for a minute or two. But I can't delay. I'll sit here. You're from the west, they tell me? How do you like our school, Mr Furey? I'm left school for the past eight years. I'm working on the farm at home. Twenty-two - that's my age. Is it all right if I call you Jack? That's what the scholars call you - Master Jack - behind your back. Please, Mr Furey, please. Your hands are so strong. I'm in a hurry to the meadow. That's Lynch's cow lowing. You're as strong as a bull yourself. My father'll notice it if I'm ... ruffled. They'll be waiting for the tea. Easy now ... take me easy ... I'm not used to ... some other time. Tomorrow night, Jack Furey. Easy. I'm not used to ... used to ... "

But there is no time other than now for it is the time of the always now. Fairy thimbles pleading for fingers, a cow lowing, the barely heard but prolific lower life of the wood, the smell of the crushed grass, the babble of the flowing stream, the shifting sunlight, bare arms, a woman's arching hips and a woman's honey all have entered into a conspiracy of passion whose urgent cry is "Yield to the Invader". There are no other options now in time and place but tumble and fumble, seek and find, siege and surrender, key and lock, man and woman. So terrible and so wonderful.

Old Grace, beginning to hum, turns towards the door of her bedroom. Josie appears at the door of the other bedroom off the kitchen - "Come to bed!" she says very softly to her husband. He growls a refusal.

"Stay then," Josie blurts in a low voice.

As if disturbed by the gently whispering, Grace turns. Now, a wraith moving in the half-light, she goes to where Dáibhí is standing, his face averted.

"Why didn't you come to meet me last night, my love?" the old woman asks. "Or the night before? I sent you a note to the school."

Close now to her son's shoulder. "Bend down your head, Jack

Furey, and I'll tell you my secret. The child I'm carrying is yours. All yours. Tom Flanagan never touched me. My marriage date to him will have to be broken, I don't care what my parents think. It was only you, Jack Furey. We can be married quietly. You'll get a place teaching up the country where no one will know us. There we'll be happy and respected. 'Twas many a good woman's story before me. I can say I took a dislike to Tom Flanagan. What do you say, Jack Furey?"

The ticking clock. The lowing cow.

The old woman draws back a sudden step. Her voice grows sharp. "Oh, no! How could I marry him? And the child yours! No one but yours! If I wronged Tom Flanagan how could I face the Almighty God? Don't dare laugh at me, Jack Furey."

Statuesque all three. Old woman, son, son's wife. The wife eases her buttocks against the dresser. The scarlet light touches her flimsy floral nightdress that is barely ample to enfold her wide hips and her large jiggling breasts.

As Dáibhí stands and makes to move away, his mother's intense voice forces him to a stop. "Turn your back on me, Jack Furey? If you do that I'll ask God's mother to strike you. The child is all yours. And mine!" Whinging a little: "Comfort me now. I got no education, only the milking of cows." Then, "Walk away from me is it? That the Almighty God may blast your limbs and blind your eyes forever. You've wronged me sorely, Jack Furey. And may God pay you off for it!"

Swaying gracefully and sobbing the old woman goes to her room.

Josie slowly raises her hand to the dresser. Takes a cigarette pack off a shelf. Lights a cigarette. Eases her body against the dresser. Her eyes fast upon her husband, she draws deep on the cigarette so that the tip glows. After a long silence, "You should go to bed," she says in a quiet tone of voice. Dáibhí continues to stand looking out the window.

The woman laughs dismissively. "She got a notion of the schoolmaster when they were both young," she says. "Now that she's doting it's coming back to her. There's no substance to it.

Let's go to bed."

Dáibhí goes to the mirror. His fingers touch his face. "She was a clever bitch to hide it all these years," he says quietly.

"She's more than that!"

Loudly. "She's a sly bitch in heat in the June woods. She has left me a bitter legacy at the end of her days."

Josie makes an amused sound in her nose.

"She has given you a knife to wound me," Dáibhí adds.

The wife pours milk into a glass. Alternately she draws on the cigarette and drinks from the glass. Then, "You're as dumb as the beast you struggled with all day."

"Use the knife!"

"I have a weapon with point and edge to it. But if you think that's something I'd like to use, you know little of a woman's mind. Somehow ... "

"Somehow?"

"I feel better for hearing what she said."

"You feel better for having a grip on me."

"Not that."

"What so?"

Sip and draw. Draw and sip. "It's not easy to put it into words. It's a riddle to which every woman knows the answer. By her feelings alone! And one which no man born can understand. Day after day listening to your mother almost drove me mad. Now it's different. I'll never put a hard word on her again."

"I'd like to drag the vessel that bore me out of her body."

"Aye! And by that same prove that you're Furey's get and no mistake. Prove it more by your hard mind than by your dark features."

The woman drinks the last of the milk. She sets the empty glass on the ledge of the dresser. She pads forward to ensure that the old woman's bedroom door is closed then moves to mid-kitchen. As she stands in silence the outline of her body is edged with the glow of the lamp. Her full breasts idle as she draws the last of the cigarette and moves to quench its end on the range-top. As again she speaks, her voice is all the more trenchant since, though accusatory, it still holds its balance.

"You too walked away from me in the wood of life! With these eyes I begged you to comfort me in my lonesome times. You were struggling with the bull of pride. You laughed and walked off through the trees."

As a sigh is heard from the bedroom Josie blurts, "She was game!"

"Game?"

"Game to carry that load all these years. And hold her head high! Underneath it, she was a full woman!" The thin ice of control almost breaks as the woman continues. "So, Furey or Flanagan, or whatever you choose to call yourself, if you breathe a word of this to her or anyone alive I'll gash your windpipe in the dark. In matters like this you're nothing to me. In matters like this she's more a mother to me than she is to you. Blood sister as well! And she's the truest daughter that a womb e'er bore. Me and you aren't fit to blacken her shoes. I'll mind her and humour her and tend her from now until the day she dies. So heed me now!"

Her splayed bare toes gripping the floor the woman prowls the kitchen. She stops to say: "Never to be mentioned again! Never! But whenever in the woods I see the grass bruised after the bodies of struggling lovers, I'll speak her name. For she's woman, faulty woman, and she's me!"

The faint sound of prayer, or of singing, comes from the bedroom. After a pause Josie plods to where her husband now sits. His elbows are on his thighs and his head is bowed on his hands. She stands behind him. Her breasts respond tremblingly as she speaks sharply. "Stir up the fire! Put the kettle on the range. Hot whiskey will dull her thoughts. And ours as well."

A faint pity-smile touches her lips. Her work-swollen hand goes out and roughly caresses her husband's shoulders and head. Suddenly arch, "What I've heard makes you somehow richer in my eyes!" Then, cuffing him gently about the ear, she adds, "Throw it from you! What is it but the world's turning wheel?"

On a shift of breeze the noise of the stream asserts itself. A cow lows softly over the darkening fields.

⟪ THE TALLYSTICK ⟫

(i)

I don't suppose that at my age I shall ever leave Ireland to visit the United States: nevertheless I shall always retain a special affection for Upper New York State together with its orchards, as it was conveyed to me in my boyhood in the quiet narration of my grand-uncle Peter Hennessy.

The Catskills and Lake George, Troy and Rome, Delaware Valley and Mohawk River - these places I continue to picture as they appear in the Fall. Then the wide landscape resembles the palette of a careless artist, its colours blue, orange, black and pale violet dominated by the yellow-green and bright red of ripe apples.

And whenever I see apples ranged in a shop window of one of my neighbouring market towns I am reminded of the old man and his unique tallystick.

The story of the apples and the tallystick I pieced together from old Peter's telling as he eked out his final years on a rocking-chair in front of the little cottage he had built in a corner of my father's land. Some scraps of the jigsaw, however, owe a debt to my youthful imagination. The tale also reveals why the taciturn sandy-haired old man, then in his late eighties, seemed constantly seated facing the northern sky. It also explains why I never saw a book or a newspaper in his hands.

[33]

In the sixties of the last century, Peter Hennessy, then eighteen or nineteen years of age, having tired of working as a farmer's boy in south-west Ireland, emigrated to the United States. First he worked as a longshoreman on the wharves of New York, but the din of the docks, added to the menace of great loads swinging above his head, had upset him - accustomed as he was to the peace of the Irish countryside. So after a time he gathered his few belongings and began to walk northward out of the city and into New York State.

He walked for several days, sleeping rough in barns and outhouses, until at last, reaching the brow of a hill, he saw below him the spread of a vast apple-growing area.

It was then full Fall, and the sight of the immense bounty of fruit almost dazzled the young Irishman. He could not help contrasting the ripe orchards stretching to the horizon with the wizened fields of home where the salt sea air had twisted every thorn tree into deformity and where, too, the apple was a rarity.

The loaded trees in the gentle undulating plain with, at intervals, knolls like female breasts and brooks like twists of silver paper, elegant weatherboard farmhouses, high-hipped red or grey barns, their ridges occasionally straddled by cupolas, white ranch-fencing lost and found in the highly coloured foliage with here and there the pale blue or grey façade of a church - Peter Hennessy must have remained for a long while on the crest of that hill deep in contemplation, the afternoon sun bright on his freckled face.

From that moment until the day he died my grand-uncle Peter was in service to the apple. I do not know what varieties he had to do with in the United States though I seem to recall names like Big Red and Yellow Northern Spy, but thanks to him, through me, even the youngest of my grandchildren can appreciate the taste of wine in Yellow Newton, can count the five knobs on Delicious, and admire the green and white translucence of Transparent.

John Henry Donaldson - that was the name of the fruit farmer who employed young Peter. With this man or his son he remained during his total stay of well over forty years in the United States.

The Tallystick

Farming in Upper New York State at that time was carried on in almost pioneer conditions. I remember my grand-uncle telling me that when the sow came in season she wandered off into virgin forest to mate with a wild boar, later to return with a litter of sucking-pigs behind her. "What did she eat while she was away?" I asked. "Apples!" Peter said shortly. "That was what gave American bacon its special flavour."

At first Peter was helper to an old handyman employed in fencing newly acquired land. He had to fell young trees, split posts, saw and plane planks - work considered quite simple. One day, when the older workman was off on some errand, Mr Donaldson asked Peter to take over on his own. Peter made such a good job of the fencing assigned him that from that day forward the farmer set him doing ordinary joinery and cooperage. This included the making of the boxes and barrels in which the fruit was stored.

Meanwhile, Peter's knowledge of apples as a crop increased. The sowing of young trees in virgin clay, the subsequent caring for the saplings, the pruning and spraying, the precautions against disease and insects, the anxiety resulting from changing conditions of weather ranging from frost and snow to storm, flood, drought and overpowering heat, the wonder of bloom, the formation and ripening of fruit, all came to a climax at harvest-time, when casual workers, young and old, canvas bags slung from their shoulders, climbed step-ladders in the orchards to gather the great harvest. After the careful handling of the picked fruit came the carting to the high barn filled with boxes, barrels and shelving. There the smell of apples and raw cider was almost overpowering.

All these operations conditioned the cycle of Peter Hennessy's year.

Harvest-time too meant that the barn was loud with the haranguing of traders, hucksters and agents of exporters, all bidding and counterbidding in a medley of languages, the lingua franca being, for my grand-uncle, initially, as for the others, a type of broken English. On the business level there was, at times, the withholding of supplies against a possible price rise, to be followed perhaps by a quick release of fruit if the market eased. But all in all this time of year was marked by the hurry and scurry of man, vehicle and beast in the yard before the barn - to be followed in its season by the ease of winter when the apple trees dropped their paper leaves and, covered in frost and snow, sank into a spectral sleep.

Winter for Peter was a season of joy; the house smelled of apple-wood and maple fires, of hops and tobacco, of aromatic cedar branches laid under carpets, while, in the kitchen, maple syrup was poured on hot biscuits, pancakes and muffins as the hired girls, their comings and goings reflected in silverware, prepared a banquet of turkey flesh, lemonade, grapes and plums, butter and sausages, chicken pies and spare ribs. On the snowpiled landscape outside the single movement was that of a bobsleigh drawn by oxen.

Winter also gave Peter the opportunity of going over the furniture of the old house - a task he relished. He could often be found in one of the outhouses repairing or polishing a large piece banished from the farmhouse as being out of fashion or cumbersome.

(ii)

The fruit farmer himself, Mr Donaldson, as I saw him through Peter's eyes, was a delicate white-haired widower; he was also a resolute man who lived alone except for the coming and going of his scholarly son. Father and son entrusted the rough and tumble of buying and selling to a huge Dutch overseer called Willem who ruled over orchards, yard and barn as if with a rod of iron.

Enthroned in the barn, Willem dipped a quill pen in a cut glass inkwell to enter the details of a transaction in a large account book.

I can see this man quite vividly in my imagination - his visored cap perched on his cropped head, his baggy dark blue clothes billowing above resounding shoes, his massive bite as he plunged an apple into his mouth, the crunch of his millstone teeth, his single swirl of the apple pulp over his tongue, then finally his trenchant spit to the barn floor. When not directly occupied with rough joinery Peter often lent a hand to the Dutchman to sort out the turmoil of the barn.

Big Willem, however, having drunk two bottles of gin at a sitting, died as a result of a fall from a horse. Mr Donaldson then asked Peter to take on the job of overseer with emphasis on the management of the barn, the sale of produce and the keeping of accounts. Peter was slow to come to a decision; the post was a responsible one. After a sleepless night the conjoined smells of apples and old wood moved him to accept. He was roughly thirty-four or -five at the time but his solemn appearance must have made him look older.

Peter's first act as overseer was to remove a long mahogany sideboard from its place of exile in an outhouse and place it in a commanding position inside the double doorway of the apple barn. He ensured that the large piece of furniture did not obstruct the passage of wagons and carts as they brought the boxed and barrelled fruit to its appointed place on the shelves. Behind this impressive counter, which he had polished until the wood had reverted to its original rich colouring, Peter presided with dignity.

For the first harvest the traders came and went as before. Only one month's credit was allowed. The second year, a minor disagreement occurred when a man called Ankatel Webster, a trader of substance who had always received extended credit from his comrade tippler, the Dutchman, queried the correctness of the amount Peter submitted. Ankatel asked to see the account book; this he maintained would solve the dispute.

Peter refused to show the book. Eventually, and with poor grace, Ankatel paid what Peter claimed was due. The next harvest was one of abundant fruit so that Webster bought a large number of barrels, later returning some varieties and taking others, with the result that the account became complicated. When payment was due, Webster refused to pay what was demanded of him, alleging that he was being wronged in the tally by some hundred barrels. He raised his voice in the yard so that the traders and fruit-pickers gathered round to listen.

Again, Peter was challenged to produce the account book as

invariably the Dutchman overseer had done in similar circumstances. My grand-uncle again refused. The buyer continued to bluster but Peter remained calm. But as his honesty was being publicly impugned his sensibilities must have been wounded. The incident ended with the angry buyer storming out of the barn, leaping onto his own wagon and lashing his horse forward. As the animal thundered off, Webster shouted that he'd be damned if he paid a cent of the amount Peter claimed was due.

That evening, when Peter, as was his wont, had gone into the parlour of the house with the day's takings he told Mr Donaldson of the incident.

"You have an account of the transactions?" the fruit farmer asked.

"Yes, sir."

"You can testify to it - even in court?"

"Yes, sir."

Old Mr Donaldson reflected for a while. Then, "I shall write to Mr Webster tomorrow giving him a further week to pay. If he fails to do so within that period of time I will bring him to court."

Webster's lawyer disputed the correctness of the amount claimed. Mr Donaldson then placed the matter in the hands of his lawyer. Legal proceedings were begun.

On the eve of the day of the hearing the fruit farmer sent for Peter.

"We are to appear in court tomorrow, Peter."

"Yes, Mr Donaldson."

"You are certain that your reckoning is correct?"

"Yes, sir."

"I understand that you have not made any entries in the old account book."

"No, sir!"

"I gather that you keep the accounts in your own way. The manner in which you do so may not be formal but you will be pressed in court to present some proof. You understand?"

"Yes, sir."

"I don't mind how tattered your notebook is so if you let me see it now it might spare us embarrassment tomorrow."

Peter paused. "Very well, sir," he said at last. Then, politely indicating that the other should follow him, he led the way to the barn, threw open the double doors and walked to the back of the long sideboard. There he pointed to a series of notches, crosses and gates chiselled on the plain wood at the back of the improvised counter.

Mr Donaldson walked up and down examining the notchings. They appeared as a series of corrals, in which were designs and diagrams. There were also some crude representations of faces and profiles. As a unit, the fretted wood could have passed as something unearthed from an Egyptian tomb.

Peter pointed to one enclosure more complicated than the others. "The Webster account," he said. "The number of barrels received, those returned. The variety, date and hour. The totals."

"Can you explain all this to the judge?" Mr Donaldson asked.

"Yes, sir."

"Very well! See to it that the sideboard is placed on a wagon and discreetly taken to the courthouse yard after dark this evening. Have the piece covered with canvas until the time comes to unveil it as evidence."

(iii)

The courtroom was crowded. Having been sworn in, Peter gave his evidence in a restrained voice. He spoke from memory, stating that so many barrels of such and such a variety of apples had been taken by Mr Webster on such and such a date, with so many barrels returned on another. While Peter was speaking the judge jotted down some figures.

Ankatel Webster followed. He strongly denied the correctness of the amount claimed. Reading from a greasy notebook he gave figures of his own which yielded a total considerably less than that given by my grand-uncle.

The defending lawyer now began to cross-examine Peter.

He began in a conciliatory tone of voice. Name, age, experience of overseeing, knowledge of identifying varieties of apple crop, bushel and barrel prices? The court knew that this was skirmishing. Suddenly the lawyer asked to see Peter's account book.

"There is no account book as such," my grand-uncle said in a level voice.

"No account book?"

"As such."

There was a murmur in the crowded room. The judge struck the bench with his gavel.

"What do you mean, sir?" the lawyer thundered. "Are there not accepted norms and standards of accounting? Are there not words and integers which when entered in a ledger indicate dates, purchases, returns, prices, quality, quantity, deductions and totals?"

As Peter sat in silence the lawyer leaned forward; he then spoke with something of triumph in his voice.

"Why beat about the bush, Mr Hennessy? I submit that as a result of the failure of your parents to send you to school in the country of your origin, you are wholly illiterate? And, as such, you are unable to keep even the simplest of accounts?"

A hush fell upon the courtroom.

Peter raised his head. He looked through the great window that admitted the light of the northern sky. He looked down at his fingers. "Your honour," he said to the judge, "you will allow me to answer in my own way?"

"Yes, indeed!"

"It may take some time?"

"Proceed."

My Uncle Peter then began: "Your honour, gentlemen of the court, my dear employer and his sterling son, neighbours, friends and customers, if I can neither read nor write, nor keep an account in the manner mentioned by the learned lawyer, it is not the fault of my parents.

"My father died in the first year of the Great Hunger: he was found dead in a ditch with grass on his lips. I was an infant at the time. Six months later, on a bitter February day, a gentleman stepped down from his coach at a stone bridge and turned over the body of a young woman with the point of his shoe. The turning of the body broke the grip of an infant's lips on the nipples of the corpse. The infant rolled over to the road and made the noise of a kitten. The infant was my brother. If I am as I am, it is because of the story of my people and the custom of the tallystick."

With a gesture of impatience the defending counsel half rose. The judge signalled him to resume his seat.

"When I was a boy in Ireland the language of the uncle who so kindly reared me was Irish. Neither he nor my brother, who was brought up in the workhouse, nor any of my cousins understood English. I heard a scholar say that Irish was brought by the Celts from that part of the world between the Black and Caspian Seas. Our forefathers, it seems, were restless people - they moved westward in search of a destined island. After centuries of wandering they reached the island promised them by their druids. With them they brought a knowledge of iron and enamel, of poetry and wonder-tales. There they knew a Golden Age."

The defending lawyer looked about him in derision.

"In eleven and sixty-nine the strangers came," Peter went on. "Even since that day, over seven hundred years ago, there has been bad feeling between our people and the strangers. My people became slaves. Our wonder-tales were mocked, our language was outlawed. The head of a priest and the head of a wolf carried the same price tag. The schools came under distant control. When I went to school for the first time and the schoolmaster asked me my name in English, I said, 'Seventy years, sir,' instead of 'Seven years' which I had ready on the tip of my tongue. Everyone laughed, including the other scholars to whom I had never spoken anything but Irish outside the school. The master came to me where I stood trembling. He hung the tallystick about my neck."

"Explain this tallystick," the judge ordered.

Before Peter could answer, Webster's counsel was on his feet. "I object, your honour," he said. "I cannot see how a recital of historic woes is relevant to the present case."

"Overruled!" the judge said. To Peter, "Go on!"

"The tallystick was a piece of timber twice the length of your middle finger; it was the thickness of a child's wrist. A piece of cord was threaded through a hole at one end of it: this cord was long enough to go round a child's neck. If a child was found speaking Irish in the school, one of the other children, an Irish speaker too, and as often as not the son of a neighbour, being encouraged to inform, would put up his hand and say, 'He's spakin' Oirish, surr'. The schoolmaster'd then take out his penknife and cut a notch on the tallystick. 'One!' he'd say and thump the stick back against the child's breast. So on through the day. As the tally grew, for children were taught to spy even in the muddy playground, the master'd cut four notches side by side and then cut the fifth notch sideways across the four so as to make it like a gate. This'd make it easy for him to count in fives.

"Once I got twenty notches. Before the end of the school day the master gave me a stroke for every notch, driving down on the palm of my hand with a sapling of ash. Often I learned to count in English when he sang out the number after every blow. But I could not then write down the numbers, nor can I to this day.

"Twasn't the schoolmaster's fault, sir, for power is power. But that's how we lost our language. That too is how I learned to keep tally."

The courtroom was silent as Peter paused. The judge nodded requesting him to continue.

"I was in school only five or six weeks in all. I ran away then and took service with a farmer. Often I had to walk nine miles driving cattle to a fair. Drenched to the skin I had to stand by the beasts on the open street of the town, aye, and maybe have to drive them home again in the evening if they failed to sell. This too without breaking my fast. At night if I was free I'd run to the nearby cabin where the neighbours gathered in to hear an old man telling rambling stories in Irish - tales of kings and queens and people turned into seals, salmon or honey-bees. I learned these stories by heart and so I grew to have a good memory: I'm maybe the last man that can recite these tales. So you see, sir, I am not what this good man said, in my sense of the word, illiterate."

The judge nodded, his eyes fast on my grand-uncle.

"Later, I fell in with a decent and learned farmer. He treated me well and taught me some joinery. He also taught Latin and Greek in his kitchen to scholars from the western coast who were preparing secretly to be off to Salamanca or Louvain and be ordained priests. Barefooted as they were - most of them grown men - I was jealous of their knowledge. But where was the use, sir, when I was dull of the alphabet? I saved up every penny and came to the United States. Here I found freedom and the right to look up at the northern sky. I was drawn to the beauty of apples, for they are often mentioned in the legends of my people. I also learned to speak some kind of proper English, mostly from listening carefully to Mr Donaldson and his son, for I have a good ear for sounds. So again, sir, though I cannot read nor write nor keep accounts in the ordinary way, in my sense of the word I claim to be a man of intellect and imagination."

"You may well be," the judge said quietly. "But more than that is needed if I am to give judgement in this case. Have you any way of proving the accuracy of your account?"

"I have a tallystick, sir," Peter said with a wintry smile.

"Where is it?" the judge asked.

"It's in the yard of the courthouse. With your permission we'll walk out into the daylight and I'll show it to you."

So, amid protestations and calls for order, those present moved out into the courtyard to where the sideboard stood shrouded in canvas. All gathered round it with the judge and lawyers to the front.

When the canvas was removed Peter Hennessy explained his method of keeping tally on the apple sales. He told what the notches stood for. He explained how he could tell the various apple-growers apart. The walking-stick with the hook - that represented Ivar the Swede; the profile with the beard, that was Heinrich the German; the hooky nose by itself, that was Ankatel Webster, the complainant in the case. Peter caught up a chisel and quickly cut lines of four and then a diagonal to indicate a gate of five. He stressed the fact that he had put no mark on the polished mahogany front of the article but only on the back which could be replaced at the year's end.

The judge led the way back to the courtroom. Everyone was silent as he gathered his gown around him, took his seat and began to deliver judgement.

The Union of States they were about to build, he said, was as yet young, and despite the worthy national aim of unity of language, purpose, will, loyalty and affection, tradition ensured that certain values of old Europe, its diversities and customs, were still relevant in the context of the New Continent.

"Down the centuries," he went on, "numeration has taken many forms. The Roman centurion counted his soldiers passing a given point by throwing varicoloured pebbles into a helmet. The ordinary Roman evolved the numbers we see on an old clockface from a simple representation of fingers and hands. The Chinese did it by brushstrokes. In its world connotation, reckoning was, at times, arbitrary - even bizarre - and varied from country to country, even from tribe to tribe. There is nothing exclusive about the Arabic numerals in common international usage today which have evolved from the counting of notched angles. Thus, Mr Hennessy's method of keeping accounts, personal and antiquated as it is, appears to me to be admissible. Accordingly, I give judgement for the amount claimed by Mr Donaldson and award him the full legal costs of the case."

(iv)

Peter Hennessy spent over twenty years in Upper New York State on the occasion of his first visit, remaining all this time in the employment of the Donaldsons. Despairing of a future for his own country, he became an American citizen at the end of the required term of residence. Rumours then reached him of a ferment among the farmers and smallholders of Ireland who sought to be owners of the land which, as tenants, they held at the whim of an absentee landlord. So Peter returned home. He found his native barony afire with agrarian unrest: a secret society called the Moonlighters shot bailiffs, maimed cattle and burned mansions to the ground.

Always a man of peace, yet conscious of the need for social and political change, Peter founded in his native place a branch of the National Land League and was elected its first chairman.

He had never learned to read or write but had mastered the art of scrawling his name in such a manner as passed for careless scholarship. His day in court had given him confidence and a further sense of authority. As League Chairman he could speak with the borrowed voice of Mr Donaldson - or the judge. This tone of voice he used to memorable effect when welcoming to his native area national leaders such as Davitt and Parnell.

The local secretary of the League was a spoiled priest. Whenever a letter came addressed to the Chairman, the little secretary snatched it away, so that Peter's deficiency was never exposed. Although all present were aware of it, it was never referred to.

When reading the minutes of the previous meeting, the secretary invariably ended his recital with a sentence which the local people still like to declaim: "Mr Peter Hennessy, our esteemed Chairman, presided over the proceedings with his usual firmness, tact, competence, accuracy, courtesy and fluency so that every member present had ample opportunity of presenting his views in the certainty that they would receive an unbiased hearing and full consideration."

While this sentence was being read, my grand-uncle, aloof as ever, would purse his lips and nod in a judicial manner as if he were about to deliver judgement in an important case. Although his Land League activities had made him suspect in Government circles the authorities of that day never interfered with him - this because of his American citizenship.

On the occasion of his first return home he remained in Ireland for ten years; during this time he acquired the site of a cottage on the farm that is now mine from my grandfather, his brother, once the infant unrolled from the clasp of the dead mother. Meanwhile, he ensured that the sapling Land League he had planted sent down sturdy roots. However, the death of Parnell and the dissension that accompanied that leader's final days troubled Peter Hennessy sorely.

Then a letter came informing my Uncle Peter that Mr Donaldson had died and that the son was now owner of the farm. The young man asked Peter to return to New York and take charge of the orchards. A sailing ticket was enclosed in the letter. Peter returned to the United States at once. He remained at his post for a further span of almost twenty-five years, finally returning to Ireland to end his days.

Peter Hennessy lived to see two-thirds of the tenant farmers in Ireland become owners of the land they had previously held so precariously. In his very old age I asked him why he had gone back to the United States immediately the son had requested him to do so. At the time of my asking the old man was seated at his cottage door with the light of the northern sky on his face and the backdrop of apple trees in fruit behind him. I saw what was probably the second smile of his life flit across his face. He took his time about replying.

"I couldn't refuse Master Donaldson," he said. "As I entered the courtroom on the day of the trial, the young man, just home from Harvard College, called me aside and whispered in my ear.

"Peter!" he said. "The judge's father, an old man who lives with him, comes from a village in the mountains of Middle Europe. I happen to know that the father can neither read nor write. Yet I have overheard the judge claim that in any sense of the word his father is a man of intellect and imagination."

🍂 THE TELESCOPE 🍂

When the train came to a halt at Heuston Station the man and woman descended awkwardly from the carriage.

From the self-conscious way in which the middle-aged couple moved about each other, and from the new but out-of-fashion clothes they wore, it was obvious that they had been married that morning. It was still more obvious from the way they surreptitiously glanced about them, pretending not to wince at the traffic din, that they were hill people from the south-west who had never been in Dublin before. The bridegroom carried the two cheap travelling cases, holding them out well from his sides as if they were buckets of milk. Passing the ranked buses at the station's end he led the way out into the city streets.

It was four o'clock in the afternoon of a late autumn day.

"Have you some place for us to stay?" the bride asked quietly.

"There are plenty of places to stay," the bridegroom said in a stolid tone of voice.

"Will we take a bus? Or a taxi?"

"We'll see."

"Is O'Connell Street down that way?"

"North, south, east, west - aye, O'Connell Street is down river. We'll walk for a while 'till we get our bearin's."

Hugging the walls they walked along the south quays in the direction of the city centre. When they came to the mouth of a street that led southwards off the quays the man stood for a while and gazed intently into it. His scrutiny ended, he walked resolutely on.

"Is it for a hotel you're looking when you stop at them streets?" the bride asked.

"It isn't."

"What is it so?"

"I have me eye out for three brass balls."

"A pawnbroker, is it?"

"The very thing!"

"And what would you want with a pawnbroker?"

"I'll tell you when we see one. You'll have to pick up your legs - they'll be all closed before we know where we are."

She picked up her legs and, keeping close to the walls of the warehouse and shops, both trundled on. They tended to cringe as the buses roared and hurtled past them on the roadway.

"New shoes are hard on the feet," she said. "The streets are hard too."

"We'll find a pawnbroker's soon."

"Wouldn't it be better to make sure of a hotel first?"

"Hotels are plentiful! Pawnshops are scarce! There's a street here in Dublin that's full of hotels. It's called Harcourt Street."

"The hotels might be full."

"If you don't get a room in one, you'll get it next door. That's what they're there for - hiring out rooms to the likes of you and me."

"I daresay you're right."

"They'll be damn glad of our custom hoping that we'll tell the lads at home that come up to Dublin for hurling and football matches."

They walked resolutely on.

"What would you want in a pawnshop?" she asked at last.

"I want a telescope!"

"A telescope?"

"Aye!"

"I thought 'twas only people at sea used telescopes."

"Anyone can use a telescope! It's for bringing things that are faraway close up to your eyes."

"I know that! And what would you want a telescope for?"

He set the bags down on the pavement and looked at her in amazement.

"Were you never at our house in broad daylight?" he asked sternly.

"'Twas always dusk or dark when I was at your house."

"Well if you were in the house where you and me will spend the balance of our days and if you looked out our front door at the crack o' dawn or in broad noon or when the sun is going down in the west, you wouldn't ask a question like that!"

"Why wouldn't I?"

"Because the finest view in all Ireland is from the front of our house."

"Is it now?"

"Standing in front of our door you can see north to the Aran Islands, east to the Broadford Hills, south to the Paps of Killarney and west to the mouth of the Shannon River. The name of our townland is Knocknareirk - which means the hill of the view."

"'Twas always dark or dusk when I was in your house," the bride repeated.

"Almighty God woman, when I have the telescope, nothing will stir in the valley of the Meelin River but I'll be able to spot it. I'll be cocked up there with an eye on me like a hawk."

"'Twill be handy so - the telescope?"

"Handy! I'll be able to pinpoint the postman on his rounds. The houses he calls to and the one he passes. The doctor's white car - I'll be able to tell who's ailing for miles around. The vet - I'll know who has a cow sick. The priest of a First Friday! Yanks in the summer! The inseminator's car - no need to hang out the red rag when the heifer is in - and on a clear day I'll be able to read the time on the steeple clock in Ballygarret. And then you ask me why I want a telescope!"

"You should have explained it to me before now."

"Since I was the big of a bee's knee, I promised myself, that when

I'd set foot in Dublin, the first thing I'd buy would be a telescope."

"Couldn't you buy one in a shop?"

"And pay five times the price for it! You must think I'm an ape!"

"You know more about these things than I do!"

"You said it there! In a port town like Dublin there are piles of drunken sailors and broken-down sea-captains selling parrots and telescopes for drink in the slack periods of the year. And I'm going to lay my hands on a telescope supposing the cat went to pound!"

They trundled on and on.

"I'm wall-falling with the hunger!" she said at last. "I hope to God we see the brass balls soon."

"We'll see 'em soon!"

"Today is Saturday! Wouldn't Monday do to get the telescope?"

"Isn't Monday a Bank Holiday!"

"I forgot that!"

"And aren't we facing home early on Tuesday morning?"

"Wouldn't it be better to ask directions?"

They stopped a man approaching them and asked where they could find a pawnshop. Too late they realised that the man was tipsy.

"Are yez busted so soon?" he shouted gleefully with a sudden lurch sideways into the closed doorway of a small pub. They didn't quite grasp the import of his comment nor the reason for his hilarity, so taking up the bags, they walked resolutely on. A glance over his shoulder told the bridegroom that the tipsy fellow, in the intervals of laughing and shouting, was pointing across a bridge as if urging them to cross to the quays on the other side of the River. This they did, and presently they found themselves in a maze of streets north of the Four Courts. Here they traipsed round and round like weary squirrels in a cage.

At last they saw the three brass balls shining in the waning sunlight. The sight roused their lagging spirits. It was some minutes after five o'clock. They mounted the mica-winking granite steps and entered what looked like a huge confession box. Alas, the pawnbroker had no telescope: he had had an excellent one for almost a year without an enquiry and then he had three enquiries in one day. He directed them to another pawnshop half a mile deeper into the city.

The bridal pair staggered on. It was almost closing time when again three beautiful golden spheres glistened above them in a dark street. Aye, the man in the pawnshop, who was about to shut the door, had a telescope, a powerful glass which opened to what appeared an enormous length. The bridegroom's eyes glittered when he saw it but bargaining was in his blood so he hid the fire in his eyes.

"Let me see the tripod!" he said.

The pawnbroker said he had no tripod.

"'Tisn't much use to me without a tripod," the bridegroom said shortly. "That article is mighty weighty. How am I to hold it?"

The bride was now resolved to play her part.

"Aye," she said. "It's useless to him without a tripod."

The pawnbroker snapped the telescope shut and replaced it on the shelf. He told them he was on his way to Wexford for the weekend and he made as if to come outside the counter to see them off the premises.

"It's like buying a beast with no legs!"

The bridegroom's complaint fell on deaf ears. The pawnbroker cut finesse to ribbons by asking them if they wanted the telescope or not.

"Of course I want a full telescope, not a half or quarter of one!"

The pawnbroker said that finished it but, of course, it did not. The countryman had a style of bargaining that could fairly be called mesmeric for a series of random remarks now seemed to transfix the man inside the counter. At long last, the money lying on his palm, the pawnbroker sighed deeply as the pair went out the door.

The couple now headed south, the bride carrying the two bags and the groom devoting all his attention to the safe carriage of the telescope. After a while she realised that he was again peering into alleyways.

"What is it now?" she wailed.

"I'm looking for a narrow alleyway."

"What do you want a narrow alleyway for?"

"To see the stars!"

"There won't be stars for a long while yet."

"Stars are always there! By day and by night! They are obliterated by the light of the sun."

"Is that right?"

"That's right! In a dark alleyway the sunlight is cut out and through my telescope I can see the stars in the daytime the same as if it were black night."

In the middle of the darkest alleyway he could find, he stood and aimed his telescope at the sky. She set the cases on the ground and sat on the edge of one of them. He began to murmur "Orion, Venus, Mars, the Plough, the Plei-a-des." Presently a messenger boy leaped off his bicycle and began to stare up at the heavens. Before long a knot of people had gathered around the stargazer. A ribald old lady accused him of watching women going to bed. A Garda squad car stopped at the mouth of the alleyway. The crowd melted. The bride took up the cases and stomped off. Reluctantly the bridegroom followed.

More by instinct than anything else, they reached the street of hotels. The fifth hotel they tried had a room. He was inclined to bargain about the price but she elbowed him to silence. They followed a maid upstairs to a low room in a converted attic. The maid never took her eyes off the telescope: she offered to carry one of the cases but the bride refused to part with any item of her burden. After the maid had switched on the light and closed the bedroom door behind the pair, she stood in the narrow corridor outside. After a time she tiptoed closer to the door and listened.

Sitting on the double bed and facing the window the bridegroom tested the mattress by bumping up and down. His fingers then caressed the telescope. Darkness had gathered over the city; from the window there was only a view of the bulk of outbuildings. The man opened the telescope and, looking through the wrong end, laughed at the minuteness of the rose pattern on the wallpaper.

Slipping off her shoes the woman sat on the other side of the bed facing the small white door of the room.

"I got a bargain in that telescope!" he said at last.

"Aye!"

"You could search Ireland this minute and not find a telescope as good as that."

"I daresay!"

There was a long pause: then he asked:

"Are you very hungry?"

"I am."

"You wouldn't think of postponin' eatin' till the morning. We could have a right good feed of eggs and rashers in the morning. I'm after spending a hatful of money on this telescope. What do you say?"

She paused for a moment, then began to speak in a blotched ironic tone of voice.

"Sure we needn't eat any more while we're on our honeymoon! Nor when we go home but as little! Won't we have eatin' and drinkin' in the view from our doorstep? The postman for breakfast, the vet and the doctor for dinner and maybe the inseminator or the Paps o' Killarney for tea. We'd get right fat on that fare, so we would, and as for myself, I'll be wondering to the end of me days whether I married a man or a telescope."

He turned in amazement to view her.

Just then she began to wail. It began undramatically but the lamentation soon gathered strength from the sound of its own blubbering. A series of muted sobs deluded him into the belief that she was about to stop - this was seen as a ruse, for the expression of her grief climbed inexorably until it reached an impressive crescendo.

Suppressing his initial temptation to view the spectacle of his weeping spouse through his wondrous glass, the bridegroom slowly closed the telescope and, setting it down on the bed, walked around the bedstead to view his wife at closer quarters. Her sobbing increased as he approached her, and his placing of his arms around her seemed only to make matters worse. At last he drew her awkwardly towards him while she, pretending to be angrier than she really was, made a half-hearted effort to shake him away from her. In the little toing and froing that followed, the telescope rolled slowly along the coverlet of the bed and crashed to the floor.

Neither stooped to recover it. She was now clasped close against him and the graph of her sobbing showed signs of taking a downward turn. To his own astonishment the groom found himself mouthing endearments he didn't realise he knew; after a while their arms around each other, they began to reassure each other in half-finished blubbering sentences.

Listening outside the door, the maid who had leaped in fright at the crash of the telescope to the floor, now began to giggle. She placed her hand over her mouth to prevent herself from being heard; then, her laughter almost getting the better of her, she tiptoed softly down the stairs. There wasn't much of a view from a hotel window in the city, she told herself as she went, but what you heard inside more than made up for any deficiencies in this regard.

ꕷ AN ENDANGERED SPECIES ꕷ

(i)

The only movement discernible on the long main street of the town is the dancing of a polished pipehead protruding from the hall doorway of the Emporium.

The Emporium, directly opposite the Bank with its two plate-glass windows, one on each side of a wire mesh gate is closed this Sunday afternoon. On the long fascia-board above the shop windows on which the blinds are drawn, the name PJ O'SHEA in ornate lettering slightly peeling in parts, spans the width of the building. A date on a side scroll states that the establishment is over a century old.

Unexpectedly the head of the shop owner, Mr Patrick Joseph O'Shea himself, appears in profile. The hall doorway on which he stands is a step above the level of the slightly sloping street. The pipe in his mouth continues to jig as he glances upstreet to the tops of faraway frosted hills, then downstreet to the dumpy steeple of the parish church.

Fine bloodveins enliven Mr O'Shea's thin cheeks: his polished toe caps, his black pin-striped suit, his stiff white collar and sober silver tie proclaim his status in the town. However, on closer examination, the cuffs of his jacket are seen to be a trifle frayed, but one would need to be a close scrutineer to detect this single flaw in an otherwise perfect presentation.

PJ O'Shea retreats into his hallway. A long-case clock ticks solemn approval. He removes the pipe from his mouth, clacks his false teeth and despatches a gentle but accurate puff of smoke in the direction of the street. His thin mauve lips then gather a gob of spittle; this he casts into the clay around a plant in the brass jardinière on the hall side-table. On hearing a faint sound from the street, he turns.

A low-sized man wearing a soiled cloth cap and a grey woollen muffler emerges from the archway of the lane beside the Bank. He looks furtively up and down before moving across the road. The newcomer waddles on soft-soled shoes. Reaching the opposite pavement he peers around the doorpost of the hallway of the Emporium. Deep in the hall the draper takes the pipe stem from between his teeth. "Ah, Bowler," he says, "There you are!"

Touching the peak of his cap Bowler Mawe leans against the door jamb. His eyes are crafty and conspiratorial.

"Nice weather, Mr O'Shea," he says cautiously.

"A bit nippy, Bowler."

"That's what it is, sir."

"You busy these times, Bowler?"

"Tippin' away. If I get a dry day I'll finish the tarrin' of your shed."

"I know that. You got my message?"

Bowler looks sharply at O'Shea's face. He scouts upstreet. He nods, then asks, "They're not gone down yet, sir?"

"Not yet. Step into the hall." Bowler comes cautiously in. After a pause, "A boy, Mr O'Shea?"

"So I've heard. A boy." After a considered puff on the pipe; "You know what to do?"

"You can trust me, sir."

"You'll be discreet?"

Bowler raised a reassuring forefinger. "I'm always around the church at christenin' time," he says. "No one takes notice of Bowler."

"Good!"

Silence falls for a while. Then Bowler ventures, "That nephew of

yours takes after the Heffernans! The O'Sheas were sensible people."
Noting a frown on the draper's face, he adds inconsequentially.
"Meany's potatoes are balls of flour."

"I'll tell Mrs Rainey," the draper says airily.

"A good woman, Mrs Rainey. You were lucky to get such a fine
housekeeper after the Missus, God rest her, died. And a widow to
boot." The pipehead dances and chatters.

Bowler had darted to the doorway to glance up the street. "Stand
back," O'Shea ordered. Bowler obeyed smartly. His eyes on the
draper's face he said, "After the christenin' I'll say, 'God bless the
child.' And then by the way no harm, 'What did ye call him?'"

"As if it didn't matter!"

"As if it didn't matter."

"Get both Christian names. Don't ask my nephew Peter."

"Both I'll get. Peter - he knows how matters stand?"

"Word was sent."

"You made it clear, sir?"

"Crystal clear."

"Cards on the table?"

"Face upwards, Bowler."

"That ape of a wife of Peter's hasn't a splink. He's under her
thumb. She'd call the child Shep if she got her way - as if he was a
collie puppy. Any man with sense would jump at a chance like that
for his child. And if he did, the same name could stay above your
shop-door."

"PJ O'Shea. On the blinds. On the message bags. On the
billheads. Everything for the child if only the father ... as I say...
would do the proper thing."

"All for the child, sir?"

"I made it clear, Bowler. 'Tis no secret how I came by these
premises. My uncle Patrick - no family either - sent out word to my
father the day I was christened. 'Name the boy for me and in the
course of time all will be his.'"

"Couldn't be fairer, sir."

"This although the two brothers never got on well with each other. But my father swallowed his pride and named me Patrick Joseph. At fourteen years I was living here attending St Mark's and behind the counter on weekends."

"You worked hard, Mr O'Shea."

"I built it up when the place was signed over. Married a niece of my aunt-in-law Maria. Not an angry word between the pair of us ever."

"Did Peter sell the home place, sir?"

"Where I was born, Bowler. With its well under the whitethorn bush. And its apple trees beside the stream. And the print of the giant's foot on the rock. Sold it for a song - on the sly. But even with that I'm still a reasonable man."

"Where in America is he heading for?"

"Chattanooga."

Both men laughed at the strange name. The sound of a motor-car was heard approaching, its horn blowing as if in celebration. When Bowler made as if to peep out, "Get well back," Mr O'Shea snapped, the pipe dancing in his mouth. Both now stood in deeper shadow.

As the first of two cars passed the doorway the watchers saw the flash of white in its front seat. The second car had slowed down; its windows were lowered and beery jeers were directed at the hallway. The vehicle seemed crowded with red faces.

Mr O'Shea tightened his teeth on the lip of his pipestem so that it seemed it would break off. "The whole tribe! Neighbours and midwife too. They must have tanked up at Deasy's," Bowler said.

There was an uncertain silence. The draper recovered his poise. He smiled wanly. "Letting off steam," he said bravely. "If things go right today, as I think they will, Bowler, you and I will have a little celebration." The draper vaguely indicated the parlour upstairs. Finger to eyebrow by way of salute Bowler said, "I'm on my way, Mr O'Shea."

As Bowler made to step down on to the pavement, the pipe came out of Mr O'Shea's mouth. "Keep a sharp lookout for Ballbearings," he warned. "That little scut knows too much."

"Leave it to me, sir."

(ii)

Bowler waddles downstreet. The November sun blears through a frosty fog. The steeple of the church barely succeeds in piercing the low hung mist. Bowler slows his gait as he reaches the triangular area in front of the church. At the window of Devere's pastry shop opposite the church, he pauses, then stands. His eyes swivel upward although he knows that as yet, he cannot be seen from any of the windows above his head. Carefully he reconnoitres the yard of the church and the cars parked about it. He glances sidelong at the window of the pastry shop on which a dark blue blind is drawn: a white strip along the bottom of the window reads, "Bats need friends." "Bloody sure they do," Bowler sneers almost audibly.

Move on, he tells himself, then idly cross the street. Stop at Hanrahan's window and pretend to read the house blessing. Here I am: "Bless this house, O Lord we pray." Slow now, and steady. Ballbearin's eyes are boring through my back. Will he connect me with the christenin'? I'll stand where the mirror ... Holy You God, is that a twitch in the curtain of Ballbearin's window? Freeze for a minute.

I know he's there. Leanin' forward in his wheelchair, the bastard. Whether or not he knows my message will be known tonight when the nine o'clock pips sound on the radio. He'll be wearin' his dark red dressin'-gown. He'll have wheeled himself out through the French window at the back of the house and on to the flat roof. His bag of silver ballbearings will be beside him and his transistor in his lap. He'll snap his catapult a few times and then he's ready.

Oh boys, he'll be ready. He'll look down on the backyards spread below him with a main back road splitting the area in two. He knows the owner of every skylight and window. He knows the habits of the occupiers by reading the switching on and off of lights. He knows all about lovers and poor sleepers. He can identify topers emptying their bladders after midnight and tinkers testing the locks on back gates. He knows the bark of each yard dog and the yowling of each cat in the area. He reads the front by day, the back by night. When he wants to tell people that he knows he drives out onto the flat roof. Coming up to the news pips at nine o'clock he'll put a ballbearing in the leather. His lips will be thin and his eyes will be shinin'. He'll spot his target. With the last pip on the radio he'll draw back the leather. Then he'll fire. Whirr. Crack. Tinkle. Roll. Slat. Ballbearin' is watchin' ye all.

Thanks be to God my lane is out of his firing range. Know what I'd like to do with him? Bowler tells himself. I'd like to hoist the bugger out of his chair and hang him by the jawbone from one of the meat hooks outside Griffin's the butcher's. All he could see then was the wall. There I'd leave him squealin' and kickin' till he died. His Ma with her wild life! "Bats need friends." Isn't that hoor's ghost a bat? Does he need a friend?

Bowler is peering through the church railings, as if out of mild curiosity. A van drawn up at the kerb ensures that for the moment he cannot be seen by the watcher at the upper window of the pastry shop across the street. Bowler is still talking to himself. Not aloud. But his lips are moving.

Paudie Joe is a fool. His drapery shop is knackered. And still he can't cop on. Still sits in his office in the middle of the shop like a spider where there are no flies. Parcels to the train, how are you! The train itself is gone. Three boutiques in town and a Men's Only. Fashion parades in the hotel. Teenagers wearin' jeans and T-shirts. Nephew Peter is right to skip to America. Have his kid hang around for dead men's shoes? PJ should flog the shop while the goin' is good. To one of them chain outfits. Live then on the interest of his money. The man is a gom, picked and painted.

The November sunlight tries to gild Bowler's face under the greasy visor of his cap. The wind blows chill through the church railings as Bowler shuffles into the yard. In the porch he places his eyes against the horizontal slit of transparent glass in the leaded and mainly translucent partition within. He peers into the nave.

The Tallystick

The ceremony is almost at an end. As yet there is activity in the sanctuary where a knot of people are gathered. Old Mary Hynes the midwife holds the infant in her arms: the long tail of the christening robe shines as does the stained glass window above. Mary Hynes is like a grain-fed pigeon. Everybody is smiling. The Dean seems relaxed enough but does he realise what it means to PJ? I'm sure he suspects. Flashbulbs, virgin blue in colour, slice the sanctuary shade. Out in the US in days to come it'll be "Pictures of your christenin' day, son. A bitter winter day in stagnant Ireland. Good job we left."

The Dean shakes hands all round. A special word and smile for Peter. Ten to one on he knows Peter has flogged the farm. The parish clerk's eyes bulge. More camera flashes. A few minutes now to sign the books. If I don't get out on the street fast they'll land on top of me.

A low hoarse call from the taxi parked outside. An arm extends through the open window of the driver's seat. Fingers click. Like you'd call a dog, Bowler tells himself. He goes over to the vehicle. The driver's face is a sleepy red. The man puts the back of his hand to the corner of his mouth. A few spasms of laughter shake him before he speaks.

"Theobald," he says.

"Jesus!" from Bowler. "You sure?"

The scarlet face struggles. "Theobald Kenneth," the driver says at last.

"PJ will go off his nog."

"Theobald Kenneth O'Shee. 'Twon't be O'Shea any more."

"He couldn't do that!"

"That I may be dead! Two ee's in O'Shee. Chattanooga Choo-Choo!" The driver yields to what is almost an epileptic fit of laughter. Suddenly his face freezes. "Watch it!" he warns.

Bowler turns to find that the christening party has come out of the church. There are more photographs. Cries of "Stand in, Molly." "Smile let ye." and "Is my hair a show?" followed by more clicks and flashes.

"Bowler!" this in a rough clotted voice. Bowler turns. The infant's father is speaking from inside the church railings. The whites of his eyes are tinged with veins of blood.

"C'mere Bowler!"

"Ah, Peter."

The draper's nephew is fumbling inside the pockets of his jacket. He drags out a wad of notes, peels off a fiver and extends it through the bars. "Drink the health of Theobald Kenneth O'Shee," he says.

"I'll do that, Peter." A smiling Bowler shuffles forward to take the note.

The father withdraws his hand. "First, you'll deliver a message?"

"I will, I will."

"Tell Shivery Pipe from me that he can stick his shop where Jack stuck the shillin'."

"I'll do that, Peter."

"Tell him I'll send him a funny postcard from Chattanooga where we'll be welcomed by my mother's decent people. And not by the lousy O'Sheas."

"I'll tell him that too."

As Bowler's reaching fingers close about the treasury note, Peter O'Shea shouts, "Feck off now, you lousy spy!"

Bowler seems to shrivel a little as he walks away. He doesn't even bother to look up to see whether or not the curtain twitches. There are ups and downs to life. The fiver is an up: a twitch would be a down. He could feel a hurt as readily as the next man. But it didn't pay to take offence. Sticks and stones may break your bones ... Agree with everybody - that way lay fivers and the drinkin' of rum.

(iii)

Back up the long Main Street. Push in the half-open hall-door of the Emporium. The side door to the shop is open: PJ must be inside at the office. The needle in the barometer on the wall shows stormy. The tall clock clucks. What's it like to be a draper? he asks himself. Day after day caged behind a counter. Soft talk for the country

people. "How're ye all outside, Minnie?" "Class of a soft day, John."
Me? I shave corpses. Pass on tips on racehorses. Clip lawns, weed
graves, replace leaky washers on taps, whitewash yards, clean out
dry lavatories, sell day-old chicks. I once got a tenner for bringin' a
bunch of primroses to a dyin' woman. Paudie Joe is a prisoner.
Sentenced for life. And he doesn't even know it.

Bowler coughs. The draper comes sidelong out the narrow
doorway from the shop. He moves with deliberate slowness. Bowler
slips on his hangdog mask. PJ O'Shea takes his time about locking
the door. Turning, his dentures clack a question Bowler waits to be
asked directly.

"Well Bowler, what's the news?"

"Not good, Mr O'Shea."

"That so?" In a well-rehearsed tone of voice. "What did they call
the infant?"

"A queer class of name, sir."

"Yes?"

"Theobald Kenneth O'Shee."

"O'Shee?"

"It's American. Two ee's."

"The christian names again?"

"Theobald Kenneth."

"I see." The draper looks around for his pipe. Finds it on an
ashtray on the hall table. His fingertips tremble as they close about
the pipe bowl.

"You're sure?"

"Positive, sir."

The pipe between his teeth and his white hands tapping his coat
pockets for his tobacco pouch, "Tck, tck," the draper says, "Where do
they get such fancy names?"

"Unless it's Theobald Wolfe Tone. The patriot. At Bodenstown."

"Could be."

"Or the Temperance priest - what's this his name was?"

"Father Theobald Matthew. A Protestant name Theobald. Must
have been a foreign drop in the Matthews."

"They're right bastards. To call a child ... "

Before Mr O'Shea can enquire as to whom Bowler has in mind the two men glance out the door. Two motor-cars have stopped almost directly outside. There are confused cries of "Chattanooga," "Jack's shilling." "Lousy draper," and "Bowler the Bum." Then, their occupants still jeering and gibing, both vehicles pull away.

"Blackguards," the draper says quietly. To Bowler, "Close the door. Come along."

PJ leads the way up the stairway.

In the parlour a coal fire has burned low. There is a faint smell of must and camphor. A red carpet has given the floor the softness of a pine wood. On the sideboard, a back mirror doubling their presence, cut glass and silver wink in the faint firelight glow. Midway on the mantelpiece a clock under a glass dome presides over four gold-coloured balls semi-rotating in lieu of a pendulum. On a low table in the centre of the room three Sunday newspapers lie unopened. Mrs Rainey, the housekeeper, has everything in order before taking her afternoon off.

"Take a seat, Bowler."

Bowler sits rather gingerly on the edge of the settee.

He looks around him: he has never been in the parlour before. Surreptitiously he takes off his cap to reveal his bald head. A glance at the sideboard mirror which is on a level with his eyes rewards him with the reflection of his head and shoulders. The baldness of his head startles him somewhat. He drops the cap by the side of the settee and draws his palm across the top of his head. He glances over the arm of the settee to reassure himself that the cap is still there.

PJ has opened a corner cabinet. "Rum, Bowler?" he asks. Bowler gasps his acceptance.

"Jamaican, Bacardi or Kiskadee?" The draper's eyes hold a brave gloss of mischief.

"The sailor, sir."

"Anything with it?"

"Blackcurrant juice."

"Don't usually keep blackcurrant. Ah, you're in luck!"

A generous tot of rum is topped up with the juice. The draper holds up the glass to the windowlight before handing it to Bowler. "Must try that some day," he says. Then, "Let me see now. Crested Ten, Redbreast or Black Bushmills for myself? Bush it is!" He pours his whiskey neat. His back to the fire he raises his glass. "Your health, Bowler."

"Yours likewise, Mr O'Shea."

The two men begin to drink. For a time there is silence.

Then the draper begins to hum tunelessly. He breaks off with an unexpected chuckle.

"Chattanooga," he says.

"Theobald," from Bowler.

"Kenneth," from PJ O'Shea.

"O'Shee," says Bowler.

"Back of the hand to breeding."

"False grandeur, sir."

"On the knuckle, my friend." The draper then adds in a sterner tone of voice. "No children here, Bowler."

"If they won't make you laugh, they won't make you cry."

"Some truth in that, Bowler." After a pause, "The USA? Five floors up, a clothes-line and pulley. Mark my words, he'll be back."

"With his tail between his legs."

"Sip your drink, friend. Plenty where that came from. The afternoon is long."

Bowler looks over his shoulder at the room door. "She won't be back soon?" There is concern in his voice.

"Mrs Rainey. Close to nine o'clock ... What's it all for, Bowler?"

"As you say, sir, what's it all for?"

"A lifetime of honest trading. Gabardine, serge and tweed. Suit lengths with the best of trimmings. Shirts, socks, ties, blankets and shawls. My uncle sold the first Paisley green and black shawls in this locality. The wives of the net fishermen were proud to wear them. The best of money for salmon in the War years. The women got uppish. Drove off to the city for clothes. The salmon got the disease. Mills of God, Bowler. Do you know what an old woman said to me in the shop last year?"

"What was that, Mr O'Shea."

"She said, 'I had my very first coort under a Paisley shawl', bought at O'Shea's."

"I bet she enjoyed it."

"Be sure she did. Is the rum to your liking, Mr Mawe?"

"It's prime, Mr O'Shea."

"In shop, parlour or dining-room we kept the best. Your health, Bowler."

"Likewise yours, Mr O'Shea."

After a shaky refilling of glasses, O'Shea leaning back in his armchair and looking thoughtfully up at the ceiling says, "That Vincent de Paul Society does good work, eh?"

"Often gave me a hand, sir."

"That Cheshire place?"

"Deservin', sir."

"We'll see. Will I tell you what's really bothering that fellow?"

"Do that, sir."

"A man was telling me in the shop. An observant man who watched Master Peter at the Races. Along came two American girls. Big chests - Vitamin C. One had "Hi-Baby" printed on her T-shirt; the other had "Have Love-Will Share." Petereen couldn't get over it. Always talking about it."

"He'd let down the wing, sir."

"What wing?"

"Like a cock after a hen, Mr O'Shea."

"That's good!" The draper tee-hee'd. "He thinks that the USA is a land of loose morals," he added with some severity. "You follow me, Bowler?"

"All the way, sir."

"The USA is a land of climatic extremes."

"So I hear."

"Due to the Gulf Stream Ireland has a temperate climate. America?

In the summer his penis will dissolve in the heat. In the winter it will freeze up and break off like an icicle."

"Between me and you, sir, he's a bit of a clown."

The draper who had still been leaning back in his chair sat slowly upright. "What did you call him?" he asked, looking over his shoulder.

"A clown, sir. White face, red nose and rings around bulgy eyes."

"Recall your status," the draper snarled. "And mine! You're speaking about my flesh and blood!"

"I didn't mean to ..."

"I take offence. You're the town bum, Bowler. I'm its leading merchant. Don't overstep the chalk. Next thing you'll refer to me as Paudie Joe. Like your fellow laners."

"The last decade in my bead, Mr O'Shea." Bowler places his drink on the floor and gropes in the pocket of his jacket. "Will I play the bones, sir? And dyddle the Blackbird?"

Mr O'Shea seemed slightly mollified. Slowly leaning back, "Play, sir!" he says.

The rib bones between his fingers, Bowler clacks an erratic rhythm. After a time, he sings, "Dyddle oy toy, diddley oy toy ..." O'Shea's face grows less severe.

When the performance ended, "Sandwich?" Patrick Joseph O'Shea asked.

Bowler vigorously nodded his assent. Then, "'Twould be nice, sir."

"Go downstairs to the scullery. Wash your hands at the sink. Use the carbolic soap. There's a towel on a roller on the back of the scullery door. Use it. You'll find the Sunday roast in the green safe. Use a carving knife; don't cut off your stupid fingers with that electric carver. Don't hack the roast. Mrs Rainey detests a hacked roast."

"Yes, sir."

"Don't steal the cutlery. There's a sliced loaf - probably in the bin. Mustard on a shelf. Top compartment of the fridge - bring up some ice cubes in a tumbler. Make a few neat sandwiches. Salad and salad cream. Cucumbers - the lot. Bring them on a tray. You like chutney, Bowler?"

"Love it, sir."

"Bring that too. Don't break your neck on the stairs. Don't forget the red soap. Glasses will be replenished when you come back. Off with you now, Theobald."

"Yes sir, Kenneth!" Bowler salutes vaguely and sways off.

(iv)

When Bowler had gone downstairs PJ O'Shea took up one of the newspapers. Opened it awkwardly. His teeth chattered. His mind seemed elsewhere as he glanced at the headlines. Presently he set the paper down awkwardly. Came to his feet and topped up the tumblers. He walked unsteadily to a window, parted the curtains and looked down. A sidelong shower of weak sleet had begun to fall. He dropped the curtain and walked towards the fireplace.

Beside the mantel clock in an ornate frame of brass foliage was a full length photograph of a woman. The woman was wearing a long dark dress with two stripes running down its front. Her right hand rested on an ornamental table on which stood a tall white vase. The draper raised his glass to the woman in the photograph.

"Your good health, Joanna," he began aloud. "You were a fine comrade. But as the poet said, 'You never gave me children to spoil my sleep with cries.' Not your fault, my dear. Possibly mine. Fault is not the word. The matter doesn't arise." The draper sipped from his glass.

"That puppy sold the old place. Sent me word beforehand that he'd give the infant the old name if I gave him ten thousand pounds. Impertinence! I thought he was joking. Told him so. Now it's 'Chattanooga,' 'Hi-Baby,' Theobald and Kenneth. You never liked him, sweetheart? 'A dodgy chap,' you used to call him. 'Any O'Shea but him.' How right you were, old girl. How right indeed."

Again Joseph sipped the drink in his hand.

"You see me now, mate o' mine? Things are grim. Once upon a lovely time everything went smoothly. Trade was brisk. We kept up appearances, Joanna. Headed the list of the Christmas offerings. Mr

Patrick Joseph O'Shea, The Emporium, ten pounds. Money was money then. Paid our accounts on the nail. Were paid on the nail. No shoddy haberdashery. Our stock straight from Rylands of Manchester. Parcels to the station. Customers got a square deal. And a Christmas box. No bums in the parlour then. Your health, Joanna."

Responding to the murmur from upstairs, Bowler had left the scullery and was listening at the foot of the stairs. As the parlour door was a little ajar he caught the drift of what the draper was saying.

"Honourable days, Joanna. Honourable transactions. Commercial travellers - what did they say? 'You have the finest store in Munster, Mr O'Shea.' Wicker baskets brought to our door in the hotel cart. The Spanish donkey between the shafts. The traveller raising the oilcloth flaps to show us the samples. Let me whisper a secret Joanna - Big Ears is listening. Pincer movements now. Outfitters and boutiques on all sides. Borrowed time. Not yet short of money, though. Damned short of pride. Ah, the mantles and the millinery. The divine hats. Confections. Your two smart milliners in black dresses. White pipings. My male apprentices selected with care after enquiries. Bound them down not to open a shop later within ten miles. Had to be in bed in the attic by ten o'clock. Warned them against spirits and bad company. Those who became village drapers still turn up to thank me. In Lisdoonvarna Spa we stayed at the Premier Hotel. When we walked up the centre of the parish church on Sundays heads were turned in respect. The pony and trap to the seaside on Sunday afternoons. Bells ringing, harness shining as we drove along. At the proper times, I sipped whiskey; you preferred sherry, dry."

As Patrick Joseph strolled to shut the parlour door Bowler scurried back to the scullery. He heard the door close above his head. The draper was back at the photograph.

"What was it all for, Joanna? For the O'Sheas to finish up like a stream running into dry sand. Standards are down, my darling. It looks as if there will be an end to everything, even to hope. Before the bum comes stumbling up the stairs, Joanna, I'll whisper my secret fear." The draper looked around to make sure the door behind him was closed. Then in a whisper: "When the radio pips sound at nine o'clock tonight, the silver balls will dance on our roof. Public ridicule, my dear. The town will ring with the news tomorrow. Up to this, the roof dance was reserved for girls who became pregnant out of wedlock, or for men who lost a law case, or who bought a boycotted house - for all those it was fair game - or so we thought. I never thought it would happen to me, nor to the memory of you. Now we're on our way out ... out ... out... I raise my glass to you for the last time, my lovely single love. Your health, Joanna."

There was a fumbling at the parlour door. The draper turned. "Ah, Bowler. Steady old horse. Place the tray down there. Have you everything? Where's the ketchup?"

"You never said ketchup, sir."

"Don't contradict me, fellow. I distinctly said ketchup."

"'Twas chutney you said, sir. There it is."

"Mm. Perhaps you're right, old man. Chutney will do. 'Pray be seated,' said Maurice Magee. "By the by Bowler - any twitch out of that curtain? At the pastry shop?"

"He goes to bed about that time every day, sir."

"Unlikely on Sundays. You're sure - no stir?"

"Certain sure. But he's a lightin' hoor, sir."

"Agreed, Mr Mawe."

(v)

Afternoon merged into evening. In the streets of the town, mauve-coloured sunlight filtered through the remnants of the November mist. The painted shopfronts turned grey-green under the street lamps that bleared from furry spheres of light with prismatic hues on their rims. The two men continued to drink. The golden balls of the mantel clock impassively described their semi-revolutions. What there was of conversation had become sporadic and guttural. From time to time Patrick Joseph snarled an order or made an out-of-context comment or joke. By now Bowler was left with only the lees of his subservience. He had grown valiant too; long since he had stopped looking over his shoulder in fear of the returning housekeeper. The draper had clicked on one of the fireside lamps and made another effort to read a newspaper. It soon fell out of his hands and onto the fender. His eye closed with a certain gesture of foolish bliss. The fire had become a fragile arrangement of white ash. Two empty bottles rolled on the floor; a further pair of bottles, deeply broached, stood on the low occasional table.

Bowler had scuffed off his shoes and was lying full length on the settee. His feet, clad in grey woollen socks with both his big toes protruding, were enthroned on one of the settee's ends. Now and again Mr O'Shea, sunk deep in his fireside chair, could be heard tunelessly crooning "Mate O' Mine." Time and again he failed to finish a verse; he would then begin all over again with "We set out together, Mate O' Mine."

Once there came a loud knocking on the hall-door below. "She back?" Bowler queried anxiously as he scrambled to get up.

PJ wagged an uncertain hand. "Usspp" he said. "Man dead in Killaneerla. Let 'em go to hell. Let 'em try a boutique for the habit, socks, black ties and underwear." As again and again the knocker sounded wanly the draper said, "Dead man no good: dead pig some good."

"On the knuckle," Bowler echoed, with a prolonged drunken chortle.

(vi)

Some time before nine o'clock a motor drew up outside the hall-door of the Emporium. Mrs Rainey, the housekeeper, got out of the vehicle. She wore a fur toque on the side of her head; a miniature Yorkshire terrier was draped over her forearm. She said goodbye to her nephew who then drove off. Having straightened the latch key with her lips she turned the key in the polished lock. Immediately inside, dog and housekeeper began to sniff. The toy dog growled in its throat and looked up the staircase. The long-case clock in the hall seemed to tick in tell-tale indignation. Mr O'Shea's bowler hat swung back and forth on its brass knob on the hallstand. Closing the door and switching on the hallway light, her index finger warning the terrier to be quiet, the housekeeper moved cautiously up the stairs. On the landing the woman turned the white china knob and quietly opened the parlour door.

The room, lighted only by one fireside lamp, reeked of alcohol. The housekeeper's eyes widened while the Yorkshire terrier, making agitated gurglings in its throat, its hindlegs working feverishly, its nose quivering and questing and its beaded eyes bulging behind tendrils of brown and black in response to the adventurous if hostile smells, tried vainly to escape from the elbow-lock of its mistress.

Mrs Rainey moved a step or two forward into the room. Sprawling in his armchair lay her employer: his jacket was removed and one wing of his semi-stiff collar was adrift like the wing of a wounded gull. Were those his dentures on the hearth-rug?

Bowler was half curled up on the carpet; a dribble of blackcurrant juice from his mouth corner had provided a dramatic bloodstain for the interlaced dragon on the cushion under his head. The chutney bottle lay uncorked on its side; the bottle had remorselessly oozed its contents. Bowler's big toes glistened high above him from their resting place on the head of the settee. And what in God's name were those bones doing there beside him on the floor? Emptied soda water bottles and toppled drinking glasses together with half-melted ice cubes, scraps of meat gristle and bread crusts littered the carpet: one corner of a dropped newspaper had charred and fortunately quenched in the fender.

The housekeeper stood for a moment in silent fury looking down at the chaotic scene.

Her premonitions had been proven correct, she told herself. Her employer had taken the sale of the old place deeply to heart. The infant must have been misnamed. She accused herself of having failed to appreciate the significance of Bowler's visit to the shop a few days previously: she had thought that he was seeking an advance of money on the finishing of the tarring of the shed. Parts of the jigsaw puzzle began to slot into place in her mind. Above all she was angry with herself for failing to remain at her post of duty on this vital afternoon.

Outwardly her anger showed itself in an odd way. At the point of her jaw there appeared a round knob of flesh the size of a crab-apple. In response to the workings of her lips this odd fruit of ire and indignation revealed obscure scribings on its surface. As the knob steadied a little her darting eyes took over to infer that men are crazy in going to absurd lengths seeking to perpetuate their names.

As if remotely conscious of a watchful and vengeful presence Bowler growled and stirred; the draper too altered his sprawl and uttered a sleepy yawn. The housekeeper crouched to pick up the nearest of the cut glass tumblers at her feet. Doing so she increased the pressure on the terrier's belly so that it wriggled furiously under the pressure of her elbow. She then abandoned the effort.

As soundlessly as she could, drawing the door behind her but not quite closing it, Mrs Rainey went downstairs. She left the light on in the stairway. Through the triangular window in the bend of the stairs she could see the almost full moon and the bright stars. There was a faint light showing at the back of Devere's pastry shop.

The kitchen and scullery too were in a mess. On its large oval dish on the kitchen table stood the hacked roast of beef, a soiled bread knife (well licked no doubt) lying beside it. In the scullery Bowler had gapped a jagged sector out of the loaf of soda bread which she had baked on the residual ovenheat of the roast. A pound of butter, sliced through its gold coloured wrapper, had chunks gouged out of its exposed flank, while stray dollops of grease on the table and floor added further outrage to the sorry tale. Even before she fully opened the already semi-opened door of the fridge, she could foretell with accuracy the fate of the half dish of sherry trifle. Tablespoonfuls had been ladled out of it and some of the cream topping had fallen in gobbets to the tiles. Breadcrumbs, lettuce leaves, knobs of chutney, smears of spilt milk, blackcurrant jam, broken biscuits and grains of Rice Crispies were strewn about. She saw marmalade glistening on the floor about her shoes.

She dropped the terrier into its basket in the kitchen and finger-threatened it not to make a sound. Its ebony nose continued to explore the alien air. Using care as to where she placed her shoes she plugged in the electric kettle and then sat down under the Sacred Heart lamp to take stock of the situation. And to plot and measure her reaction and action in the days ahead.

The tell-tale knob on her jaw recurrently formed and disappeared as she counselled herself to think out each step with the utmost care and to proceed in a manner that held no elements of her present fury.

First of all, she could ill afford to fall out with her employer. Properly handled, this episode could be used to increase her influence in the house. For years she had puzzled over what the Missus had said to her on her death-bed. "Look after the Boss, Angela: men are fools." What exactly had the dying woman meant to convey? Was she herself being urged to entice PJ into marriage? To compromise him so as to keep other adventuresses at bay? If she wished to draw PJ closer to her, now was her time - he was wrongfooted while she herself was armed with the emotional weapon of outrage. She could even give notice. But then again he might accept. And where would she be then? A highly charged if restrained scene involving sniffles and reconciliation might be the surest course to take.

Having Bowler in the parlour was too much. He had to be banished from the house. If she heard that he had talked in the town she would make him suffer.

She finished a cup of tea. And quenched the kitchen lights. Left the door to the hall slightly ajar. She liked to sit in the faint glow of the votive lamp to hear the news on the radio. A few minutes to nine, she raised her hand to turn on the set when the thought struck her. Was it possible that Ballbearing knew? Was that crazy young man already waiting on his flat roof. his thin face alive with evil anticipatory glee. His transistor radio turned on in the pocket of his dressing-gown. His eyes identifying every flicker of light in the higgledy-piggledy world of stalls, workshops, bathrooms, annexes and sheds below him and the diurnal story that went with each little building. His frail body tautened to convey "I know, I know," and to announce another victory for a man whose world was the width of a chair.

As yet the radio gave out gentle Sabbath music. The house was quiet. An occasional open eye on his mistress, the pet dog was almost asleep. Through the kitchen window the housekeeper sensed a typical November night. Stars were silently on show. As the seconds ticked away the crab-apple appeared on Mrs Rainey's jaw. The radio music stopped. The long-case clock in the hall gave a low whir as if clearing its throat prior to striking. Then came the six radio pips to break the silence.

(vii)

Almost at the same time all the house clocks struck the hour. The faraway chime from the parlour, the magisterial tones from the hall, the plebeian note from the workaday kitchen timepiece all proclaimed almost in unison the hour of nine o'clock. PJ had taken care that all the clocks kept accurate time. There was a cessation of sound. Before the newscaster could speak the woman rose and turned off the radio. She stood and listened.

Then came the first sharp crack on the slates and the high hard rolling of a missile on the roof above. Again and again the sound came, ball succeeding ball until it seemed to the listener that the marksman was shooting ballbearings in two or threes. The housekeeper heard a thump from the parlour indicating that Bowler had struggled to his feet. He was moving out on the stairs. Irregularly stumbling on the steps as he over-cautiously descended, he was cursing, fumbling and muttering.

Bowler's footsteps ceased: he was obviously fully aware of the crack, slat, rattle, roll and drum of the cannonade. A sharp crack and the tinkle of falling glass accompanied by a sharper expletive and the housekeeper knew that the triangular window on the landing had been shattered close to where a befuddled Bowler had been peering out. Then came what proved to be the final fusillade of missiles sounding on galvanised roofs, noising along eaves-chutes and rolling along channels to come to a metallic rest on the gratings of the yard. In response to her pet dog's frenzied yappings Mrs Rainey could hear McKecknie's Alsatian howling in the deal yard and Hanrahan's greyhounds baying and bloodcrying as if rabid for game.

The firing ceased. Bowler resumed his downward plunge. The housekeeper heard him miss his step in the darkness (God grant he break his neck, the woman prayed) and land with a tangle of thumpings and curses on his buttocks. At last, the soft click of the lock on the hall-door indicated that Bowler had recovered and left.

So much rubbish got rid of, Mrs Rainey told herself. Now to adopt an immediate plan of campaign. Patience was called for until the Boss was in bed. Using the flashlamp she would pick up the ballbearings that had rolled on to the shore gratings in the yard. In the morning she would decide whether or not to place one of the silvery balls in the eggstand which Mr O' used with his boiled egg at breakfast. To convey that she knew what had happened. If he got cross about it she could pretend the missile had been there for months - this ruse would entail using one of the best china eggstands from the top shelf of the dresser. Not that much subtlety was called for - neighbours in whose yards errant balls had landed would ask mock-innocent questions. For these she must have a ready answer.

Donovan's, the Hardware Merchants, would quickly glaze the broken window: the receipt for the replacement she would place discreetly before Mrs Devere on her next visit to the pastry shop. The amount would be paid without comment. While waiting in the shop she would read the environmental slogans on the wall or window. "Save the Whale," "Preserve the Tiger," and "When did you last hear a Corncrake?" Mrs Devere was a conservationist and Chairperson of the local branch of WABS - Women Against Blood Sports. She had carried banners at coursing meetings. Reputed to be of gentle blood, her deep-set eyes watered a little when speaking of endangered species of wild birds and animals.

There was a sound of barely-heard fumbling from the stairwell. That would be the Boss - God grant he may not break his neck. The blick of a switch from the bathroom was accompanied by a faint glow of light on the yard wall. Then came the distant blurr-blurr-bluish as the draper soused his face. Later she heard the sound of a trickle of water falling into the lavatory bowl above, followed by the flushing of the toilet. He would now struggle up to his bedroom, blearily fold his clothes across a chair and roll painfully into bed. In the morning nothing would be said: the Boss would appear somewhat thinner than usual and his face would be a fiery red. The broken landing window would tell its own tale.

When the housekeeper heard the bedroom door slam rather loudly, the crab-apple on her chin began to disappear. She resolved to set her alarm clock for an earlier hour and clean up the parlour before PJ came down to breakfast. She cancelled her decision to collect the ballbearings in the yard and perhaps the missile on the stairs at such a late hour. The parlour was important; the windows had to be opened top and bottom to get rid of the reek of tobacco and drink. There was also the matter of the fallen dentures - she could leave those on the washhand basin in the bathroom. Yes, morning would be better.

She quietly mopped up the mess in kitchen and scullery. She sat on a chair and waited for her employer to settle down. She felt calmer now. Although she knew that an uneasy night's sleep lay before her she had to plan carefully for what lay ahead. Her attitude towards various people had now to be clarified. This involved her own future.

Her own nephew and his wife? She had no illusions about them. The pair were interested in the little reserve of cash she had prudently set aside. She would continue with her visits to the country but would blow hot or cold as the occasion demanded.

Bowler? He had to be silenced. Pressure to finish the tarring of the shed was one of the ways to go about it. Better still to mention that an ornamental plate was missing from the parlour; she could hide the plate in the sideboard and "discover" it later - there was an Old Testament precedent for the hiding of a gold cup in a sack of corn.

Ballbearing was a problem. A communal affliction to be borne.

She had seen him downfaced once only: at Mass one Christmas morning sitting in his wheelchair beside the holy water font just inside the church door, where he was anonymously shrouded in rugs. A perky lassie from the new council estate had dipped her fingertips in the font and then instead of crossing herself, had called out "Ballbearings". As he turned his head she hooked the nail of her middle finger to the tip of her thumb and flicked the holy water into his grey eyes. "You bastard!" the girl had hissed. She had then sailed serenely up the crowded nave of the church. Ballbearing's eyes, slitted with hatred, had followed the girl until she genuflected and entered a pew.

The country O'Sheas could be written off - they were going to Chattanooga wasn't it - in the United States. Early in the morning she must discreetly enquire what they had called the infant. She wouldn't have been surprised if that gligeen Peter had named it Rumpelstiltskin. Other vague persons, including the glazier from Donovan's, had to be probed and if necessary warned obliquely against betrayal.

(viii)

Mrs Rainey continued to ruminate. Her posture indicated that she was making progress. Once she would have relished the challenge of restoring balance to the Emporium. Her future was tied irrevocably to that of her employer who might even mention her in his will. She did not wish to end her days in an old people's home. The years had taken their toll, yet she dared not falter now. She might try to sail through all obstacles with superficial serenity. She might not even bother placing the ballbearing in the eggstand or hiding the plate in the sideboard. As the late Canon Boyle, her first employer, was wont to say, "There is a law of minimal intrusion which should never be overlooked."

The reflected light on the yard wall went out. The Boss was in bed. A few minutes further in reflection and she herself would tiptoe up the backstairs to her own bedroom.

A pang of worry took her on the realisation that she had not made sure that the Boss's pipe was safe in the parlour with no danger of setting fire to the place. She reassured herself with the reminder that if this had already started she would long since have smelled smoke. She dared not venture up the front stairs now for fear of waking her master.

Mrs Rainey came to her feet. Bade the terrier goodnight. Every step up her own stairs was a minor ordeal. Halfway up she paused to identify a source of irritation: what stuck in her craw was the attitude of the old couple in the pastry shop. With their pale hands and their paler smiles. Earthwatching if you please, while above their heads their chair-bound son was townwatching by day and by night, seeking to shatter an environment that possessed communal peace.

Endangered species! Tigers, whales and hares clamouring to be protected while almost everyone she knew in the town answered to the same description. The Boss, Bowler, a quaint survival, the Deveres. (Once the old couple died, the Ballbearer would be clapped into an institution.) The Dean with the ecclesiastic world trembling about him - it could be that Peter O'Shea with his Chattanooga and Rumpelstiltskin was the only wise person among the lot of them. Unwittingly as it may be, not knowing what lay before him, the challenge of a new environment might conquer his innate sense of stagnation and sheer laziness.

Come to think of it, she mused as she paused in her bedroom while peeling off her stockings, did not an elderly housekeeper belong to the same endangered class surely moving on the same road to extinction. The last of a line distinguished by loyalty, service and dedication was now being displaced by microwave ovens, pre-cooked meals from the delicatessen shop and by the duvet which had rendered the ancient craft of bedmaking almost obsolete.

Yes indeed, she told herself, like it or not, she belonged to a most endangered species. With one important proviso, that if all came to all she considered herself every bit as worthy of preservation as a corncrake with its raucous rattle flawing the peace of a summer meadow, or a bat with its implied sense of velvet terror defiling the innocence of an evening sky.

🥀 TESTAMENT OF A SEWER RAT 🥀

(i)

"All Nammocks are mad!" our parents kept telling us. We four lads didn't think so. We continued to listen open-mouthed to what Mr Nammock had to say. He could talk for hours on the most extraordinary subjects.

"The sewer is the hallmark of civilisation," the old jeweller declared, his white beard tilted to catch the light from his shop window while behind and above him clocks of all shapes and sizes ticked their approval. "At the precise moment that man, using his bare footsole covered his faeces with sand, civilisation had its rude beginning."

("Stone mad the Nammocks! Don't you say you haven't been warned!")

Squatting on the shop floor around the old man's highly polished boots we continued to look up at the jeweller's biblical head. But even as we listened, our ears were sieving the noises of the street outside. For this was the troubled Ireland of 1920 where violent death was commonplace.

"Because of the offensive odour," Mr Nammock went on, "progress in the disposal of human excretion was slow. Polite society ignored the problem. However, in the context of even a town sewer there is adventure and beauty."

(Adventure and beauty? Only a dotty Nammock would say a thing like that!)

At this point in his narration the jeweller inhaled snuff from the back of his hand and then went on. "As late as the last century, so as to neutralise the foetid stench from the River Thames, sheets of burlap soaked in lime covered the windows of the House of Commons. Even then, out of a sense of spurious gentility, the public remained silent.

("Mark my words! That gooky jeweller will one day land the four of you buckos in serious trouble.")

Toni spoke up. He mentioned the men's privy that straddled the stream of the sewer just before it emerged from beneath the market wall and discharged its greenish slime through the archway into the river. "That place stinks," he blurted, pinching his nostrils. We three followed his example, at the same time humming on a note of disgust.

"The odour is natural," Mr Nammock chided. "Wind from the bowel has nine properties; gas, scent and music; disgrace, dishonour and shame; ease, peace and comfort." After a pause, "And it is inflammable."

(It was inflammable. We later proved the old man right by means of a singeing experiment.)

"The correct word to describe such a privy is a garderobe," Mr Nammock continued. "A garderobe is a crude cubicle set above flowing water. For centuries, closets of this type festooned the parapets of London Bridge."

"Crazy as cuckoos the Nammocks" - we had been amply warned. But, our parents conceded, Mr Nammock was intelligent - too much so for his own good. See how he became a watchmaker and jeweller! Started off by taking to pieces his own watch and those of his fellow-internees in Frongoch Camp in Wales where he had been interned as a result of his taking part in the 1916 Rising. We were to humour him, of course, but not to heed him. To be blunt about it, he wasn't the full shilling. At this the speaker spun a forefinger at his temple.

After a ruminative cackle, "The White House in Washington had its first bathroom installed as late as 1840," Mr Nammock went on. Then, as his beard sank on to his stiff shirt front, he lapsed into silence.

We lads also fell silent, pondering what the old man had told us.

We four were inseparable friends. There was myself, Bernard or Barney Gallivan, the youngest of the four at fifteen years, with Sylvester, or as we called him, Silvo Dee, whose father was a railway porter, the eldest of us at eighteen. In between, at sixteen and seventeen respectively, were Toni Bartarelli, known locally as Toni Kelly, who on the death of his Italian-born father in New York had been packed back to Ireland to be reared by his widowed grandmother Kelly, and the last of the four, Brud Barrett whose father, a semi-butcher, killed, skinned and sold the quartered flesh of newly-dropped calves and kids.

At the local Seminary, despite our different ages, we were classmates.

There we studied Latin and Greek, Mathematics and the then imperial versions of History and Geography. Influenced by the tensions of that hour, Silvo had ambitions to be an officer in the first army of a free Ireland, Brud wanted to be a surgeon; if that goal were beyond him he aimed at being a country bonesetter holding a market-day clinic in the backroom of a bar. It was common local knowledge that Toni's grandmother offered up rosaries in the hope that her grandson would one day become a priest. As for myself, I wanted eventually to join the Indian Civil Service with the secret resolution of continuing to serve under native rule once the British Raj had fallen. Failing that, I would aim at a post in our own Civil Service.

Raising his head, the old jeweller broke in upon our reverie. "We know a great deal about the stars," he said, "yet what happens in the sewer, twelve feet below the floor of this shop is a mystery to us."

As he tapped the floor with his shoe-sole to emphasise the

comment, all the clocks in the place, striking, whirring, chiming and cuckooing almost in unison sent us four lads scurrying for the door.

The hour of the evening curfew had stolen up upon us. And already - another few seconds and we would have bumped into them - the double file of khaki-clad Yorks had left their barracks in the nearby Square and were now firing warning salvoes into the air. Our eardrums, till then attuned to the sound of clocks striking the hour, were suddenly harshly resonant with the sound of volleys of rifle fire crashing in the narrow street.

(ii)

Our curiosity aroused, we stood on the clay bank looking down on the archway of the sewer.

The summer effluent from the underground stream was meagre, so that at times the tumbling turds were halted for a moment or two on the edge of the stone-paved culvert before easing lazily over and down into the pea-green pool a few feet below.

In retrospect I see this moment of pause as a turning point in our lives.

Silvo was the first to leap downward and inward onto the drier paving stones on the floor of the culvert. Brud followed, rejecting Silvo's arms outstretched to receive him. Toni accepted help in his leap from both Silvo and Brud, while all three gripped me as I careered wildly downwards, thus saving me from tumbling backward into the cesspool.

Hopping from dry stone to dry stone we followed Silvo into the greenish interior. As we did so, the noise of the marketplace above grew fainter - the bawling of calves, the squealing of suckling pigs, the barking of dogs, the yelling of farmers, carters, china-sellers, and cast-clothes men became a low pitched murmur that merged with the faraway hiss of river water flowing over the mill weir a little distance down river from the town.

Lord, how the place stank! We now pinched our nostrils in earnest as in the jeweller's shop we had done in mockery.

Gradually, our eyes growing accustomed to the gloom, we advanced cautiously. Above us thin stalactites watched our progress.

A channel to our left came from under the marketmen's privy. This closet was reached by a series of stone steps leading down the clay cliffside from the corner of the market wall. Inside, it had a sagged flagged floor with four doorless bays, three of which had a worn beam set along the edge of an upended flagstone so as to provide precarious purchase for the users' buttocks. The inmost cubicle had lost both flagstone and beam - consequently there were occasions when an unwary or tipsy user of this recess had fallen backward and become jammed just above the stream on the edge of which we four now looked upwards over one another's shoulders. Due to the rusted and porous nature of the galvanised iron roofing, the interior of the privy was invariably either damp or half-flooded.

This was our first tentative venture into the subterranean world of our town.

On later occasions, a blazing paraffin-soaked sod of turf providing us with light, we penetrated even deeper under the streets. Presently we entered a central chamber - a kind of junction-box of streams with lesser culverts radiating uphill in different directions. Since the streams from these culverts ran by the walls of the chamber before converging and draining off at the one lower archway, a paved area of dry stone was left in the middle of this hall. Here we set up our headquarters, furnishing it with orange boxes and a few old milking stools; we also drove brads into the wall; on one of these brads we hung a rather large wicker bread-basket salvaged from the town dump. We fastened it at a height which we reckoned was above flood - or indeed rat-level. In this hall, squatting on our boxes or stools, we tried to reckon our exact position as regards the world above us.

We estimated that we were close to the foundations of the church which stood in mid-square. The culvert to our left as we entered the hall probably came from under the hotel, while the opening to our immediate right possibly came from under the Geraldine Castle on the clifftop which guarded the ford in the river which curled beneath its ruined walls. We liked to conclude that this passage was the one chanced upon by the English forces during the Geraldine rebellion in 1600 and which was extended by them right beneath the castle where, having proven their presence to the defenders by tapping on its roof, they threatened to blow the building to smithereens if the garrison did not surrender without conditions.

Mr Nammock, tears slow-trickling into his beard had read us an account of the siege from the pages of an old volume called Pacata Hibernia or Ireland Pacified.

There were times later, when, seated in our subterranean chamber, the stench set aside rather than forgotten, the green mainstream enfolding its tributaries, the torchlight lost and found on our faces and on the olive-coloured outlines of a pig's head which we had affixed to the front of the bread-basket, when we glanced over our shoulders in fright as if to see approaching us the ghostly figures of thirteen of the defenders of the Castle who had been hanged on a gallows almost directly above our heads.

Nor did we consider it odd that the Ireland of 1920 was no less disturbed than the Ireland of 1600. Above us in the town and countryside around it, Black and Tans, Royal Irish Constabulary, Auxiliaries or "Auxies" (educated rascals these, demobbed ex-officers for the most part) together with the Yorkshire regiment fought sporadically with the Flying Columns of the IRA fronted by the quasi-political organisation Sinn Féin, which at that time operated its own police force and law courts.

For us youngsters, however, all this turmoil provided choice entertainment. Law and order were non-existent, so that the opportunity to plunder was too good to be missed. We embarked on the second stage of our adventure when we decided to steal whatever we considered was worthy of being stolen. After all, we had the ideal place to conceal our booty.

(iii)

Silvo led the first raid. He and Toni set off together while Brud and I waited in the sewer. When they returned, Silvo had a long white cardboard box under his arm; opened, the box was seen to contain a few dozen stubby fine-toothed combs as they were called, each one inscribed with the outline of an elephant.

The four of us then, standing just inside the archway of the sewer outlet, our faces aglow with the light from the evening west, began most diligently and laughingly to comb our matted heads of hair. Presently, the white space between the two sets of teeth on each comb was blotched by the blood and bodies of nail-flattened lice.

We continued to pilfer, loot and steal. We shoplifted books from the town's single bookshop and from the local library - titles by Arnold Bennett, Ambrose Pierce, GK Chesterton and Hilaire Belloc. One book among our loot which I recall distinctly was "Saïd the Fisherman" by Marmaduke Pickthall. On a lower literary level we stole Sexton Blakes, Buffalo Bills and Billy Bunters. We then moved on to acquiring carpet slippers, a barmbrack, some tins of Van Houten's cocoa and Zambuk ointment, a scouring brick called Monkey Brand, packets of Thin Arrowroot and Boston Cream biscuits, confectionery in the form of Vanilla Slices, Liquorice Laces, Coconut Macaroons and Magic Spot Balls of which one in twenty contained a new halfpenny piece. We pilfered coils and curls of discarded film from under the screen of our primitive cinema (how these films stank and smoked when set alight in the sewer), a truss which, in turn, each of the four of us tried on for size, several hurling balls, a box of carbolic soap, a dozen elastic belts in the rebel colours of green and gold (Silvo was kicked in the stomach by a Black and Tan for wearing one), a roll of salted ling and a pair of steel-rimmed spectacles which Toni set askew on the snout of the stolen pig's head so as to give it a comically wise and even oriental appearance.

We also stole the bank manager's tomatoes and the parson's peaches. We raided every orchard within a radius of three miles of the town. To Grandmother Kelly who baked enormous apple tarts for us, we spun a tale of a grateful farmer who had given us the run of his orchard for having recovered a heifer of his which had strayed on Big Fair Day.

About this time too, I came into the possession of an airgun. Whether I bought it out of my meagre savings or my clerkish father had given it to me for my birthday - an unlikely purchase for him - I cannot now recall. It fired a fairly heavy pellet shaped like an hourglass. From the sewer-arch we had target practice firing at the wagtails strutting like waiters on the sleazy stones at the water's edge.

To this day I break out in a cold sweat whenever I recall the use - nefarious and hilarious - to which we put that airgun.

(iv)

For some time previous to this, we four lads had been in the habit of taunting a huge hill farmer whose nickname in the countryside was Acre of Arse. He could be heard at a great distance shouting "Hupp!" at his mule; he was also given to yelling overbearingly at others who frequented the crowded marketplace.

The moment we saw Acre drive in by the northern gateway we scrambled to the top of the wall at the lower end of the market ready to drop down into Coffee Lane if he tried to chase us. Having brought his mule to a halt, a little distance from and below where we squatted, Acre ponderously dismounted from the seat-and-guards of his common cart. Then, slipping the rope reins over the mule's head, he swung its loop upwards until it gained purchase on a stone projecting from the top of the wall. From under the rim of his sweat-stained hat the whites of his eyes kept rolling in our direction.

Silvo began the taunting.

"Acre of Arse," he said just above a whisper, at the same time pretending to look in a different direction. Having repeated the taunt a few times he would suddenly shout "Hupp" as if giving vent to a loud hiccough. The mule then threw up its head in fright. The other three of us took up the "Hupp" chorus in various pitches of voice, upsetting the mule completely. Toni, an excellent whistler, could even mimic the percussion of the man's full nickname.

The Tallystick

At first, Acre pretended to take no notice of us; generally, after casting a mad-dog look upwards in our direction, he would move off among the loads of hay and turnips. Then, having first unlooped the reins from the stone, we shouted "Hupp" at the mule until it wandered free to cause trouble in the thronged market. Later we leaped down from the wall and meshed cautiously through the crowds until, having found where Acre was, our jeers reached him from various points of the compass.

One day, Acre, large and shambling, whip in hand, his trousers baggy about his buttocks, his piggish eyes darting here and there as he prowled among the hay-loads, came up behind Silvo as he was about to steal "scollops" or thatching withies from one of the great-hundred bundles in which they were sold.

As Silvo turned at the sound of a harsh "Hupp!" Acre lashed him again and again across the face with his whip, leaving criss-crossed weals on Silvo's forehead, nose and cheeks and almost blinding him in blood. With each lash Acre shouted "Hupp" as if he were flogging his mule. If onlookers had not intervened the incident could have had serious consequences.

Silvo's face, when at last he staggered away, was savagely striped; at home he made a lame excuse to explain his condition. Later, squatting on the boxes deep in the sewer, we plotted revenge.

A few weeks later, on market day, Brud, Toni and I were deep in the culvert when Silvo came splashing in. Snatching the loaded airgun from Brud's hands he moved under the lintel of the flow from under the men's privy. There, crouching, he stood in the swiftly flowing water. Soundless and in Indian file we followed. Then, above the hiss of the racing water, we heard coming from above us the grunts of a big man straining at stool.

Silvo froze when the plop of falling faeces came; he then moved forward a cautious step and brought the rifle butt to his shoulder. Peering upwards in the gloom I could see the white estate of flesh that had earned Acre his nickname. As Silvo fired and we sensed the pellet drilling deep into the bland buttocks we yelled "Hupp" at the top of our voices. Roaring with laughter, floundering, splashing and clawing at one another's jackets and ganseys we stumbled, staggered and leaped in our haste to be first away from retribution. As we scrambled to safety under the rampart of the market cliff, we could hear the anguished howls of Acre far behind us.

That afternoon, the laughter choked in our throats on hearing a rumour that a countryman had been shot dead in the men's privy. Later, to our great relief, we heard that Acre was alive but that he had had to limp his way home to the hills hobbling painfully at his mule's head. Later still we heard that in the early hours of the morning he had had to send to the nearest village for the dispensary doctor. She was the first "lady doctor" in the area and the imagined picture of her probing deep in the buttocks of the huge man sent waves of laughter through the countryside. "She drove round on him for an hour before she found the point of entry," was one of the comments that evoked guffaws.

(v)

Mary Monday, a foundling waif, now earns a place in this testament. This because, unwittingly, she proved to be a cause of fragmenting the comradeship of our adolescence.

But first, a mention of the contrast between the odd peace obtaining deep in the sewer and the bizarre chaos of the streets above in the Ireland of that hour. Central in this contrast a crazy humour was sometimes mingled with black tragedy.

Humour? By careful pacing above ground we were able to locate exactly the exit pipe from Mr Nammock's yard lavatory or closet. When the faint clanking sound of metal above our heads informed us that the old jeweller had risen from his wooden throne and was now pulling the chain, Silvo, his head cautiously close to the pipe outlet, played "A Nation Once Again" on his mouth organ. Later we found the old rebel in a transport of joy as he told us of the mysterious music he had heard issuing from the bowels of the earth, and which most certainly presaged the freedom and unity of Ireland. On another occasion, moving ever deeper into the sewer, we watched boiling water spluttering and hissing as it issued from a melted lead pipe pouring down from a house which the Auxies had set on fire as an official reprisal for an ambush; the arched stone vault above our heads was too hot to touch and the air stifling with the smell of stewed ordure.

We even penetrated to a point under the hotel, a building then occupied by the Auxiliaries: as erratic members of Fianna Éireann the outlawed scout movement of the day, Silvo and Brud argued as to whether word of our discovery should be sent to the flying column, so that by exploding a landmine beneath the building, vengeance could be extracted for the hanging of the castle garrison in 1600. Brud was all for telling his cousins the Barretts in the west, who kept a safe house for men on the run, but Silvo calmly overrode him saying that if the explosion took place our part in the operation would almost certainly be discovered. Brud was sullen for days afterwards. During the bitter argument that followed, Toni and I could only look on in awed silence.

By now it was clear that, judging by local happenings, national events were moving to a climax. Girls who consorted with the Yorks were stripped naked, their hair shaved off and their bodies tarred: with luck they would later be released on a country by-road. Din Doolan, an ex-British naval rating who had lost an arm in World War I while taking part in a raid on the German U-Boat base at Zeebrugge in Belgium, was found lying dead at a kerbside, shot out of hand because the old warrior had considered himself above the rule of curfew. I myself while taking shelter from a shower in a newsagent's doorway saw the corpse of a young member of the flying column roped by the feet to the tail of a Crossley tender. As the vehicle began to move I saw the body trundling and swishing from side to side as it was being dragged along the waterlogged roadway.

But, make no mistake about it! We four revelled in the turmoil. Communal fear and everyday risk had engendered a sense of closer comradeship, even of brotherhood in our relationship with one another. That was, until Mary Monday entered our lives.

(vi)

It is odd to consider how a normal life of sorts can assert itself in a time of abnormality. Just as Derby Day with all its traditional colour is held even at the height of world conflict.

There was nothing unusual in the fact that a bunch of fairground folk with a set of shabby amusements and games of chance pulled into a corner of the marketplace. Having had their airguns confiscated by the Tans, the newcomers were allowed to ply their trade - but only after the tattooed owner had proven that he had fought on the British side in the Boer War.

The showman and his wife slept in a battered caravan: on early afternoons and on Sunday mornings a thin girl of sixteen or so turned the handle of a barrel organ which twanged out an unrecognisable tune. She also took fares at the swingboats while the pock-faced showman managed the merry-go-rounds.

The girl slept under the caravan on a bed of sacks. Her bedmates were a foxcub on a chain and a scruffy German shepherd dog.

The girl's name was Mary Monday.

Whenever the showman and his wife were away, Mary Monday allowed Silvo and myself to remain on the swingboat for as long as we pleased for the price of a single ride.

Even today, over sixty-five years later, I tremble when I vision myself low-crouched on one seat of the boat, my rope dangling before my pale face, my hands glued to the bars, while towering above me, his powerful fists gripping diagonally opposite bars, Silvo swung and rocked the boat higher and higher until for a terrifying tick of time it hung almost upside down, its movement checked by the chamfered ridgepole that held the whole shuddering contraption together. Just as I had reconciled myself to the fate of crashing head foremost to the ground, the boat yawed downward, scooping my stomach hollow as it fell, again to soar upwards on the other side to be stalled for a further hellish second at the highest point of the opposite swing. And so on to the end of the ride.

Through chinks in my terror, I glimpsed below me the peaked face of Mary Monday.

She was gazing upward with admiration at the feats of the tall blond-haired young man on the swing, and, I daresay, with contempt for the coward crouching at his feet! It was with a sense of release from panic that I welcomed the moment when the girl raised the free end of the heavy wooden brake and, indicating a strength unvouched for by her frail forearms, took the brunt of the blows as recurrently the brake came in harsh contact with the underside of the boat.

When some days later, I saw the girl quietly move the wooden ring which Silvo had pitched on to a coin-studded black shawl, so that it then completely encircled a florin which she handed to Silvo without glancing up into his face, I realised that by this token she was conveying her love.

At first Silvo seemed coolly amused at the girl's interest in him. Later he told me that she had been abandoned as an infant and that the orphanage nuns who had reared her had named her for the Virgin Mary and the weekday on which she had been found. The family with whom she had first been boarded-out had proved unkind so she had run off and joined the fairground folk. I wasn't quite sure how Silvo got to know all this, but I do recall that he seemed to be speaking to himself rather than to me when he mentioned the matter. Then abruptly he stopped talking and did not refer to the subject again.

There came a quiet afternoon when the marketplace was almost deserted. Silvo, seated on a low stone by the weighbridge, began to play a slow air on his mouth organ.

Spying down from our upstairs gable window, which looked out over the market, I saw Mary Monday, her hands clasped behind her head, lying on her back beneath the caravan.

For a time she remained motionless and was obviously listening to the music; then, carefully raising herself on her elbow, her face almost hidden behind the spokes of a wheel, she began to watch Silvo. Pricking up their ears the dog and the fox-cub watched too.

The girl cringed a little on hearing the boss open the caravan window above her head: he too watched Silvo for a minute or so before turning away to mutter something to his wife.

Without raising his eyes, Silvo seemed to sense that his love signal had been received. Slamming the mouth of the instrument recurrently on the taut trousers covering his thigh, he strode off towards the upper gate that led to the centre of the town. From behind the rag curtain net on the caravan window the showman watched him go: from her bed of sacking the girl's dark eyes under her bush of unkempt hair were also fast upon him.

I raced around to a front bedroom window to learn what Silvo was up to: he was dawdling behind a cart just outside the market gate, where, I guessed, he could be seen from the undercarriage of the caravan but not from the window above it. Back again at the gable window I watched for some time until, at last, Mary Monday came cautiously to her feet, and, crouching somewhat, and taking a line where she could not be seen from the caravan, moved quickly towards the alleyway at the lower end of the marketplace.

Later I learned that Silvo had gone along Market Street and, hurrying around by Bank Place, had entered the archway that led down to Coffee Lane. Thence he moved up the steps on the clay cliffside, timing his movements so that he met the girl just as she entered the alleyway.

On this the first occasion of their meeting it seems that they merely spoke to each other for a while - the girl then hastened back to the caravan. A few days later, as with my terrier I hunted for rabbits among the furze bushes on the opposite side of the river, I saw Silvo framed in the sewer archway with the girl on the clay bank above him. Silvo, his arms outstretched, was smilingly encouraging her to jump: she hesitated for some time, then leaped trustfully into his arms. Hidden behind a clump of furze I saw Silvo clasp the girl close, his hands caressing the slim length of her back and buttocks. Then the pair, eagerly joining hands, moved into the interior of the sewer.

When, as tactfully as I could, I hinted to Toni and Brud that we should avoid going to the sewer for some days, Brud, his dark eyes blazing, was furious. It was clear that he had learned what had happened. "He had no bloody right!" he kept blurting. Toni was philosophical. "We couldn't sustain it forever, could we?" was his comment. I felt only mildly betrayed: nevertheless we three avoided the sewer and in varying measures were distant or offhand with Silvo when we met him. He seemed amused at our attitude.

When, as is their custom, the fairground people unexpectedly moved on, leaving only some litter in the shape of torn jumpers and paper bags to indicate that they had ever been in the market, I urged Toni, our peacemaker to meet Silvo and see how matters stood. Brud was opposed to this but Toni went off just the same. On his return he told us that Silvo now had a parabellum pistol which he had uncovered in a dump on the cliffside. The weapon was brand-new, he added, and had obviously been smuggled in from the United States. It had a detachable stock which fitted neatly to the shoulder: the weapon was loaded through the butt with a clip of bullets. Sitting on an orange-box a little distance inside the sewer arch Silvo had fired a few shots at ducks foraging on the outfall of sewage on the river - "just to frighten them" Toni had said. "He asked me to try a shot but I declined," Toni added later and then said, "He seemed so morose and strange that I was half afraid of him."

After this, we three tacitly agreed that the time had come for us to go our separate ways. What we did not know at the time was that events outside our control were to reinforce our unspoken agreement.

(vii)

Almost before we realised it the National Education Board Examinations - the Senior Grade for Brud and Silvo, the Junior Grade for Toni and myself - were upon us.

As we sat silent in the examination hall puzzling over the Greek paper we heard a sudden flurry of shots. An eerie stillness in the streets was followed by the sound of erratic volleys coming from different parts of the town. The school porter put his head in the door of the hall to whisper hoarsely that the District Inspector of Police had been shot dead a few hundred yards from the college gate and that Tans, Auxies, Constabulary and Yorks were careering through the streets firing at anything that moved.

The Examination Superintendent grew pale; grabbing his hat from a hook beside the doorway, he rushed out the door of the examination hall down the back stairway, raced through the orchard, tumbled over the wall at its lower end and puffing as he pelted across the fields was just in time to catch a train about to leave the station.

It took us a few moments to realise that his absence could be interpreted as an educational bonanza!

Silvo was the first to come to his feet. Whistling coolly through his clenched teeth he marched to the adjoining college library presently to return with a Greek grammar, a lexicon and translations of the set texts. There was a scramble to crowd around him; the exception was Brud who, scorning to crib or copy, worked on in sullen silence. We completed our answer papers in an orgy of shouting, prompting and comparing as Silvo instructed us to make deliberate minor mistakes in grammar and offer slightly different versions of our translations so as to convince those marking the papers that the standard accurately reflected our prowess in that branch of the classics. All this to the accompaniment of salvoes of firing from the roadway outside.

Silvo also warned the porter, if he valued his life, to keep his mouth shut. Finally, Toni was despatched to the College Residence just across the road, to inform the Very Reverend President of our plight. Toni hid behind the gate pier and looked up and down several times before finally dashing across. By this time the firing had ceased.

The President tut-tutted a good deal. He came and looked suspiciously over his glasses at our mock-innocent faces. Finally he collected the answer papers and inserted them in a large envelope which he sealed and signed in our presence and had Silvo add his signature as witness of his having done so. He then despatched the porter to learn if the Crown forces had been recalled to their barracks and encampments. Finally he announced that the Examinations would continue on the following day.

The following morning we found that Mr Nammock had been pressed into service as Superintendent of Examinations. The old jeweller, accompanied by an elderly sergeant of the RIC spent his time peering out of the window and turning a deaf ear to the whispering that went on behind his back. Now and again he looked over his shoulder with obvious distaste at the policeman seated in the porch who, with his forearms on his thighs, kept looking into his cupped hands and stiffening with a start at every sound in the neighbourhood.

The examinations at an end, we four left the college.

Silvo strode alone on the footpath ahead of us: Toni, Brud and I walked some distance behind. We were oblivious to the happy-sad yells that came from the country lads cycling past, some of whom like Silvo and Brud, were leaving for the last time. What had my two older friends to show for their six years at College? I asked myself. A few Latin tags, a smattering of Greek, some pidgin Irish, poems by Shelley, Keats and Byron consigned to memory, a nodding acquaintance with logarithms and calculus, and, in History and Geography, that overpowering sense of an empire on which the sun always shone.

"Where do they go from here?" the query came unbidden.

Unexpectedly there came a truce to the guerrilla fighting. We didn't quite know whether to rejoice or not. When the members of the flying column, their limbs red and raw with hayshed itch, some of them trudging along on leaky boots, the more fortunate riding in common carts or tub-traps, but all still carrying their guns, drifted into town, they were cheered - half-heartedly. For now these remote heroes were revealed as being sons of neighbours, many of whom had odd nicknames.

And as we tried to come to terms with our disappointment, events in London gathered momentum.

At No. 10 Downing Street, David Lloyd George, flanked by the finest diplomatic talent of that day, faced a bunch of Irish delegates, some of whom had been on the run for over six years. And (or so we heard) at the critical moment when negotiations seemed fated to break down, placing the draft of an Anglo-Irish Treaty on the table, the British Premier said, "If the Irish delegates do not sign this, within three days we will unleash upon Ireland a terrible and immediate war."

For days the delegates argued among themselves.

"What? Accept Partition and the taking of an oath to His Britannic Majesty?" was countered by, "But it may well be a stepping stone to unity and freedom."

At last, their nerves frayed, each delegate in turn signed the document. Before affixing his name, one of them looked up and said prophetically, "I am signing my death warrant."

Lloyd George smiled tolerantly. Then, gathering up the signed documents, he went off to sleep with his secretary.

(viii)

Once again, Ireland was in uproar.

Drums! Torchlight! Conflicting voices!

"By Christ, I will never agree to a partitioned Ireland." "But Britain may keep faith." "You fool! It's the old trick of divide and conquer!" "For the first time it gives us control of our own affairs." "I tell you that if we accept this Treaty brother will wade through brother's blood."

The flying column was divided. Free State or Republic? Unity or Partition? Loyalty to Ireland or an oath to a foreign power? It seemed only a question of days until the Irish were at one another's throats. Calmly, their bands playing "The Girl I Left Behind Me", the army of occupation marched out of four-fifths of the land.

At our final meeting in the sewer, Brud shouted the old slogans at Silvo: "Ireland unfree shall never be at peace!" "You will never quench the Irish passion for freedom," and "England has sown her laws as dragon's teeth and they have come up as armed men."

Silvo sneered. I had to hold Brud back. Toni clung to Silvo as his patience broke. In the confused struggle the torch fell into the flowing scum. We stumbled and splashed outwards towards the light of day.

That evening, as darkness fell, Brud left home and moved west to where the old column, now purged of its pro-Treaty members, had joined with the remnants of broken columns from other areas. Silvo slipped north and rowed across the wide estuary, to where, on the opposite shore, the newly formed National, or Free State, army controlled a considerable area. Toni told me that he was returning to the United States to be re-united with his mother and, for the first time, to meet his stepfather, step-brothers and step-sisters. Personally, I was bewildered - not the least so politically: one day I was an out-and-out Republican: the next day I was a pragmatic Free-Stater.

Angry words breed acts of anger. The delegate who foretold his own death was among the first to die.

To the west, after a Free State raid across the estuary the riddled body of a young man called Barrett was found in a sea cave.

Rumour had it at first that the dead man was Brud: later it was learned that the body was that of his cousin and that Brud himself had been lucky to escape with his life on the night of the raid. Later still the faintest whisper named Silvo as one of the raiding party.

One morning we woke up to find the Republicans in possession of the town. Dressed in trenchcoats and wearing cloth caps which they sometimes wore back to front, they swarmed through the streets. Well armed with service rifles and an assortment of handguns, they wore crossed leather bandoliers of ammunition. They took possession of the bank, the hotel and the now deserted police barracks. In the barracks yard they began making landmines: I watched as snuff tins were filled with iron nuts, bolts and scrap-iron, all of which held a stick of gelignite in place. A hole punched in the lid of the tin through which a fuse was passed, the fuse-end gently inserted in a detonator and therein crimped gingerly by the front teeth of the mine-maker. When the detonator was inserted in a pencil-made hole in the end of the explosive, the lid pressed home and the can set in a timber butterbox of fresh cement - the mine was ready for action.

A little later I saw Brud lead a party of men through the town: he was pointing out shops and stores where bread, beef, bacon and tinned food were quickly commandeered in the name of the Irish Republic. Silvo's mother, her arms crossed on her breast, stood in her doorway watching him with contempt.

For the following four or five days the Irregulars or "Diehards" as the "Staters" called them, tightened their grip on the town and surrounding area. Then word filtered through that the "Staters" across the estuary had taken possession of a river steamer and were preparing to cross. The Irregulars felled trees across roads and destroyed culverts and smaller bridges between the town and the shore so as to delay the advance of the "enemy". The shopkeepers kept their premises half-open half-closed. From time to time they glanced out apprehensively at the almost deserted streets.

By long tradition the next day marked the beginning of the Quarant Ore or Forty Hours' Adoration. This was usually held in the Convent Chapel and grounds. On this day the children of the parish, dressed in their First Communion and Confirmation clothes, marched in solemn procession in front of the monstrance bearing the Host exposed: the monstrance was carried by the old parish priest resplendent in copious cope, and walking slowly under a scarlet canopy with golden coloured tassels. The previous year we four comrades had been chosen to act as pole-bearers of the canopy and later had earned the severest reprimand from the seminary president. This was because Toni's winking at one of the girls strewing rose petals on the pathway before the priest had caused all of us boys and girls to be taken with fits of giggles.

Despite the tension in the town most of the mothers brought their younger children to take part in the procession. The usual route around the convent grounds had been reduced by half and the hymn-singing of the nuns and the veiled Children of Mary was tremulous. The priest having returned the Host to the altar turned to address the congregation in the crowded chapel.

"Go to your homes at once," he quavered. "Before long there will be trouble in the town. Once again we have fallen foul of an old engine of destruction."

As they hurried home, the people saw the first flames crackle through the windows of the bank, the hotel and the barracks. I cycled west to the outskirts of the town just in time to see the boardroom of the old Famine Workhouse being set on fire. Through a small latticed window I saw that Brud and two other republicans had just finished piling minute books and ledgers into a heap in mid-floor. I then heard the approaching tapping of rifle fire. As a whistle was blown Brud spilled the contents of a petrol tin over the pile. Stepping back he flicked a lighting match on to the heap, which after a modest beginning of flame, suddenly went up with a huge roar of "Wow".

As I backed away from the window I saw Brud in the company of other armed men hurrying towards an archway leading to the rear of the building and face for the hill above the town. Brud's face was smoke-red and his dark eyes were glaring. He turned and saw me. "I'll get him yet!" he shouted over his shoulder as he moved out of my sight.

I cycled home through clouds of smoke drifting down from the burning buildings.

A handful of republicans set up a false resistance firing from houses which offered a safe line of retreat. There followed an odd silence in the town in which the more venturesome of the citizens opened their front doors a cautious inch or two. I watched from my bedroom window which looked down on Market Street: just as the Yorks had done when enforcing curfew, two files of Staters, one on each pavement, each soldier bearing his rifle at the ready, moved warily below me. I could not suppress a surge of pride to see them dressed in green uniforms - the first native force to be so arrayed since the days of Henry Grattan. They even had lorries - and an armoured car!

I then saw the tall figure of Silvo, dressed in the lighter green of a lieutenant, leap down from one of the vehicles and call the weary lines of men to attention in mid-road. As he strode along inspecting the rifles, his right hand rested on the butt of the parabellum which now nestled on a low slung holster on his thigh.

A town lounger standing on the kerb, his tongue on his lower lip, his eyes a-shine in anticipation of drama, watched Silvo move along the line. His inspection finished, Silvo marched smartly back to where the lounger still stood. I saw Silvo's lips move as he asked a sidelong question; I also saw the lounger's thumb indicate the hill that lay behind the houses. Suddenly Silvo's cold eyes were upon me where I stood half-hidden by the lace curtain on our bedroom window. His eyes flashed me a warning. "Keep your distance," they seemed to say. "I cannot now tell friend from enemy."

I let the curtain fall before my face.

As events were presently to confirm, the Republican withdrawal from the town proved to be a successful ruse. For when, on an order from Silvo, the soldiers of the Regular Army leaped to their vehicles to follow the Republicans into the hills, they drove straight into an ambush on the roadway beside Floyd's place three-quarters of a mile above the town.

Ours was a three-storey house. With my head out the front skylight of the attic I could look over the roofs of the lower houses on the opposite side of the street. I watched as the file of army lorries with its armoured car and a few nondescript vehicles hastily commandeered, moved slowly upwards on the hill road towards the grove of trees on the crest of the hill beside the burnt-out shell of the Floyd mansion. As I continued to watch I could barely make out the stocky figure of a young man crouched on one knee behind a pampas clump on the edge of the lawn where he could not be seen from the road.

As the first of the vehicles moved cautiously into the trees, nothing seemed amiss. The crouched man had his fists locked together on some object. Other vehicles including the armoured car followed slowly. Suddenly as the off-road watcher threw his full weight downward a crude splash of flame was seen. The armoured car bucked and lurched like a crazy horse. A second or two later the roar of the exploding landmine reached me. The roadway above was hidden beneath a lazy cloud of smoke. I saw the man who had set off the mine run away. Still moving in a crouched position as he ran, I had no difficulty identifying the runner as Brud.

Soldiers threw themselves out of the vehicles that as yet had not entered the grove of trees. They hurled themselves against the foot of the fences and the low demesne wall. Rifle fire and the stammer of machine-gun fire was so muted by distance as to resemble the sound of carpenters beating a tattoo on timber. Now and again came the splash and crunch of an exploding grenade.

This went on for some time. Then I saw a Model-T Ford being driven crazily (it must have been reversed in the recess of Floyd's gateway). From the smoky arch of the trees, the car came swayingly down the sloping road to the town.

The vehicle rocked heavily on its springs while a cloud of white road dust rose up behind it. At times it was hidden from my view on the hillside road but again and again it reappeared, ponderously but surely coping with the steep fall of ground. As it was lost from my view at the entrance to Michael Street, I pelted downstairs, raced out the back gate, crossed the market and sped through an archway so as to be in the Square before the vehicle arrived.

As it drew to a shuddering halt in the shadow of the mid-square church I saw that its canvas hood was scraping along the road surface behind it so that it resembled the wing of a wounded crow. It brought with it a smell of hot engine and explosive. "A priest," the driver shouted, as he jumped out and called to a group of Free State soldiers who came running out of the Post Office.

I was one of the onlookers who closed in around the car. I peeped over the low doors: in the front seat a bareheaded private soldier lay slumped over, peacefully dead. His fair freckled skin was translucent: his red hair glistened as with health. On the back seat a second private was also canted over on his side as if he were taking a midday nap. Beside him, his face upturned, sprawled a young officer with mud-matted blonde hair. His face was blood-speckled and his blood-smeared left hand was thrust inside his unbuttoned tunic where the jagged outlines of a wound could be seen in his breast. He was moaning in a way I had never heard a man moan before. Blood from the wound draining through the fingers had spread to form a wide black stain on his tunic. Turning my head sideways I saw that the officer was Silvo.

There was a commotion on the edge of the circle of onlookers. Then through a gap in the watchers, the old parish priest tottered forward. His capella half off, half on, the red tassel of his askew biretta brilliant in the afternoon sunlight, he almost fell as he was pushed by one of the soldiers. When he came close to the motor-car the old man's fingers had difficulty in unrolling his violet stole: when at last he succeeded in doing so he had difficulty holding the strip of silk to his lips so as to kiss the cross on it. A soldier snatched the stole from the trembling fingers and slamming it around the priest's neck and shoulders spun him around to face the vehicle.

Adjusting his spectacles, the priest peered in at the dead soldier in the front seat. His fingers made a fluttering movement indicative of futility. He then faltered to the rear seat and looked in. Seeing the calm dead face his fingers again fluttered. Hearing muttering from Silvo he shuffled around the back of the vehicle and bent down over the car door.

Silvo's lips barely slurred: "Bless me Father for I have sinned." He then began to mutter-mumble his sins.

The soldiers who had come up braced their rifles across their chests. "Back, you bastards!" they shouted as they thrust roughly against the onlookers.

As I staggered backward I could not help over-hearing, "Stole combs ... shot a diehard ... rode a girl in the sewer."

Again, "Back, you bastards!" from the soldiers.

I saw the priest's lips move in the rite of absolution. His hand traced the Sign of the Cross over Silvo's face. Then, his fingertips touching Silvo lightly on the forehead, the old man retraced his steps to attend to the others. To the soldier who tried to bar my way, "He's a friend of mine," I said, indicating Silvo.

Silvo was breathing coarsely. I put my face close to his. "Silvo," I said softly. When he did not respond, I put my lips closer to his ear. "Silvo," I said again. With a great effort he barely raised his eyelids. "It's Barney," I whispered.

The glazed eyes opened a further fraction. A bubble of blood began to form on his mouth. His bloodstained right hand had fallen on to the empty holster on his thigh. I noticed that the index finger of the hand had crooked and was twitching about an imaginary trigger. His lip-corners twisted in the ghost of a smile. "H ... uup!" he muttered faintly. The bubble of blood broke. He died then.

Above me the clock under the steeple began to strike the hour. I turned away to face the first of manhood and to pick up the pieces of a broken Ireland.

🥀 NO MOUSE 🥀

When the huge craggy-faced man entered the crossroads bar, conversation ceased at once. The three or four customers seated on stools at the long counter seemed to bend lower over their drinks.

Kicking the legs of a bar stool into place, while his eyes covertly roved left and right, the newcomer conveyed a truculent challenge to those present.

From behind the bar the publican turned with a muscular smile. He raised his eyebrows in unspoken query to confirm what the newcomer wanted.

Receiving an almost undetectable but contemptuous gesture of the big man's hand, the publican began to pull a pint of stout. From time to time his eyes looked up from the froth-filling glass to glance at his latest customer.

The man was seated alone; his face glowered as he turned his powerful calloused hands over and over as if to ponder the clefts and creases on his palms and fingers. From under his frayed shirt-cuff the blue-splayed flukes of a tattooed whale protruded on to the back of his hand. Now and again the flukes offered a semblance of movement as the big man clenched and unclenched his fist.

The almost-filled pint glass was placed aside for its froth to subside. At last, the filled glass before him, the big fellow threw some coins on the counter: receiving his change he began to chink the coins between his fingers with a sound that conveyed menace.

Still no overt conversation. The man took the first slug of his drink.

The door leading to the kitchen at the end of the bar suddenly burst open and the face of a Down's Syndrome boy appeared. He seemed to be about thirteen years of age. His widely-spaced eastern eyes surveyed the scene. Suddenly recognising the latest customer his head jerked, and in an uncoordinated way he shambled forward, launching himself at the big man now with such violence as almost to dislodge him from his stool. The craggy head swivelled sideways and the craggy face broke into an ill-fitting but indulgent smile.

"Big Dan," the boy chortled. "Dirty man. Wash he face, fryin' pan."

The expression on the weather-beaten features grew a shade more indulgent. Big Dan kicked a second bar stool into place beside him. The boy clambered awkwardly and sat upon it. Nonchalantly the man lifted his pint glass and placed it under the boy's jaws. The boy buried his nose in the glass and gulped and swallowed noisily. He wore a broad moustache of cream-coloured froth when Big Dan indicated that he had had enough.

The boy settled his bottom comfortably on the stool.

A query creased his face. "Fishin'?" he said.

"Show me you," the big man growled.

The boy began to cringe. He tightened his body and bunched his shoulders forwards so as to hide the tell-tale spread of dampness on the flies of his trousers.

Big Dan would have none of it. With rough gentleness and determined tuggings he disentangled the lad's legs so as to reveal the wide stain of which the boy was ashamed.

"Why d'ya do it? You're a big boy now?" Big Dan growled in a low voice.

"We go fishin'?"

"I won't take you fishin' if you keep wettin' yourself like a bloody baby. You hear me?"

"Up at the bridge - fishin'."

"I'll throw you into the goddam river if you do it again. Forty times I told you to unzip your flies, take it out, and piss. Let me show you."

"No, No!" in great agitation. "He bite you."

The publican took no notice. The other drinkers didn't even glance around. A newcomer who had entered the bar and had stopped to watch the odd pair was subjected to a fusillade of stares from all present.

Big Dan had his mouth close to the boy's ear. He spoke in a hoarse whisper, "Listen, you stupid little bastard, get this into your head. You must take it out and slash your water against a ditch or a wall - into the river or anywhere except down your trousers. If you do it again I'll give you a belt in the ear that you'll bloody well feel."

The boy was sulking. Head down, he eyed the man with an odd upward glance.

"Your lesson," Dan said. He spilled froth from his pint out the counter. Smoothed it out to make a little plaque of froth. With his forefinger he wrote C...a...t on the cream blackboard. "C...a...t," he said, "Wha' word is that?"

"Cat," the boy said in a surly tone.

Dan traced the outline of a cat's head on the froth. The boy grew gleeful at once. His lips worked. "Cat kill 'im." he said.

"Kill who?"

The boy's eyes were on his wet fork. "Kill 'im bad," he muttered. "All blood, his head."

Big Dan's stare roamed from the boy's face to the water stain. His eyes gradually registered awareness and realisation.

"Who say?" he whispered in the lad's ear.

"Nanna, Mamma Kate, Josee."

"Go upstairs. Wash yourself. Change your trousers. We'll go fishin'. I've the rod at the house."

The gentle boy shambled gleefully back into the kitchen. "I go fishin', Big Dan," he shouted as he thundered up the stairs.

The man waited until the noise of the lad's boots had died away.

He got up suddenly and kicked the half open kitchen door fully in. The womenfolk inside, the grandmother, the mother and the yard woman all looked up. Concern was written on their faces.

"What kind of stupid bitches are ye?" Dan shouted. He called on Christ and the Mother of God to punish them. "Why did ye tell him to call it that?"

The grandmother spoke, "Not to shame us in front of the people," she said with trembling bravery.

"Could ye get another name for it?"

"What will we call it so?" from the mother.

"What d'ye call it is it? Call it prick, dick, mickie, Patsy Fagan, John Willie, number one or penis."

"Penis!" the grandmother said with scorn.

"Any bloody thing ye like except what you call it. That frightens him out of his wits. The same fright is on an elephant or a stabled stallion. If ye call it that again, ye'll answer to me."

No one stirred. Dan crashed his way back to the bar. Standing, he gulped the remnants of his drink, wiped his mouth and turned to growl at the other customers. All were listening although no one turned.

"If ye see me at a gateway or behind the bushes with the boy don't get any wrong ideas in yeer heads. All I'm tryin' to do is teach him. Before Jesus, if I find one of ye sniggerin' behind my back he'll pay for his snigger with a mouthful of broken teeth."

Still no one appeared to take notice. The publican blandly worked on. If he did glance up it was at the moving flukes on Big Dan's uplifted wrist below the rock that was his fist.

Hearing the din of boots coming down the stairs, Dan strolled out the doorway and walked away. The boy came lumbering after him. They went past the trailing laburnum in flower and the soiling shawl of lace blossoms spread on the blackthorns. At the crossroads they turned left and began to move down the road that led to the river. Old Joanie The Stone, basking in the sunshine and seated on the big stone beside her door, did not look up as the boy squawked in her direction. "We killa trout," he kept shouting. The old woman seemed deep in an ancient reverie.

A breeze stirred the young sycamore trees and revealed the wine-coloured stems beneath the leaves. The first ash leaves were clean against the northern sky.

Dan's roadside cottage stood close to the stone bridge. He lived alone. His fishing rod, with a cast of trout flies stretched on its length, hung on wooden pegs under the eaves and above the door and window. The silver glint of the body of a Bloody Butcher and the gold body sheen of Wickham's Fancy hanging from the cast caught the midday sunlight. On the little gravel and stone strand below the limestone bridge, Dan unhooked the Butcher and gently whipped the air preparatory to casting over the white water breaking from under the nearest of the three arches.

Tentatively drawing the flies a few times through the flowing water downstream from the nearest of the two piers, Dan allowed the lures to drift through the froth dappled ale-brown water. Glancing sidelong he suddenly realised that the boy beside him was clutching the fork of his trousers and seemed to be in pain.

"Hell!" Dan muttered as if to himself, "the sound of the flowing water will set him off." He signalled his moving down a little distance towards the tail of the stream. His boots clattering on the stones, the boy followed. At this point the little river was slightly wider than it was at the bridge. Dan cast expertly: the gossamer of his casting line together with the olive green of the fishing line made a flying S in the sunlit upper air before the tail landed close to the opposite bank where the deeper and darker water lay. As each cast began Dan threw a backward glance to ensure that his flies did not become entangled in a broom bush in flower behind him and below the clay river bank above the gravel.

The boy was hunched close to the angler's left side. His fist was still tightened about his crotch and his widespread eyes continued to watch the rise, fall and passage of each cast. A foolish salmon fry took the dropper close to the shore and fell off the hook close to the boy's shoes; it slipped through the boy's fumbling fingers and was gone like a flash.

The Tallystick

Near the far shore a trout rose and turned over in the water leaving bubbles behind it as it dived away. The "yowp" accompanying the sound of the vacuum of its descent was followed by a similar "yowp" from the excited boy. Dan was calm; he had seen the yellow belly of the fish and had already judged it to be about a pound and a half in weight. Again he landed his tail fly accurately among the drifting bubbles: so lightly did the lure land that it might have been a midge falling naturally on to the surface of the water.

On the third such cast Big Dan hooked the trout. Holding the rod upright so that its tip looped spasmodically under the strain Dan ensured that hook and barb were fixed deep in the mouth of the fish.

The boy beside him danced awkwardly with excitement as he watched the frenzied trout fight for freedom. "Kill 'im," he kept shouting. Dan handed the boy the rod. The boy took it awkwardly: standing behind him and holding fast to both boy and rod, the big man began to step backward so that the trout was more skulldragged than played back onto the gravel.

The boy was shrieking with delight. As the fish clattered on the stones he made as if to throw the rod from him and hurl himself on the trout. Dan grabbed the rod just in time. Holding it aloft he swung the fish inward so that the lad could catch it without becoming entangled in the other flies. To the accompaniment of confused cries the boy would almost clutch the fish, but then, inexplicably at the moment of tightening, his fingers about his struggling prey, the trembling fingertips would draw back. "Kill 'im," Dan continued to shout but the boy continued to draw back until at last, exhausted by its death dance on the stones the trout lay limp and still.

It was only then the boy dared to pounce and claw the highly coloured trout against his grey shirt. "Take out the fly and kill 'im," Dan ordered as the fish continued to wriggle. It took the boy some time to remove the fly: he then thrust the head of the fish into his mouth and cracked it behind the gills with his powerful teeth. The trout gave a convulsive shiver and dangled limply along its arc.

"Wash your hands," Dan ordered.

The trout still between his teeth the boy crouched at the river's edge. He splashed his hands to left and right and then, rising, dried them cursorily on his trousers. He then stumbled to the back of the strand and broke off a strong twig with a fork on its end. Hooking the trout by its gills on an arm of the fork he held it aloft. "I eat him," he crowed. A few scales from the salmon fry that had escaped, glistened on his wet jaws.

"Home now," Big Dan said. Holding the rod before him with its cast of flies flying from its tip, he made to move up the little road by which they had descended to the river bank. Looking back over his shoulder he saw that the boy had thrown the fork and fish on the stones and that his two hands were clasped tightly on his crotch. The lad's face was contorted. He looked quietly at his big companion.

"Undo your zip," Dan said quietly. The boy winced between emotion and physical demand. Twisting and moaning he looked from his hands to Big Dan's face. Dan took up the trout on its twig.

"Undo your zip or I'll throw it back into the river," he said.

Blubbering now. "No, Big Dan. No. I eat 'im."

Sternly. "Do what I tell you!"

Ever so slowly the boy took the metal tab of the fastener between forefinger and thumb. With a glance of agony at the man's face he lowered the tab a fearful inch. From his expression it seemed as if he found the tab red hot.

"Go on," Dan shouted.

A car had stopped on the bridge above. The face of a man appeared: he was leaning on the parapet of the bridge looking intently down.

"Don't mind the car," Dan shouted at the boy. Then upwards at the watcher, "Shag off!"

The face disappeared. The car moved slowly away.

"Now!" Dan had again turned his attention to the moaning boy. "Down with it. Down, down!"

Fearfully the boy obeyed. The flick of a grey shirt could now be seen in the gaping flap of the trousers.

"Come on you little bugger. Take it out. Quick or I'll ...." The man pretended to throw the fish into the water. "No, Dan, No!" Hysterical now.

Dan looked about him. As on a sudden thought he crashed towards the broom bush in flower with the flat sloping bank of bare clay beside it. The clay surface had been made smooth by the waters of winter floods.

Big Dan picked up a twig, snapped it to a point, and with quick strokes began to trace a pattern on the clay table. The head of a cat with pointed ears and slanted eyes took shape under the end of the stick. Then were added a few strokes for whiskers and teeth. A laboured smile of recognition and release appeared on the boy's tortured face.

"Cat kill 'im," he said.

"Good lad," Dan said as the lad's fingertips began to search and his member appeared in the opening of his trousers.

"Run behind the bush and let go," Dan ordered.

The boy shuffled and staggered behind the bush of broom. He stood there under a curtain of willow catkins drooping from the bank overhead. He glanced from the man's face to the scrawled outline of the cathead.

Dan turned away to watch the weaving of the water. Now and again he glanced up at the bridge above him. Behind him then he heard the strong hissing on grass and the sound of spattering on a hidden pool. He waited patiently until the noise ceased. "Put it back now," he said quietly, "and zip yourself up."

The boy obeyed. He turned to face the man. He looked down at his dry flaps and back again to measure the man's reaction. Then, "No mouse," the boy said, his lips working with joy.

"That's right," Big Dan said hooking the Bloody Butcher on the cork covered handle of his fishing rod. He turned and began to walk toward the narrow mouth of the boreen.

With a chortle of delight the lad crashed across the stones to pick up the twig fork with the fish dangling from it. Holding it aloft in triumph he began to blunder after his companion. Out of an eye corner Dan saw that the boy's hair and cheek were coloured with the yellow pollen of the catkins while a silver scale or two from the salmon fry still shone on his wet chin.

As the pair trudged up the narrow laneway to the road above the boy began to chant:

"Dan, Dan, dirty man,

Wash he face, fryin' pan."

Dan's face had cracked into an odd grimace which remotely could be construed as a smile.

🌺 THE CROSSING 🌺

— Excuse me. — Yes, miss, miz? — Do you think we'll get on the ferry boat? — Doubtful. — How many can it take? — Twenty-five, twenty-six at most. — How many in the queue? — Thirty-four. — Oh!

    — Let me see. Three, six, nine ... you're number 25. I'm 26; with a sea like this he might only take 20. — So, again, it's doubtful.

    — Did you come on the island this morning? — Yes. — A bad crossing? — Dreadful. — Must you go back today? — Yes. — At number 26 my chance is poor. You're slim for a woman, I'm heavy as a man. You'll be taken. — I see.

    — There goes a shower. Hissing across the sea. They should have had some sort of shelter here on the pier. — Yes, indeed. — We're lucky to have a ferry boat. This island is remote even by West of Ireland standards. — So I've discovered. — In the old days we had to come out by currach. If the sea was rough we could be stuck here for a week. Hey, grab a corner of this showerproof or you'll be drenched. — Thanks. That's a heavy shower. — It'll pass in a minute. Crouch. Put your back to the pier wall. There, what did I tell you? It's gone. — Do you come here often? — An odd weekend now. To keep my tongue used to the Irish language. — You speak Gaelic? — At times I don't know whether I'm speaking Gaelic or English. —

You like it here? — The best of company in the island pub at night. Where are you staying on the mainland? — Hotel Keevaun. You Irish? — Born in Ireland, went to the States in my teens. — You on holiday? — Well, yes. To see my mother too. My sister was to come with me. She got a tummy upset. I came alone. — I see.

—What is island life like? For a man, you, I mean. — Monastic, but great. — Great? — Plain food, a hard bed, fresh air, a few drinks, a few songs, no phone, no cars, a basking shark. — Company? — International. Mostly one night stands Excellent. — Excellent? — An island breaks people down into their constituent elements. Like mahogany. — Mahogany? — As in old hotels. It makes people talk to one another. Also a cure for insomnia. — Mahogany? — It soaks up the emissions of the spirit. Glass and chromium repel. Watch that pool of water. — The sea looks rougher. — How much so one never knows until one is out there. But it's rough just now.

— Where do the visitors come from? — Everywhere. Young Swedes and Germans chasing traditional music. That boy with the blue anorak is from the Pyrenees. Those two women there are Dutch schoolteachers. Middle-aged virgins. — A term of contempt, virgins? — I use the word loosely.— Loosely? — You trying to trip me up? — The way you pronounce certain words confuses me. — Okay. Three or four mixed doubles. Americans from Vail, Beloxi, Minneapolis and Sleepy Eye, Minnesota. — Any Irish except yourself? — Yes. Dropouts who suffer from the delusion they can write. An Englishman cohabiting in a tent with a pair of French women. — The man in tweeds? — An inspector of Irish here to check the progress of the Irish-sorry-Gaelic, summer college. — You! Where do you stand? — A middle-aged drop-out. Trying to square the Irish circle. — What do you mean? — Trying to solve the riddle of my identity. A fanatic because of the over-compensation of my secret doubts. Hey, duck! — Wha..? — Down, stupid. Here … it … comes. — I'm drenched. It poured over me like a, like a … — I should have warned you. Now and again the sea breaks against the pier behind us and pours over. — It broke the queue. — Take the towel out of my hold-all. Dry yourself. Are you ill? — I was ill this morning crossing. Thanks for the towel.

— You wear light clothes. — Didn't realise … any trace of the boat? — Not yet. Another wave due. Prepare to … dive now. Ooh, we've been under the Niagara. The others took a beating. — Tell you what … squat. — Ground is wet. — You'll be wetter by the time we get ashore. — Is that the sun? — It certainly is. — I feel better on my feet. — Stand so.

— How do you spend your day on the island? — You want to forget the ordeal before you? — Right. — Well, here goes. I get up about 8.30. I'm staying in a cottage. Shave sometimes, brush my teeth, take a shower. — A shower? — This is the first year the islanders have had electricity. It has revolutionised their way of life. As yet it has not eroded anything. — Please continue. — I dress. Singlet and jockey brief, shirt, sweater, denim pants, old sandals. — Breakfast? — Hot fruit juice first, porridge then, which I make myself, a big slice of home-cured rasher, an egg lightly fried, home-baked brown bread and Coarse Cut Irish Marmalade. You bored? — Quite the contrary; it makes me forget the sea. Then? — After breakfast I feel marvellous. I walk up the twisting boreens between the rough stone walls. Peep over them to see little fields like rooms. Find a mushroom. Am looked at by cows. Oh, there goes the mail boat. — Will it call here? — No, it's too big for our pier. It goes to the two larger islands. Besides even if it were calling as we call it, the currachs would be moving out to meet it. Look right through the mist very faintly, that's our ferry boat. — It's not big enough for that sea. — The open deck is a nuisance in bad weather. — Please continue your life on the island. Anything of significance?

— I am on the hillside, at its highest point. Looking at the western ocean. — You are alone? — Completely alone. In the daytime that is. — I see. — The islanders have built crude catchments of tilted flat rocks to collect rainwater for their beasts. I lie on my back on one of these. I enjoy the sun. Shading my eyes I read. Slowly savouring each word. — What do you read? — Poetry mostly. — What poems? — "The Net" by WR Rodgers. "Byzantium" by WB Yeats. "Lament for Art O'Leary" in translation, it's by Eileen Dubh O'Connell. American poetry too. Rhoetke or Berrigan. — Berrigan, the priest? — I get mixed up. Are there two Berrigans? Something about burning draft cards. — Correct. — Rhoetke was on this island. Mad about geraniums. — I never knew that. You write? — Scribble. A compulsive venting of the fermenting cask of my passion. — Lunch? — This is prosaic. — I don't think so. — Midday meal is called dinner. Lunch is something you put in your pocket. — I see. — Packet soup, none the worse for that, bacon home cured and Enfield cabbage, mustard, boiled floury potatoes, home butter, a jug of milk, then cream on jelly, a cup of tea and four thin Arrowroot biscuits. — No one else stays in your cottage? — A Government official, the richer hikers. — Male or female, the hikers? — This and that, or this and this. Or that and that. — Afterwards? — Nap for an hour, then take my togs and towel, chat in Irish with my Woman-of-the-House, stroll to the beach. Swim. Loll. Only three or four others there. — It sounds idyllic. — It is idyllic. Then I watch out for the ferryboat. See who comes ashore. Assess the talent and the prospects for the night. — Then? — Walk on the cliff edge. Pick a corsage. — A corsage, for whom? — For myself, hearts' ease, wild iris, trefoil, wild orchid, cowslip, gentian and sea pinks. — Smells nice, even now. — Correction. The corsage might be for a special companion. — A lady? — Could be. — One of the already noted talent? — Could be. It's incredible to men what flowers do for a woman. — Where? When? — Out of the pub at midnight and up into higher ground. — Yes? — On an errand of intimacy, a woman, often by the implication of murmur, leads her male companion to higher ground. — Why? — So as to be in a position to enfilade the area below her. — Enfilade? — To ensure that there are no interruptions. Also ... — Also? — To see, as in an island context at night, the village lights here and there on the black ground below. — Also again? — To see the white lacy hem of the breaking sea on the far and farther dark. — Then? — She relapses into utter womanhood.

— This is your theory. — With qualifications. — You stand beside her; what do you say? — I say, "We both participate in the Crusoe syndrome. We are alone on an island off another island, off yet another island off the island of Ireland, off the greater island of Great Britain, off the land mass that stretches from Finisterre to Vladivostok. Utterly alone." — Little need to reply. — Correct. — That is your final card? — Not quite. — Continue. — I seek the furthest star with a companion star beside it. I point them out, let her draw her own conclusion. — Excuse my giggle? — Yes? — Nothing. There has been no wave over for some time.

— It's swelling behind the pier, not breaking. — The evening meal? — High tea. Cold meat or hot rasher. — Then you go to the pub? — To drink lager beer, not much. I'm intoxicated before I enter. — Inside? — I chat with my island friends. — About what? — Crops, politics, weather, the antics of other visitors. — Antics? — "*Bhfuil fhios a't?*" *duirt Beartlaí Joe liom cúpla lá ó shoin - ag cur síos ar chuairteoirí a bhí sé. Tagann gach aon sort amach anseo. Bhí beirt Lesbians sa phub an oíche eile. Gach aoinne ag breathnú orrab'*. — I don't understand. — Another islander said to me the other day, "All kinds of people come out here. Two Lesbians were in the pub the other night. Everyone was gawking at them." — That's naïve. — He was talking about Lebanese. — I see. — The caravan is open. A cup of coffee? — Fine. — Won't be two ticks. Hold my place.

— Watch it, it's scalding. — Thanks. That's good. — They get great amusement from the visitors. One of a pair of Cockneys questioned old Pawrick the other day; I was standing by. "Do you know your patches from each other?" he asked the old man. Pawrick thought he was referring to the patches on his trousers. — I see. — I muttered in Irish that he was referring to the small fields. Pawrick muttered, "*A Chríost, cad a dhéanfaidh mé leob seo?*" "Christ, what'll I do with these people?" Then the Cockney asks, "How long are these patches laid out?" "About three hundred years." "Thought you'd mix them up, see?" "We don't."

—The boat is coming. — I can't see it. — It'll come around the headland any minute. — How do you know? — The men at the gable can see it. Old Marge is out on her deckchair. She's a trap. — For tourists? — She tells me what they ask her. — What do they ask her? — "*Bhfuil fhios a't cén cheist a chuir bean díobh orm inné?*" "*Níl fhios a'm, uaimse."* *"Céard a itheas muid?"*. Asked you Marge, what ye eat? What answer did you give her? "Gaineamh." — You told her ye eat sand? — That's right. — There she blows, the ferry boat.

—Very few on board - islanders only.

— Dear God, the boat is jumping and crashing down. — Here she comes. — That woman on board is green and pale, pregnant too. — They'll lift her ashore. They're used to emergencies. That's our boatman with the beard. See the orange peel floating at the foot of the steps. The sleazy steps. Take care. Prepare to board.

— Looks as if he'll draw the line after your Number 25. — Goodbye. I'd feel safer if you were on board. Could he stretch a point? — No concessions on our island. — Will there be a delay? — He'll turn around. He has a second crossing later in the evening. Off you go. You're the last. I'll wave to you. — I wish … I hope … hey! What's he saying? He's counting. Take a single. Any of you people care to take a single? All pairs. You all sure? Well, that lets me in. Down the sleazy steps. Leap over the orange peel. To where the lady with the eyes … For good or ill, here I am.

— I'm glad you're here. I feel safer. — Sit up there by the bulkhead. I'll stand here and prop my back against your knees. — I obey, master. — Tell those knees to stop trembling. And those teeth to stop chattering. — Please. — What is it? — If it gets rough may I grip you? — Sure! Brace yourself. Off we go. Goodbye all you up there on the pier, the disappointed and relieved. Fare ye well, slán beo to the island as we face the harbour mouth and the foul temper of the open sea.

— What is your name? — Woman, just now names are meaningless. As is the place we come from. Labels provide an identification of sorts. But between here and the precious shore beyond there is need only for the common nouns, man, boat, woman, wave and sky. — Pick up the thread. — Of island life? — Yes. — Oxygen, in all its purity, drinks for drowsiness, song, anecdote, banter, wildness, comradeship. — When the pub closes, the higher ground? — I know at a glance when a woman is ready to cast off the first of her seven veils. — Yes? — I could pass a thousand women, make eye contact, and say No No No a thousand times. Then suddenly, Yes. Yes. Yes. — With certainty? — Yes. It argues a lost sense. It vouches for reincarnation or chemical congruence. — You are on the higher ground? — It is midnight. She is beside me. She is from anywhere, from nowhere. I do not seek to silence her. — No? — At this stage I would prefer to open the thighs of her mind rather than those of her body. — Always on higher ground? — Almost always. But there are shore women, rock women, dunes women, chapel women - even pier women. The mention of pier women makes you smile? — Chapel women too. — Chapel women guide me towards the chapel. If I turn out to be a rapist they hope to be able to cry out for the priest who lives close by. — What do you do all this time? — We walk or talk for hours. Intervals of silence in which we see through the darkness the sea, the lights in the little habitations, the sky, our past lives and our futures. — You talk on what? —We probe, cogitate, clarify, discuss, drowse in one another's arms, maybe prompt, contradict, try to bridge the chasm between reality and dream. We also may discuss the merits of books. That depends. — What books? — "Leisure the Basis of Culture" by Pieper, "Being and Having" by Gabriel Marcel, the philosophy of Marcus Aurelius. — And all this time the bodies are quiescent? — That's the last of the seven veils. Fantasy comes naturally to women. Brace yourself now. We are leaving the mouth of the harbour. Hold on ...

— Dear God, that was a dreadful wave. — The boat is broadside to the Atlantic as we turn for home. This is tricky - hold on. — He'll never, he'll never ... — Grip me. — Jesus, here it comes. My nails are going through your hand. I'll never ... — We rode it. We're siblings in distress. — My God, here's another. Right above us. As big as ... she's hurt, that woman is hurt. She was flung ... — Catch my wrist, Sister. — Sister? — Hang on, woman. — Woman? — Listen, all of you, don't fight the sway of the boat. Steady on your feet. — Another wave. Sacred Heart of Jesus, Flower of Mount Carmel, Immaculate Virgin. Here ... it ... comes ... O Crucified Christ. — Brace and relax. — I'm inland, inland. — Spread your legs. Clasp my hips with the inside of your thighs. — Star of the Sea! Mother of the Son of God. — Hang on, there's another ambling alp of water.

— Remember O Most Gracious Virgin Mary, that never was it known ... — Here's a beauty. "There's a wife and wee ones waiting." — How can you sing when we're about to go down, down, down. — "To the One who walked the water once to bring us safely home." Down she comes. Grip, all of you. Hey Sister, what'll you give me if I bring you safely home? — Anything! — Body and soul? — Yes. only don't let me ... "implored Thy help or sought Thy intercession was left unaided" ... It's that terrible silence. — As we go up, the propeller rides clear of the waves. Then there is no sound. When again it hits the sea the sound resumes. — I'm so much trouble. — Trouble? This is glorious. — Are you crazy? Why don't you pray? — I pray in my own way. — Is it God's way? — I could die in a lousy hospital ward. Stippled with bedsores, stinking with methylated spirits. Incontinent fore and aft. Family at my bedside. No one caring a goddamn about me. So if I'm to die, hold me quick ... — O Mother of the Word Incarnate - a monster wave ... Lord Jesus I was sure we were gone. — Let me die in a dramatic coign of vantage ... — You mean? — I emerged from between the heaving thighs of a woman. If we go overboard clutch me closer. As we are swept away spread your legs about me. — The biggest wave yet ... in Thy clemency hear and answer me ... — Now or bloody never, all of you hold on ... over us ... over us ... Ifff ... Hhh ... we're through ... out there, a two-backed beast on the crest of the last wave of all in this insane medium. I shall give the final howl of love for life to balance my first mewling cry of entry. Down then, you and I together in a bag of bubbles into what for me may be an end and for you a beginning. — You shall bring God's anger on us. — God's approval! — How far to shore? — Five waves more. I could have duped you. — How? — I know exactly when we enter the lee of the Little Island, I could have waited until we were at a certain point. — Yes? — Could have stretched out my hands so over the sea and chanted, "Be still you mad bastard," and you might have said, "What manner

of man is this," et cetera et cetera. Only two or three waves more. So
dame dear, clutch me now. If you scream I shall slap your hysterical
face. Grip me utterly. Up, up, up, do your worst, we defy you, O
Wave. Ah, the silence. Come and gone, crested in flecks and froth,
toppled and fallen down. And still we live.

— Thank you O Bountiful Virgin. — Thank me, O beautiful man.
After a hot whiskey in Clancy's you'll feel better. — I don't drink. —
I'll ram it back your throat. — We shall see. — Trail your fingers over
the side when the last wave crests. — Why? — Like a child touching
a corpse, to banish fear. — I'm sitting in sea water. It has been a
dreadful experience. — It's been wonderful. You and I have reached
a common high plateau of energy. — You think so? — You have just
now come to know water in one of its many guises and
manifestations. — Water insane! — There are a thousand other forms
of 2HO. They range from ice-cream to the iceberg, from the thermal
spring to the turnip, from the waters breaking from a mother's womb
to that which oozed from the red side of Christ. See, you didn't mind
the last two waves. Here comes the pier. Steady. Up the sleazy steps.
Blessed be bloody terra firma ... *in saecula saeculorum.* Amen.

— Aye, Mrs Clancy, a rough crossing. Two large whiskeys please ...
hot. — I told you, I don't drink. — How's himself, Mrs Clancy? As
you say, the devil looks after his own. We'll be over there in the
corner of the lounge. — I have never tasted alcohol. — It's medicine
today.

— I am driving a car. — So am I. It's parked outside there for a
week. Sit down till we both get back to normal ... Hello, Angela.
Intellegesne Latinam? Off to Brindisi or Palermo? Sister, when you get
that whiskey inside you you'll feel good. Here it comes; a swirling
lemon moon and hmmh, the aromatic smell of cloves. Okay. Mrs
Clancy. Lady, watch the hot glass.

— Say *Sláinte,* woman! — *Sláinte.* — In yielding to the fumes of
the whiskey I may become loquacious, even pugnacious. — I
understand. — Hope you do. Sip slowly, let the steam rise into your

brain-box. And explore the five senses, the five gateways to knowledge. — The five senses?

The five senses! Seeing? You see the sea, the hillside, a lighthouse, a woman. The sense of touch. Man the striker, woman the stroker. The ecstasy of the fingertips. Hearing? The laughter of women, a traditional song being sung, a whisper, a fart, a shout. Smelling? Let me inhale this fragrant glass. Smell-ing calls on me to pause. O Sister mine. By the sense of smell alone, a man his activity unimpaired by smoking or antiseptic or whiskey, can differentiate the many moods of women. Am I boring you? — Not yet. — Fear sweat, hate sweat, anticipation sweat, jealousy sweat, body-oil sweat, the permanganate of potash smell of menstrual blood, the neutral smell of saliva, the ammoniac smell of urine - can all be detected by primal man, dog man establishing contact with bitch woman - shall I shut up? — I've no comment.

— Hearing? Too boring to exemplify its permutations and combinations. Raucous or sound sweet. I keep reverting to tasting which I am now experiencing. Watch me, enjoying to the full. I recall what the old priest said when he was blessing the bridal pair. "When one of you weeps," he said, "may the other taste salt." Three cheers for the crossing and the whiskey that follows it. Thanks, Mrs Clancy, for taking my signal. If you don't fancy it, Miss, Lady, Woman, Dame or Sister, I'll down the pair of them. Cash on the nail! Pay the woman or leave the bed. What harm if I flood the carburettor. — You're going to drive? — Think I'm a fool? Mrs Clancy has a bed upstairs for me. An old hand here. Told you I'd be loquacious. — You're doing all right. What month is this? — August.

—August is a squirrel. — A squirrel? — An image squirrel. Stores up images for cold winter. Images of The Crossing. Of hot whiskey. Sinful and sorrowful, O Mother of the Word Incarnate. — Don't laugh, please. I thank you for your help. — We're still at veil number three. — I am more acceptable to you now? — Yes, the crossing has broken you down into your constituent elements. — You foresaw it? — Partly. Ever hear of Gerald Massey? — No. — Neither did I. A friend who sends me quotations included one of his. — Repeat it, please. — "Not by appointment do we meet delight or joy; they heed not our expectancy. But round some corner of the streets of life, they of a sudden greet us with a smile." — Says nothing about a rough crossing. — For God's sake don't be literal or obtuse. — Pugnacious? — And with good reason. — I agree; I am not the same person who went to the island this morning. — Outwardly you are the same, a little more windswept perhaps but inside the head there is a radical change. You must learn to yield to the troubled waters of life. Let me savour the moment. — Where are you off to now? — To higher ground. First let me polish off these drinks. — Like that? — Like that. Care to travel? — I'm not sure. — You're safe with me. The thighs of the mind. — I'll drive. — Think I'm drunk. — A little, yes.

— Isn't that view something! The cliffs to the south, the crescent of golden beach on the horizon. — The island? — From here it's misty. Gives no indication ... — Nor does the sea seem angry. — Except at the headlands. See the great waves bloom up, remain static for a fraction of a second, then fall back into the sea. No sound to be heard from here. — All is remote. — Be silent, woman.

   — That enough silence? — Yes. — You have already addressed me as miss, lady, dame, woman and sister. — Which do you prefer? — Sister is correct. — You have brothers? — It's more than that. I am a sister in religion. — A nun? — Yes. — Well, well, what do you know? Sorry I don't wear purple socks and say I'm an archbishop ... Ladies and gentlemen, we have here in this vehicle an archetypal example of the post-conciliar virgo consecrata. If I were sober I'd say that you were a boab. — What is a boab? — A bit of a bitch. — You call me that? — You kept it up the sleeve of your whatever it is all the time. — And you protest? — It's not cricket. — You said we would be anonymous in name and place. — Come to think of it, so I did. But ... — But what? — One night at a private social. A bunch of women round the little bar. Gin-and-limes. Vodka and whatever. Tia Maria's and Marguerites - the ones with salt on the rim of the glass. Want me to continue? — Why not? — Unfettered female chat. High doh in the discussion of sexuality. Hair down to the floor. The young barman, silent up to this, looks up and says, "Cut it out!" "Why should we cut it out?" the women say. "I'm a priest," the bartender says. — What happened then? — Hell broke loose. The dames called him a patent bastard. "You're an impostor," they said. "If you are a priest you should be in clerical garb. The worst kind of eavesdropper. You're just as bad as a layman pulling on a chasuble and going on the altar. Get away!" they shouted, showing their scarlet claws. He skedaddled fast.

— That is why you call me a boab. — Exactly. — The word nun intimidates you? — Right. — I am also a woman. I see, hear, smell, taste and touch like a woman. Menstruate like one too. — Too bloody pat that answer. — I've rehearsed it. — Night and day I bet, especially night. — True! — Boudoir and benediction. Semaphoring taboo and inferring Peekaboo. Know what you are? — No. — For a start you should have had scarlet fingernails. — Do I have to run away or you'll stone me to death? I still say that I'm a woman, despite vows and a veil. Want me to carry a framed legend on my chest? Taboo.

— I'm going to upset you. More. — I doubt it. — There's a story by Camus. It's slightly blasphemous. — Let me hear it. — That Christ did not die on Calvary. That he escaped to the high temple of Isis. And there ... — I know the story. It is allegorical. It seeks to reconcile Christianity and Paganism. It's a classical conundrum. Nowadays it's expressed in novelettes like "The Gypsy and the Virgin". It's used also in the exclusive brothels of Paris. We nuns are omnipresent. When Pizarro encountered one of the great pagan religions of America he came upon corrals of consecrated virgins. In every age we have been there. — Your day is done, my dearest dear. — Not quite. A new appellation, I notice. You married?

— Yes. — So you also are a boab, with bastard replacing bitch? — *Touché*, as the scholar said. It's different for a woman. — Why the double standard? — A woman is the vessel. A man's body forgets. A woman's remembers. — Isn't that what feminism is all about? To redress the unfair balance. — There are lawful means of redressing the balance. Why do you laugh? — I have painted you into a corner.

I am now advocata diaboli or some such. — You're more cunning than I thought. — Every woman is. — Fall silent, wench. — You ask for mercy? — Something like that, if you wish it that way.

— It's nice here, madam. — Quite nice. — I feel completely at ease. Do you? — Yes. — I was about to say but ... — Say it. — Before you fall asleep tonight on your virginal couch examine the inner blades of your thighs and say "Today you've held a man." — You're now a prurient little boy. — What do you nuns talk of in the convent? — Everything. — Love and passion? — That too. — Your vow of chastity? — Does it bother me, is it? — Yes. — At intervals. I was eighteen when I took my first vows. Chastity was then a vague possession if not a negative one. — You surely must have? — Odd cinema gropings didn't count. Our screams of wantonness as we gaggled home in the dark from the circus or even the parish mission. — You speak of these things yet? — Of course. Objectively. We giggle. They're part of the mosaic of conventual life which has immense compensations. — Sublimation? — It does exist, even if you don't believe me. Time for us to be going. Time for you to sleep it off in a backroom in Clancy's. — I agree.

One thing, Madam. Will you recall the crossing? — Yes. — In its total implications? — Of course. It's pabulum for the imagination. The lawful imagination. — That's that, so. — That's that. — I propose to kiss you now. — That's okay by me. — What kind of kiss shall I give you? — You are a man. But there it ends. — Agreed. Here goes.

— You taste of whiskey! — We both do. — You turned out to be a sensitive man. — In what way? — You never pressed me as to my name or where my convent is, home or abroad. — That was the bargain. — Bargains are sometimes broken. — So that's all? — That's all. Goodbye, dear man, dear friend. I shall remember the crossing. — Me too, madam, miss, lady, dame, woman, sister ... — Wench? — That too. The last word is yours. — Goodbye.

❧ THE REVENANTS ❧

It could be argued that in an age of silicone chips, microwave ovens and genetic engineering witches do not exist. However, they do. Without a witch or two it would be a lack-lustre world. If a society for the preservation of witches is to be established, it will not be before its time.

For all the world it happened to be the Feast of the Dear Departed. Just before midnight Old Maag was trudging her way home from a cottage on the edge of the town where there had been a turkey gamble - a rural diversion in which the winner of a series of card games of Forty-five receives a scrawny turkey as first prize. Old Maag was in foul humour for she had won only a single game in a long evening of gambling.

Those playing with Maag never made bold on the old beldame, for she had the reputation of enquiring by improper means after things lost, hidden or to come. Rumour also credited her with having spilled the hot blood of a cockerel on the ace of hearts and of having held up the card at the Consecration of the Mass so as to procure luck of the wrong kind.

Maag never praised the living: she invariably praised the dead. At times she scolded or upbraided the dear departed or spoke to them with amiable irritation, just as she would address a kettle reluctant to boil or a door that would insist on blowing open without apparent cause.

Conflicting thoughts contending in her brainpan, Old Maag staggered alone in the darkness. There was a fitful wind but an erratic moon. Of a sudden she stopped at the graveyard gate on the edge of the town. She glanced sidelong at the ranked crosses faintly showing in the meagre light. Black Harry, her Lord and Master pricked her. She stood irresolute for a while, then pushing her head between the bars of the gate she began to intone:

Gentle ghosts gone like foam
Some of you sadly, wanting at home.

As the words left her lips, a coconut rosary beads hanging from a spike of the gate began to melt into dripping chocolate.

There was an echo of hypocrisy to the complaint. The cry of a widow at the edge of her husband's grave as her eyes secretly sieved the mourners in search of a new man. A husband bemoaning a dead wife while inwardly cheering for conjugal liberty. There was a further echo in the hag's chanting - one tinged with malice and a desire to upset the normal condition of affairs.

The Good Provider also heard the incantation as He hears the chirp of every sparrow in the ivied eaves of creation, the rusty whinge of every peacock in the gardens of the Eastern World, the minor modal song of each black-backed whale under each island cliff in the Northern Hemisphere and that unbelievable medley of minor sounds with which the air is replete, though largely unheard by pure humans.

The Provider left off this whimsical painting of new varieties of butterflies and parrots. As He listened to the reiterated call of the Old Lady, a smile framed his pearly teeth in the recesses of his curling beard. To Himself He said softly, "I'm a little tired of cant. I'm tempted to teach someone or other a lesson."

"Just the very night to do so," He added.

Maag tried to withdraw her head from between the bars of the gate. Her head was a prisoner. So was the rest of her old body. At first she refused to panic. She told herself that she was among her own. Above her was a heavens of scudding moonlight.

As midnight chimed rustily from the steeple of an old church in the town, the clay on the surface of a grave a short distance from the gate began to heave, crack and part. It did so utterly without sound. Faintly at first, but gradually growing clearer by the second, there hung and whirled a little mist of ectoplasm, that viscous substance, if substance it can be named, which exudes, seeps, or emanates from the body of a spiritualist medium during trance and which now through the whim of the Provider was percolating through the cracks of the grave. Gradually, as Maag watched it with intensity, the spinning shape became edged with prismatic hues, the whole writhing and wriggling as if balanced on a tail not unlike that of a huge tadpole or the play-top of a giant child.

This primal shape became still larger: it then almost imperceptibly divided into three parts which wove back and forth, in and out, up and down, until, not unlike a pupa or chrysalis they changed into rather human shapes. These shapes assumed the forms of an elderly man with an aureole of silver hair, a buxom woman in her late prime and a girl who had obviously just emerged from puberty into young womanhood.

Maag watched this, the whites of her ancient eyes showing at intervals faint blue in the fitful light of the sky.

There was nothing even vaguely eerie about the three personages now standing on the pathway. They could have been late family mourners come to pay respects to a common grave. Their clothing, if clothing it could be called, seemed to be a kind of institutional grey. The elderly man was seen to be carrying a black walking cane on which silver mountings glinted at intervals.

The trio drifted towards the gateway where the eyes of the imprisoned Maag recognised Old Malcolm Dunn whose nickname was Sagacity, his daughter Lizzie Grigg, née Dunn and his grand-niece, Mary Josephine Lavelle. The girl, a first year University student of biology, had drowned in the quarry pool having fallen in while picking whitethorn blossoms in early May, an undertaking which everybody in the countryside knew was most unlucky.

At the squeeze-belly stile, although the gesture was completely superfluous, the elderly sage stood aside to allow the two females to precede him. Lizzie Grigg, who went first, paused to offer Old Maag a hostile stare as if to indicate the measure of her resentment at the disturbance of their eternal rest. The old witch closed her eyes and turned her head away.

The revenants then drifted off towards the town leaving behind them the serried crosses and headstones, the squat spotted tombs, the sprinkling of marble angels with bird droppings on their heads; presently they reached the poor radiance of the first of the street lamps and later still moved along the pavement of the main street of the country town.

There was no one abroad: from the recessed doorway of the town bank a cigarette tip glowed and faded; at the same time a button or two on the young Garda's tunic took and lost the gleam. The Garda poked out his head, swivelled it to glance up and down the street - it was obvious that he was less concerned about seeing than being seen. To the Garda the fluent passage of the triform on the opposite pavement could have been a drift of fog or turf smoke. The younger woman kept looking about her. Dreamily, as if sleepwalking, she tagged a little behind her companions.

A brindled cat scurried out of an archway; stopping short before the shapes it made a horseshoe of its back and spat-hissed upwards in their direction. An old stray sheepdog sleeping on a bakery grating on the pavement roused himself with a deep growl and made a semi-circle on the roadway to allow them passage. An inevitable owl from the ivied castle tower rustled its wings above them as it crossed in the upper air of the street.

The revenants turned off the Main Street and entered a narrow row of tall houses of faded red brickwork, their fronts flush with the line of the street. Outside one of these houses Sagacity, who was leading the way, stopped and turned to his companions.

"Things have changed," he said in a deep minatory voice. His daughter Lizzie Grigg nodded grimly. Mary Josephine looked up at the house with an anticipatory smile.

"Discretion is called for," Old Malcolm said severely. "Also tact and control. Daughter," he added, addressing Lizzie. "Bear in mind that you are merely wife of the First Part."

Lizzie pursed her already tightened mouth. As her father raised his hand to lift the heavy knocker, he paused to look up at a first-storey window over which dark blinds were drawn. Turning again; "A wife of the Second Part now shares what was once your conjugal couch," he said. With a glance at Mary Josephine he added, "There is also the new wife's nephew named Andrew Soople. A young man of twenty-three. An electrician."

Mary Josephine's lips came easily apart. "I danced with Andrew once," she breathed.

Sagacity knocked on the door.

All three waited. There was no response.

"Louder!" said Lizzie Grigg.

"Please," from the grand-niece.

Old Malcolm knocked a little more loudly than before.

In the first-storey bedroom above their heads, Judy Grigg née Soople, second wife of Billy Grigg, her pneumatic form squashed against her husband's back raised her head from the pillow. As the knocking again re-echoed through the house her fingernails clutched her husband's breast.

"That our door?" she gasped.

"Dineen's," Billy growled through half sleep.

The knocking came again. It sounded like thunder. "Someone is dead," Judy gasped. "Go down Billy Grigg and see who it is."

Billy cursed under his breath. He swung slowly out on to the floor. Too sleepy to recall that the window was paint-bound he tried in vain for a moment to raise the sash. Dragging on a long brown cardigan and cursing still more vehemently he shuffled downstairs in old carpet slippers. Reaching the front door he bent his head.

"Who's out?" he muttered.

"Open, you fool!" Lizzie shouted from outside.

Billy's first reaction was to growl, "Where's your bloody key, woman?".

On the sudden realisation of the true state of affairs he drew back from the door and made the sign of the cross on himself. Cautiously indeed, the while reassuring himself that he was still half asleep, he drew the bolt, twisted the knob of the lock and opening the door on its safety chain, peeped out. "Whassit?" he asked.

Like three cold draughts of air the shapes brushed past him in the little space allowed. Then as they stood in the hallway, Billy Grigg managed to gasp as if in confirmation of his wildest conjecture. "Holy Christ, it's Lizzie, Ould Sagacity and Mary Josephine herself out of the Quarry Hole." Again he blessed himself feverishly.

Lizzie drifted into the kitchen followed by her father and the young woman. As wife of the First Part she groped on the dark wall just inside the kitchen door. "Where's the light switch?" she asked peremptorily. "It's to the right of the door now," her former husband answered, a bullfrog of bewilderment in his throat.

Lizzie switched on the dim light. Looked around her imperiously and proprietorially. Peered at the Consecration Certificate above its now quenched votive lamp. A new certificate indicated that the house had been re-dedicated to the Sacred Heart in the framed oleograph above. No mention now of herself or her two fine sons in Wyndmoor, Philadelphia. Lizzie, folding her arms across her breasts as if in preparation for a battle, took a seat adjacent to the fireplace. Mary Josephine was already seated.

Billy stood framed in the doorway. His face was chalk white; after an appropriate silence, "What brought ye?" he asked hoarsely.

"Wanting at home," sniffed Sagacity.

"Remains to be seen," Lizzie commented.

The girl made a pleasant humming, purring sound in her nose.

"We buried you decent," Billy was addressing his first wife.

"You could hardly leave me overground," the woman countered.

"What way are you, Malcolm?" Billy asked his ex-father-in-law.

"Perpendicular," the old man said.

Mary Josephine continued to smile vaguely. Her head was held a little to one side. She appeared to be listening to sounds coming from upstairs.

"Herself will get a shock," Billy ventured.

"That she might for fear she mightn't!" Lizzie sneered.

"Is there someone upstairs besides Judy?" from Mary Josephine.

"Andy Soople, Billy's nephew. An electrician."

"A cuckoo," Lizzie sniffed.

"I danced with him in Ballybay," the young woman said.

"Judy gave up her widow's pension when she married me," Billy said.

"Or was it her Old Age Pension?" from Lizzie.

"What age is Andy now?" Mary Josephine asked meekly.

"Twenty-three," from Billy.

"Married?"

"No!"

"I was twenty when I tumbled in," the girl said, not without pride. "I'm still that age."

Billy became alert to footsteps on the stairs. He hurried out into the hallway. Feverish whispering was heard outside. Cuff-huffling and a sense of consternation. Voices. "Dead?" "Alive." "Come in and see." Peering and peeping. Advancing and retreating. Urgency and mystification. Then, "Are you out of your mind?" and "For God's sake call Andy." The faces that peered were coloured red from the red bulb above them in the hallway. And from natural or supernatural agitation. After considerable tugging, Billy led in his wife Judy. She resembled nothing more than a nanny-goat on a halter. She groped just inside the kitchen door, gripped a chair and sat on its edge. She wore an out-at-elbows cerise dressing-gown. She spread her fingers across her mouth and gawked. She made no attempt to greet the visitants. "You, Divine Lord," she kept repeating as she blubbered. The dribbled spittle leaked through her fingers and ran down the back of her hand. "Mine," Lizzie said, addressing her father and indicating the cerise dressing-gown. She looked up at the mantelpiece. "Where's my blue vase?" she demanded.

"The cat," Billy gulped.

"A cat with butter-fingers maybe," Lizzie said. She looked up at the walls of the kitchen. "Such a daub," she added with a grimace. Her stare settled on a paler rectangle on the wall. "Your stickyback is gone, Dad," she said.

"In the attic," Billy put in.

The First Wife glowered at the range.

"My Rayburn is gone too," she commented.

"This one heats four radiators," Billy said.

Judy had come to some kind of terms with herself. With a superhuman effort she asked with all the sweetness she could muster, "Will I wet a pot of tea?"

"Are you able?" Lizzie said.

"That's enough," her father chimed in.

"She can't keep it bottled up," Mary Josephine ventured.

"Strong or weak?" asked the wife of the Second Part.

"Strong," said Sagacity crisply.

Billy grabbed the chance to escape. "I'll plug in the kettle," he said. In the scullery he filled the kettle and looked at himself in a mirror hanging over the sink.

"What dimension am I in now?" he asked his reflection. "What did I have for supper? With God's help, it's only a nightmare. If it's for real, I'll roll with the punch. I'm not to blame. All I did was marry a widow when my prime wife had gone over. Now she's back, the prime wife that is. I mean to say, I mean to say, I mean to say, this doesn't make me an extra-marital canoodler does it? I mean to say, am I bigamist or eejit? Eh? It's twenty past one o'clock in the morning in a small sane Irish town and here are three come-backers looking for tay. One of them died of a superfluity of wisdom, another died of enmity and another died of romancity - the last a girl who tumbled down through the blackthorns and choked on green scum and frogspawn. I mean to say, a man's brain should not be subjected to such enormities. My moral stance was sound," he assured his reflection.

The kettle had begun to sing. Billy clattered ware onto a large tray. "Imagine," he continued in a mumble, "after where she has been and seen, what bothers her now is the colour of the kitchen wall. Is it Nile Green or Woodland Verdure? Eh? They're bloody well not going to sleep here tonight. I mean to say, if this got out, look how it would affect my standing in this town. If Judy doesn't scoot 'em, I'll find some way of doing so. If only people kept hens in their back gardens nowadays like they did long ago, the cockcrow might call 'em home. By golly, but that gives me a bloody good idea. Hurry up kettle and boil!"

Click went the control of the electric kettle. Billy continued to sing in a low voice at the point where the kettle left off.

Still muttering to himself Billy, bearing the tray laden with tea things, returned to the kitchen. "I should have put a stronger bulb in the kitchen - the light might put the skids under 'em. 'Wanting at home' my royal Irish arse. Have I everything, tea, milk, sugar, biscuits? Myself is the crackers. Maag had a hand in this I'd swear. That's what I get for refusing to buy her pishoguey home butter. Get up Tom Coffey and drink your tay."

The three revenants looked down morosely at the tea tray. Billy began to fill the cups. "Shamrock tay," Lizzie said. "Three leaves only." As Judy made to bridle up, Andy Soople appeared in the doorway. All fell silent. He wore a vivid silk dressing-gown.

Mary Josephine put up a ghostly hand and patted her ghostly hair. Lizzie looked from the girl to Andy. Billy flashed a look at Judy. Sagacity closed what was formerly the aperture of his mouth.

All the others saw that Mary Josephine had eyes only for Andy. Andy had electric eyes only for Mary Josephine. Billy made some unheard mumbles of introduction. No one offered to shake hands.

The group was frozen to tableau for an appreciable period of silence.

"Can you bake meal bread?" Lizzie stabbed at Judy.

"With caraway seeds, yes."

"Not if you soak them first."

"My scones were famous."

"Someone told me they were like birdlime."

"Once you have a good oven you can bake anything."

"Can't beat oven and radiators together."

Sagacity made a sound like the warning cough of a mortal. Billy gestured to the untouched fare on the tray. "I daresay you'll have to go back before long," he said.

"We were thinking," Sagacity said solemnly, "of staying around for a few nights."

"I'd love that," said Mary Josephine, her eyes on the flowered dressing-gown.

"And where would you stay?" Billy asked.

"After all the ullagoning you had," said Lizzie with severity - she was addressing Billy, "the least you might do is put us up for a few nights."

"Can't stay here," from Judy. "All the rooms taken up."

"Might stay with real old friends, then."

"As you please."

Sagacity turned to Billy, "Do you still keep pigs?" he asked in an effort to raise the conversation to a more placid plane.

"There's a by-law now against keeping pigs. At a pinch we might put up Mary Josephine," he then added.

"All or nothing," from Lizzie.

"Three musketeers," the sage said.

"My coffin wasn't up to the mark," Lizzie said, glaring at Billy. "And I always told you I detested a brown habit."

"We searched the house for your Child o' Mary cloak and veil," Billy countered. "Couldn't find it."

"Pawned perhaps," from Judy.

"Water under the bridge," Sagacity said dismissively.

"Would any of you like to go to the toilet," Judy was addressing the revenants.

"Toilet?" all three said together. Lizzie put their common scorn into words. "Do we look like people who go to a toilet?"

Since it seemed that no one was interested in having tea, Billy took up the tray. He went out to the scullery and stole open the door leading to the small back garden. Nothing there but shadows, high stars and stillness. A small upper window of the living-room was open so he could hear the conversation in progress inside.

"I got Andy to install a new bathroom suite in pale rose," Judy was saying.

"Chamberpot to match?" from Lizzie.

"The Master room is en suite," Judy countered.

"I built up this place," Lizzie said. Indicating Billy, "When he comes across he'll be buried beside me."

"No guarantee," from Judy.

Out in the meagre garden Billy plucked a blade of grass. He licked the insides of his thumbs and closed them about the grass blade. Placing his lips against the slit he blew a cock-a-doodle-doo. Malcolm alone seemed to heed the bugle call of eternity implicit in the mock cockcrow. The others took little notice. The wives were at it hot and heavy. Mary Josephine's eyes dreamed on. Then lights flickered in the eyes of the young electrician. Billy crowed again. The call now seemed to be making some impression.

Malcolm indicated that it was time to return to their proper home. Mary Josephine drew close to Andy. "Do you ride a motorcycle?" she breathed. "A little," he murmured.

Lizzie played her final card. Outfacing Judy she said, "You've small claim to a man if you haven't a child by him; without a child all you have are words and paper. My sons in Philadelphia won't see me wronged."

The cock crew the third time. "We'll be off now," Sagacity said. His two fellow revenants indicated assent. The older man cleared his throat with a measure of finality. All prepared to listen. Billy stood in the doorway of the kitchen.

"Our visit here has been a wound of eternal law, a lesion of time and space," Malcolm began - "the result of a whim rarely indulged in by the Provider. Why He chose us as exemplars I cannot explain except perhaps that we are ordinary folk and thus are typical. If I hold aloft the flame of a ha'penny dip I cannot illuminate the summit of Mount Fuller. The common head louse, *Pediculus capitis*, cannot be expected to solve a quadratic equation nor a rhinoceros to do crochet. The Provider, the Prime Instigator, obviously has a keen sense of humour, how else could He endow humans with the ability to appreciate and reconcile the more bizarre elements of human life consequent upon which recognition the zygomatic muscle of the upper lip responds in a series of nervous spasms - a minor epileptic fit in fact - a phenomenon which mortals, limited in the matter of precise terminology, call laughter. Superficial observers marvel at man's exploration of space but express little wonder at the fact that the common elver, equipped with only natural radar no bigger than a pinhead, can crawl 5,000 miles of slime on the ocean floor to find its way to a pool in the stream below the town."

"You never lost it," Billy said in admiration.

"Hitachi and Mitsubishi make powerful machines," the girl whispered in the young man's ear. "There's also the Moto Guzzi."

The young electrician had closed his eyes, tightened his fists on imaginary handlebar grips, and was shuddering in imaginary speed.

Sagacity glared at the whispering girl and the shuddering electrician. "'Wanting at home' is a misnomer," Sagacity went on. "We are intruders," he said including the other revenants in the declaration. "Once the game of a person's life is over a new hand of cards is dealt. In this game we have no further part. If the greatest loss to family or nation or mankind were to return in response to the plaint of a hag or the love ache of an adolescent, the revenant would cause an upset. I go further," he said with severity. "We are dirt! Inasmuch as dirt has been defined as displaced matter, a piano in a cornfield is dirt and a cowpat in a drawing-room equally so. A whore in a convent, a virgin in a brothel - dirt! But if piano and cowpat, whore and virgin exchanged places, *pari passu* as it were, the result is harmony. Let us be on our way."

The trio of revenants drifted towards the door. Mary Josephine moved last; as she passed the young man she whispered in his ear, "Faster, my love. Myself on the pillion behind you. Like Oisín and Niamh riding to the land of the Ever Young."

When the revenants reached the churchyard gate they found the old gossip still enstocked between the bars. Her face was white and drawn; her eyes shone like those of a snared hare. Her rump stuck out behind as if somehow she had managed to achieve a position of repose.

Sagacity poked at the old woman's buttocks with his walking cane. Although the ferruled end passed through her flesh without causing pain, the old woman winced, squealed and twisted. As with an odd laugh, Old Malcolm poked again, the crone turned her neck so awkwardly and indeed so fortunately as to release her head from the bars of the gate. The old woman tottered backward, dragged her trailing shawl over her shoulder and staggered away through the mid-road darkness.

Sagacity led the way through the stile. Mary Josephine lingered; "Safety last," she whispered with a final look backward at the dim cut-out of the town skyline. Following the others, she extended her arms and then drew them close to her breasts as if hugging them about a young man's waist. She shuddered as if in response to the shuddering of a machine.

Reaching the grave the three forms stopped. A cloud covered the moonface. "Ready, steady, go," the Sage intoned. Three swirls of paint colour gathered momentum, grew larger, then tapered to the shape of large spinning tadpoles. Then all three forms merged into a single unit and slowly screwed down into the grave. The final glint, indicating that they had been there at all, could have come from the silver mounting of a walking cane or the ray of the moonlight tweaking a gleam from the broken glass of a wreath on an adjoining grave.

This episode which townspeople are wont to describe rather quaintly as a "caper" was observed by the Provider who was watching out of one of His myriad eye-corners. There He was peering down over the ambo of the universe and taking it all in.

"I still have the old touch," He mused. "This reconciliation of opposites constitutes a form of relaxation I should indulge in more often. I possess splendid resources. What with spheres and stallions, volcanoes and vesicles, redwoods, rooks and ravioli, puffins, plasticine and politicians, asparagus, anatomy and algebra, the litany of material to hand is truly endless. To blazes with stasis - I favour kinesis," He said with a rare burst of emphasis.

Then, thoughtfully, "I'll have to keep a closer eye on what's afoot on PE. Fission and fusion in the nuclear sense indicate the pride of my creatures. Knowledge yes, but sagacity to use it also. I mean to say, I mean to say, all this genetic manipulation, clones of a basic nature, in vitro experiments, the uterus as a hostess, embryo banks, untimely rippings, chromosomatic aberrations not to mention human-beast hybrids as prefigured in mythology by the centaur Leda and the Swan - all this might merit a little attention from my Good Self.

The Provider paused. "I'll have to keep a more watchful eye on my matchstick subjects," He said. Then with an omnipotent smile, "I might even steal their thunder by cross-fertilising there with here as on a Superb Occasion I did in the long ago of what they call time."

The Supreme Personage mused in silence for a while. Then aloud, with no one to hear Him in the vast echo-chamber of space, "Young couples keep reminding me of what has proved trustworthy over the centuries. Yes, yes, yes, but nowadays they appear to be sliding off the gold standard of Old Love ... I must scribble the letters OL on the back of my hand to remind me that that mystical, almost metaphysical attribute is currently under siege and that I must do something, something ... about it."

"Drastic? - No! Dramatic? - No! Punitive? - not quite!" Then, "Corrective." He added with a smile, - "that's the word I was looking for."

❧ THE TIME OF THE WHITETHORN ❧

It was May. In the countryside around the Maternity Wing of the County Home the whitethorn blossoms stretched row after row to the horizon.

In the front parlour of the cutstone building two girls worked. One, Betty Carrigan, a slim city girl, flicked the furniture with a duster: the other, Mary Kish, a girl of stronger build vouched for the countryside in the way she energetically polished the floor. After a time Mary Kish sat back on her heels to survey the results of her efforts. Softly, as if to herself, she began to sing:

I wish, I wish, I wish in vain
I wish I were a maid again
But maid again, I ne'er shall be
Till cherries grow on an ivy tree.

"For God's sake drop it!" Betty Carrigan blurted. "You'd swear no one ever had a kid on the wrong side of the blanket before except me and you." Then, "Ssh! Here's Mother Gabriel."

"Come along, Mary! Keep on polishing. Betty, be sure not to leave dust after you this time," the nun said as she entered.

"Very well, Mother Gabriel," meekly from Betty.

"I left a letter somewhere out of my hands. For the life of me I can't find it … ah here it is on the mantelpiece. Ye…es. I see. Keep busy girls, the devil finds work for idle hands to do," the nun said as she went away.

"Polish the floor! Dust the furniture! Put out the ashes! Don't chip the statue!" Betty mimicked, then suddenly laughed aloud.

"What are you laughing at?" Mary asked.

"At the face me man put on him … "

"What man?"

"Him that fathered me child. The time I asked him out to the Feather Bed."

"The Feather Bed?"

"That's a mountain. It's in the County Wicklow."

"Did having the baby trouble you at all?"

"It did at first. Keep an eye out till I light a fag. But of course the money me brothers squeezed out of him helped to heal me wounds. Mary Kish, will I tell you a secret?"

"Yes."

"Betty had a little lamb before … over in Rule Britannia. The first dozen are the hardest … "

"I never knew you had a baby before."

"For God's sake don't shout it off the rooftops. Ssh, here she comes again. Where the hell'll I throw the butt?"

"Smoking! Smoking!" Mother Gabriel commented mildly as she entered. Then, "Here's a nice spray of whitethorn. I'll put it in the vase … at the foot of the statue of the Virgin Mary. Looks pretty doesn't it?"

"Gorgeous, Mother … " Betty said.

"Mary doesn't think so," the nun said. "She probably knows the old superstition that it's unlucky to bring whitethorn blossom under a roof. You're from the city, Betty Carrigan: Mary and I are from the country. Run along to the kitchen, Betty, and prepare a tea tray for two."

"Tea for two?" Betty paused to consider. Then: "Very well, Mother," as she went.

Mary Kish and Mother Gabriel were alone. After re-reading the letter the nun pushed it deep into her sleeve. She went to the window and looked out over the foaming vat of the countryside. Raising herself on tiptoes she watched an elderly man, dressed in a severe black suit and having a slight limp, stump purposefully up the driveway. She looked back at Mary Kish.

"May is the loveliest month in the year," the nun began ... "Everything is so ready. I'd like to know about yourself, Mary. And about the father of your baby. Today ... now ... please ... I have a reason for knowing."

"He was a servant boy at Langford's. The one fellah ever in my life! We had it med up to marry."

"What happened then?"

"A troublemaker came between us. She said I was loose. I was not loose! Now he's gone foreign and I'll see him no more."

"Can you go home when you leave here?"

"No!"

"The whitethorn may bring you good luck instead of bad ... If a second chance came your way I'd advise you to stay in the countryside. You like the woods and fields?"

"Yes, Mother."

"Another thing, love is not always passion. There are quiet aspects to love. Food shared. A home. A fire lighting. Don't let pride or folly deprive you of these if the opportunity occurs. I have to see someone now. Finish off the polishing. Tidy yourself, I shall be back to you again!"

Viewed from the window, the countryside lighted by a weak sun, seemed covered with snow. The white of the blossoms added a glare to the brightness of the parlour ceiling.

"I bet she was drawing you out," Betty said when she returned and found Mother Gabriel gone.

"She was talking about the country."

"I seen a pigsty once, and I didn't eat rashers for a year. Then I seen snails walking on cabbage - Ugh! Before long you'll be free ... Then work your head and your hips ... "

"What do you mean?"

"The world is wide for a woman who's wide. Yeh understand?"

"I wasn't made for cities and noise. The nun says I might get a second chance."

"Once a culchie, always a culchie! Hold the bone and the dog'll follow you."

"You want me to be a class of a ... ?"

"You might as well be that as the way you are. The city is great! The warm nights! The dance-hall stinking with sweat. I'll turn on the transistor ... You and the man closer than close ... The music sending you straight up into the Kingdom of Heaven." She is now at the window. "There's someone at the front door. A middling old fellah dressed in a dark suit. Gabriel is opening it. I'd bet 'twas he wrote the letter."

"Once I sat with Jimmy in a wood," Mary said dreamily. "We were so quiet that the animals and birds came back. They took no notice of us."

"When I'm free, I'm off to some sunny corner of the world where no one knows my name. Watch me and me hips, Mary Kish."

The music-lilting and finger-snapping of Betty came to a sudden stop as Mother Gabriel and her visitor entered the room.

"Do out the dining-room!" the nun said sharply.

"Yes, Mother!" both girls answered as they left. Betty looked quizzically over her shoulder as she went.

"Take a seat Mr ... ?"

"McFerran. Michael Joseph McFerran."

"Of course," Mother Gabriel said evenly. "The parish priest has it all here in his letter. Excellent character, a widower, no family, a good home, eight acres of land, a bank account ... Mr McFerran, you're what we used to call in the old days, 'snug'."

"As you say - 'snug'."

"May I ask why you have come here to look for a wife?"

"Does the name O'Donoghue mean anything to you?"

"Dear, dear! Are there children of that union?"

"Six!"

"And they're happy? Yes? There are compensations for an old meddler like myself! Have you considered, Mr McFerran, that the girls here are what is known as 'fallen'?"

"'Fallen' is a good word. It implies 'rising'."

"Well said! I must press you to be still more frank with me."

"I shall be frank! The fact that the girl is here postulates that she is fruitful. There is also in me a desire to be looked up to, to be respected ... I am weary of hired help."

"Gratitude should not be confounded with love ... Patience now ... we shall see. The girl I have in mind is called Mary Kish. She was here when we came into the room."

"Dancing?"

"No, polishing. A country girl. From the other end of the country. The child is a boy."

"Other arrangements must be made as regards the child."

"Very well! Shall I stay and explain? Or would you rather speak with her alone? Alone? Very well."

The nun is at the door. "Mary Kish," she calls out.

"One moment please. Come along in. Betty, go to the kitchen and make the tea. Stay here, Mary. Mr McFerran wishes to speak to you. Listen carefully to what he says. Don't you think, Mr McFerran, that the whitethorn is wonderful? Mary thinks that it is unlucky, she has country ways like ourselves. It may be lucky for her ... that is if there's such a thing as luck at all ... Excuse me. I'll be back in a little while."

There is an awkward silence in the room when the nun has left. McFerran glances at the girl, then looks down at the polished floor. Mary sinks to her knees and with a shy upward glance resumes her work. Both are ill at ease.

"You are ... Mary Kish," McFerran says at last.

"Yes, sir."

"Please, sit on the chair. Mother Gabriel won't mind. That's it. What age are you?"

"Twenty-two, sir."

"You are not from this locality?"

"What have I done, sir?"

"Please sit down. I'll come to the point. I live in the village of Cleeny. Not young: not old - I have a little land. I keep two cows. I have means and a house ... with a woman it could be a home."

"What has this to do with me?"

"Please bear with me! My wife is dead. I have no family. With Mother Gabriel's permission I have come here to look for ..."

"For what?"

"For a partner ... a wife."

"Why do you ask me?"

"Seeing your circumstances and the uncertainty of your future ... "

"My future bothers you?"

"Not exactly ... perhaps I should not have put it that way ... "

"My future is my own! To make or break. You hear? The world's wide for a girl who is wide. And while I have the hips and the humour ... "

"You talk like a ... "

"Like a what?"

"Like a trollop! I offered you security, a place in society, a chance to redeem yourself ... "

"My body is young. I can have any man I want."

"Any man can have you! That's what you mean, isn't it?"

"You're twistin' my words. Marry you, is it? You're the last man in Creation I'd marry!"

There was a tense silence as Mother Gabriel entered the room. She was followed by Betty bearing the tea tray. Both newcomers took in the situation at a glance, the nun with a composure born of years of crisis, the city girl with a quick tightening of her eyes. The nun sighed deeply as McFerran came to his feet.

"Now. Now!" Mother Gabriel began. "We can't have you leaving us bad friends, Mr McFerran. Besides, see the rain falling on the whitethorn blossoms. The countryside never looked so wonderful - never since the year of my profession. That will be all, Betty."

"Would the gentleman like some more scones?" Betty asked.

"That will be all, Betty," the nun replied sharply, then turning,

"Mary, I advise you to stay. Much depends on your ... oh dear, dear. The foolishness of youth ... she has left us ... Drink your tea, Mr McFerran. Please sit down. Did you say something?"

"I came on a definite errand. I don't mean to come again."

"Go on, please! Is there something I can do?"

"The other girl? You called her Betty."

"I do not recommend her."

"Will you allow me to speak with her?"

"Given time, Mary Kish would see matters in a different light. No? Very well. You understand my attitude as regards Betty Carrigan? I'll call her in. Would you like me to remain?"

"Yes, please remain."

"Betty. Betty Carrigan," Mother Gabriel was at the door. "Come in for a moment.!"

Walking like a cat, sure and unsure by turn, Betty Carrigan entered the room. Her darting eyes were fully alive.

"Sit down, Betty!" the nun said. "I wish to speak to you. We both wish to speak to you. This gentleman, a widower without encumbrances, has come here, as have many men from remote villages before him, to seek a partner, a wife. As a city girl you may find this somewhat unusual. But there it is! He offers a woman a home and a place in his community. You understand?"

"Yes, Mother."

"I think it is fair to say that I first recommended Mary Kish. She did not accept this gentleman's offer. If you'd like time to think it over. Yes? What is it?"

"About ... about the child?"

"That is a separate matter. It can be arranged ... It has nothing to do with Mr McFerran. Speak up, girl!"

"He'd always be throwin' it in my face that I ... "

"Mr McFerran?"

"If in the course of my married life I offend in the matter indicated I shall later humbly beg my wife's pardon."

"Well, Betty?"

"When does he want me to go?"

"Today." McFerran said. "Now! In the bus you will sit directly in front of me. When we reach a certain cottage I shall touch you on the shoulder. You shall stay at O'Donoghue's until matters are arranged."

"Betty?"

"It's all right, Mother."

"Very well! Get your coat and case. Say goodbye to your baby."

"I'd rather go now ... "

"As you wish! Is that you, Mary Kish? Polish the small table. The rain has stopped. They tell me that meadowing was never better. Goodbye, Betty! God bless you. I shall write to your father. Goodbye, Mr McFerran. I wish you both every happiness."

The old nun closed the door and returned to the parlour. She found Mary Kish standing at the window watching the pair move down the driveway. As backdrop to their going the sunlit rows of the whitethorn blossoms stretched to the horizon.

Mary Kish turned to look back into the comparative darkness of the room. She saw the nun's fingers arranging blossoms at the foot of the statue. As the nun looked up their gaze met and interlocked. The girl's face broke; untouched by her fingers the tears moved slowly down her face.

"You're sorry now, Mary?" the nun asked in a low voice.

"Yes, Mother," barely audible.

"So am I, girl. So am I."

The nun did not move; she continued to watch the girl with wisdom, patience and understanding in her eyes.

🥀 APPLES FOR SALE 🥀

It was the throwaway remark of an old tramp that sent me there. "Moneeshal," he said with the oddest of smiles, "is full of lovely daft people."

The description had continued to nag in my memory. So that early on the morning of an August Bank Holiday I drove off to see what kind of a town had merited such an unusual description.

There it was at last; a fairy tale castle above a deserted town, a sluggish river under trees, a square, rather a rectangle, of Georgian houses with, at one end, a hotel its gold-lettered name winking at me from a profusion of Virginia creeper - that was Moneeshal.

I parked my car and entered the hotel.

The lounge or bar was an old-fashioned place. A countryman sat on a high stool, a half-consumed pint of stout on the counter before him. He had an impish twist to his greasy tweed cap and his eyes were semi-closed as if he were recovering from a bout of hard drinking.

At my request the barmaid-cum-receptionist, who had emerged from an office off the bar-room, served me with a glass of beer and a sandwich. With a disdainful look at the countryman she then retreated into her office where a radio was broadcasting a commentary on a Race meeting. My fellow customer opened his eyes to verify that she had left a few inches of the office door ajar. His ear was cocked at an acute angle of listening.

As the race commentary ended I saw the countryman eyeing me from under the peak of his cap.

"No one in town," I ventured.

"Not a sinner," in a tone of complaint.

"Why?"

The man looked at me scornfully. "Race Day in Trabane," he said sourly. "Missed my lift. An' I havin' a dead cert for the fourth race." He glared up at a clock behind the counter which showed the time as half past one.

Silence for a while. My companion again strained his ears to listen to the muffled broadcast from the inner room. As the tempo of the commentator's voice quickened and the name of one of the horses was repeated in a tone of mounting excitement, the man leaped from his stool and began to shout a fancied racehorse up the straight towards the winning post. He snatched off his cap and began to whip his own buttocks with its peak all the while roaring at the top of his voice. The barmaid, her face frozen in an expression of disapproval, stood in the door of her sanctum watching this antic.

There was so much confusion of sound as the race ended that I was not sure whether or not my friend's fancy had won - but as the final result conveyed in quiet tones from the radio he slumped gloomily on to his stool and cast his cap onto his head.

The girl returned to the office. The countryman took a consolatory slug out of his pint glass and growled.

"Every mother's son on the racecourse except Eejit Me." He had cocked his ear again to the renewed murmur of the radio.

He was soon off his stool again. He now stood in mid floor, patted his cap on both sides until it bore some resemblance to a hat and opened an imaginary leather bag. He began to shout in a loud voice. "Six to four the favourite. Two to one bar one. Ten to one the field." He looked through imaginary binoculars, wetted his fingertips and altered a chalked figure on an imaginary bookmaker's board.

Like a character in a Swiss-made clock the barmaid was out again.

Two other figures, an elderly American tourist and his wife, were standing in the doorway of the lounge. Both wore rimless spectacles over which they peered in genuine concern as the "bookmaker" roared onwards. The woman leaned against her husband as if seeking protection. She then guided him upstairs with slow careful steps.

The barmaid was poised to attack, when from the Square outside there came the sound of a car horn. The countryman dropped his racecourse role as if it were a red-hot coin; he rushed to the window, swore a gleeful oath, knuckled the pane and signalled frantically to someone outside, ran back to the counter, drained his glass, wiped his mouth on his sleeve, pummelled his "hat" to the shape of a cap and raced for the door shouting, "I'll catch four of the races."

There followed the sound of gleeful cries from the Square outside followed again by the slamming of a car door and the noisy revving of an old engine. The town reverted to silence.

The barmaid looked at me, then at the window, her lips curling in contempt. She retreated to her hideaway. As she went she slapped her buttocks once in mimicry and scorn. I was left to finish my modest meal in peace.

"A journey in vain," I told myself looking around the silent lounge.

I sauntered out on to the Square. An old beagle lying on the pavement came to its feet, bleared at me with rheumy eyes, then scornfully circled and lay down again. The town itself seemed under a spell; the castle seemed sunk in the sleep of centuries. "A journey in vain," I found myself repeating. I should have known that on a Bank Holiday, everyone, like myself, had decided to be elsewhere.

I strolled along the pavement on the lower and sunny side of the Square pausing now and again to admire the traditional shop fronts or the tall private houses across the broad thoroughfare from me. At the point where the houses ended I crossed the road and now facing back towards the hotel resumed my inspection at closer quarters.

The names on the fascia boards indicated an almost equal division between planter and mere Irish. Although nothing stirred, I had the impression that I was being watched.

So powerful was this impression that on one occasion I turned quickly and scanned the upper windows of the houses; apart from the twitching of lace curtains, which could have been caused by a gentle draught of air, there was no sign of life.

I stopped outside the doorway of a tall house. An unpruned rose-tree and a boot-scraper inserted in the wall beside it vouched for some kind of grandeur gone to seed. The heavy hall-door was ebony black and the brass knocker and doorknob, together with the lock facing, were solidity itself. Hanging from the doorknob by a rubber band was a scrap of irregularly torn cardboard on which something was scribbled. At first I thought it was a warning against fresh paint: when I looked more closely I saw that the notice read - "Apples For Sale".

There was something whimsical about the scrap that held my attention. Obviously there was some life behind its hanging there on such a somnolent day.

A brass bell-pull was sunk deep in the stonework at one side of the doorway. I flirted with the idea of pulling it, but came to the decision that something less formal was called for. The door itself was open a few inches offering a glimpse of a cream hallway within. I dismissed the idea of using the ponderous door-knocker; if I did, who knows what malignant or benevolent genie I might summon. So mounting the single semi-circular stone step I placed my fingertips on the door and pushed it cautiously inwards. The cardboard notice pendulumed a gentle welcome.

The linoleum pattern in the hallway was of imitation parquetry, slightly worn at the joinings. A huge mahogany hallstand with a foxed inset mirror confronted me; it bore a pile of moth-eaten fur coats, some silver-mounted walking-sticks and a hunting horn. A brass dinner gong rested on its glove box. The carpet on the broad stairway had seen more affluent days; at the joints of tread and riser each step was controlled by a strong stair rod of dull brass. There was a spacious landing above.

I looked around me. At the aspidistra in its jardinière before the window from which the light was almost occluded by the neglected rose-tree outside. I raised my voice. "Anyone there?" My call echoed in the emptiness.

Silence.

"Anyone there?" I called in a louder tone. For a moment there was no sound. As I was about to mount a step or two of the stairway I heard the squeak of shoes on the landing above. Looking up I saw a low-sized old lady, with apple-red cheeks and what could have been a neat thatch of white apple blossom hair. She was leaning on the banister of the landing looking down at me.

We stood there, taking one another's measure. I gestured towards the door. "The apples," I said lamely.

At first there was no indication that the old lady had heard me. She remained crouched over the landing rail, smiling down at me as if she had brought off some kind of coup. After a short interval of puzzlement her index finger beckoned me to come up the stairway. When I reached the landing she looked at me in a kind of arch satisfaction. Then, her tongue on her lower lip, she said "Yes?" and signed for me to follow her into a spacious parlour to the front of the house.

I saw small teacups and saucers on a side table. The table was laid for two. Close to the curtains of one of the front windows stood an old armchair with a straight severe back. A point of vantage, I told myself, whence a person could, without being observed, note the comings and goings of the broad street below. Sniffing the vague mustiness of the room, I found the smell of stored apples.

"Tea?" the lady asked in an eager-to-please tone of voice.

I nodded; my hostess plugged in an electric kettle and hastened into a smaller room off the parlour to emerge almost at once with a cake stand with tea-cakes, slices of fruit-cake and scones upon it. For the little space of time she was absent I examined my distorted reflection on the convex surface of a silver teapot.

A white linen napkin spread on my knees, and my little finger elegantly cocked as befitted the occasion, I sipped tea and nibbled a brittle scone in the company of the old lady. She sat opposite me on the edge of her chair, eager to totter to her feet if there was the slightest indication that I needed another queen bun or a "hot drop" of tea in my china cup which she replenished from the silver teapot, taken from under a large teacosy. As she drank, her eyes kept watching me over the rim of her teacup.

During a pause in the little meal she said suddenly, "I knew Honey Fitz."

The statement was so much out of context that I faltered in search of an answer.

"The President's grandfather?" I asked on my recovery.

"Yes," she said. "At that time the citizens of Boston had a custom in connection with the celebration of St Patrick's Day."

"Custom?"

"The most recently arrived girl in the city from Ireland would lead the parade. She'd march side by side with the Grand Marshall Honey Fitzgerald. I had arrived there on March 16th so I was selected to walk by his side. My small hand was in his hand as we marched along."

"An honour," I said.

"Yes, indeed."

"On the platform on Boston Common, before everyone, he lifted me up and kissed me. Then he said, 'This Irish colleen who arrived yesterday is welcome to the land of the free and the home of the brave.' The crowd cheered like anything."

"That was a bigger honour."

"Ever hear of John L Sullivan?"

"The boxer?"

"The heavyweight boxing champion of the world. I met him too, in Roxbury Mass. The men there told me that when he came to an Irish bar, he'd shout, 'Bellies to the bar, boys!' Then he'd treat everyone present."

"I never heard that."

The old lady giggled. "He visited Ireland once. Crossing a field to see the place where the cabin of his forefathers once stood, he put his new patent shoe into a fresh cowdung. He was disgusted. He looked down and said, 'I don't blame Grandpaw one bit for quitting this goddamn site.'"

The old dame and I laughed heartily together.

"Ever hear of Paderewski?" she asked me.

"The pianist?"

"Yes indeed. Prime Minister of Poland too."

"You knew him?"

"At that time I was companion to an old lady of the Rockefellers. She owned a villa on the shores of Lake Geneva in Switzerland. I used to go there with my mistress every summer. Mr Paderewski owned the villa next to us. My mistress and I would often visit there. I'd give a helping hand to Mrs Paderewski, just to pass the time and be neighbourly. She bred different breeds of table fowl - hens and ducks from every country under the sun. She had a hatchery on the edge of the lake. Am I bothering you?" the old lady asked archly.

"Not at all." I said.

"One day Mr Paderewski was in the drawing-room playing the piano. Mrs Paderewski had asked me to dust the room. I came in by the French window with my feather duster in my hand. 'What is it?' he asked, as I stood there. 'Excuse me, Sir,' I said, 'but will you be long more there - I want to dust the piano?' I was young at the time.

"His hands dropped to his sides. He swung around on the piano stool and looked at me crossly. 'Young Irish girl,' he said. 'If you sit there quietly I will give a personal recital on this instrument. If I were asked to give a similar recital in Covent Garden, London, do you know how much money I would be paid for what I propose giving you for nothing?'

"I have no idea, Sir," I said.

"One thousand golden sovereigns!" he said. "Do you believe that?"

"I do, Sir. But will you be soon finished with the piano?"

So engrossed was I in the variety of subjects and personalities the old lady described for me that the afternoon slipped by without my noticing its passage. She transferred a clear and often humorous description of the life of a young immigrant in some of the major cities of the United States in the early years of this century. Her lively description of the festival dances held by the various Irish County organisations - she and her companions often rushed from one dance to another - indicated laughter and banter born of modest flirtation with lads of her own age from every part of Ireland.

Despite her age the old lady's voice was vibrant and versatile. She was a good mimic; her voice ranged over accents high and low, rural and urban, Irish and American and even over broken continental according as the anecdote demanded. There were times when she laughed secretly as she mentioned in passing the name of young men she knew, some of them with, to me, almost unpronounceable continental surnames.

The single symptom of extreme age which she betrayed was the chatter of the bottom of her teacup against its saucer when she was agitated or indignant. This was very much in evidence when she told me a secret of the sinking of the Lusitania.

"There was widespread anti-Irish feeling at that time. It was during World War I and the world press neglected no opportunity to vilify the Irish people," she declared, the while her teacup chattered.

"One newspaper printed a story that a cowardly Irishman, masquerading as a woman, had occupied one of the last precious seats in a lifeboat of the Lusitania in order to save his own skin. The man was not Irish," the old lady declared. "At that time I lived with a rich family in an exclusive enclosure in Upstate New York - a walled-in area complete with a guard house to screen all visitors. Not fully aware at the time - I learned later - I was part of the conspiracy to hide the culprit. He certainly was not Irish. The false story went through the world and is repeated to the present day."

Together we drank cup after cup of tea and consumed pyramids of tea-cakes. Now and again I made movements preparatory to leaving; each time a further exciting anecdote on the part of the old lady compelled me to stay. As we talked, the afternoon slipped by. I began to hear the infrequent passing of traffic in the Square below, and concluded that people were now returning from the beach or the Races. At last I rose, determined to take leave of my hostess: it was then I mentioned my errand.

"Apples?" she said with a gurgle of laughter.

"Yes, the apples."

"Ach, they were only an excuse."

"An excuse?"

"To coax you in." The woman was bubbling with good humour. "The minute I saw you strolling along the opposite side of the street I knew you were a stranger. An enquiring one too, otherwise you wouldn't be here on a day like this. 'What brought him here?' I asked myself. I was lonely like many more." As a postscript she added, "They're all jealous of me now."

"Who are jealous of you?"

But now she was crouched, rummaging under the large table in the room. I helped her to drag out the heavy cardboard box of apples which had a piece torn from its side. Like herself each apple had a blush of scarlet to match the high blush on the old lady's cheekbones.

"Who are jealous?" I asked again.

She had gone into the smaller room murmuring, "I have a bag somewhere." She found the bag; returning, she began to fill the white tissue paper bag with apples, placing each fruit in the bag as carefully as if it were an egg. Presently the receptacle was bulging full. She gently pushed aside the treasury note in my extended hand.

"The notice said the apples were for sale," I said with what little severity I could muster.

"Put the notice in your pocket when you're leaving," she said. "And please pull out the door. Off with you now," she ordered gently.

Her twinkling fingers pooh-poohed the idea of payment. She led me to one of the large front windows of the room. Standing beside the tall-backed chair and drawing aside the lace curtain an inch or two, she signalled that I should look over her shoulder. "Don't let them see you," she whispered.

I peeped through the aperture. Apart from the odd vehicle passing below, I could see nothing of note. I gestured my mystification. The old lady placed her index finger before her lips.

"They're behind the curtains of the windows," she whispered. "Mostly old women - one-agers with myself. Men too. Retired bank managers and insurance officials; an old school inspector and the likes of that. They've seen you coming in here and they're waiting for you to leave. And they're hopping mad that an old woman like me was too clever for them."

"Where are you from?" I whispered.

"I'm from up there in the hills. But I spent a lifetime abroad. I'm here now retired in my granddaughter's house, with everybody at the Races."

After a peep out, she added with a grimace. "They never accepted me. Too proud even to salute me. They call me a blow-in or a runner. The cheek of them. Here twelve years and I'm still a stranger."

The old lady's eyes were firm upon me. "Will you do something else for me?" she asked.

"If it's in my power."

"When you reach the middle of the road, turn on your heel and raise your hand like this to say goodbye. I'll be standing at the window to wave goodbye to you too."

Down the stairs I went to glance back at her ladyship leaning over the banister above. I kept a firm grip on my bag of apples. I took the notice off the doorknob, folded it once and slipped it into the pocket of my jacket. Out onto the open Square I went, facing for my parked car on the lower side, my head held as high as a soldier of the Queen. Out of an eye-corner I saw that, as yet, there wasn't a stir out of the curtains of the tall windows of the place.

On the crown of the road I turned. I raised my right hand above my head to bid goodbye to my hostess. She was standing in full view with the backdrop of the curtains behind her. As I waved my hand I remotely spied the lace curtains twitching in the other windows of the Square. I knew then that I had a wide audience. Some impulse made me yield to a vengeful surge of pride, so I waved still more vigorously. At the saluting base above me, my fair lady was twinkling her hand in farewell.

But alas! Pride goes before a fall. Unconsciously with my left hand I held too strong a grip on the paper bag of apples. So much so, that my fingers, especially my thumb, which were moist with the sweat of the day, went through the flimsy paper of the bag. Too late I sensed the slippage. In an effort to avoid a calamity I clutched the bag still more tightly, bringing my right hand into play as I did so. Despite, or possibly as a result of, my desperate clawing with ten moist fingers, the light paper bag disintegrated and tore to flitters in my hand.

For a moment or two I must have looked like a juggler attempting an impossible feat. At the end of my contortions only one apple remained in my hand; the rest had escaped in every direction. And as they hopped and rolled away they conveyed the impression of being quite gleeful at their new-found freedom.

Standing in mid-roadway, I must have looked a fool clutching shreds of paper and a single apple to my breast.

What was more humiliating still - the tall windows above me were now alive with laughing oldsters - mostly women as I had been informed. And in a refinement of irony there was my apple lady, eight of her fingers pressed against her lips and her eyes glittering with mischief, for she too had joined in the communal titter at my predicament.

My first reaction was one of anger born of betrayal. By this time, too, several of the cars were moving slowly, drivers and passengers obviously enjoying my discomfiture while pretending to avoid squelching the fallen fruit. Presently I had a sizeable audience; I noticed the barmaid's head at the window of the hotel bar. The elderly American pair now halted on the pavement, obviously did not know what to make of the scene, while the grizzled beagle at their feet sniffed the air and yawped idly at an apple that had rolled to the kerb beside where he lay.

And if this were not enough, a shirted figure wearing a cloth cap sideways thrust itself out of one of the open windows of a slowly moving vehicle. Ignoring me, the newcomer, his uplifted hand clutching a swatch of treasury notes, shouted up at the window where my hostess stood, "Mary Willie, I won a bloody packet at the Races. C'mon to the hotel, girl, and we'll celebrate."

As my apple lady twinkled her fingers by way of recognition and genteel refusal, the driver jerked the car forward so that the joyful punter, whom I quickly recognised as the jockey-cum-bookmaker of the hotel bar, almost fell out onto the road beside me. At the same time I saw the barmaid's head disappear from the hotel window.

But I was not easily fazed. I'd show 'em - if 'twas the last thing I did. Imperiously directing the desultory traffic I strolled about collecting the scattered apples. When I had an armful I walked slowly to my car and spilled my load into the rear seat of the vehicle. Off with me then on my rounds again. Most of the apples had rolled down to the kerb where my car was parked; a few had rolled beneath it, and I had to go down on my hands and knees to retrieve them. Believe it or not, one or two had rolled fifty yards from the scene of my downfall.

My collection ended, I found that it coincided with a break in the traffic stream. I then took my stand at the open door of my car and, with one hand on the steering wheel, surveyed the scene with what I hoped were eyes of triumph and challenge. At their posts by the windows the oldsters were watching me closely.

Then something quite unexpected happened. My apple hostess grasped the two clasps on the lower sash of the large paned window at which she stood and raised it slowly. It cost her an effort to do so and the cords and rollers squealed in protest. She stood at the open window, her eyes enfilading the square. Then joining her hands under her chin she began to clap most formally. It took me a moment or two to appreciate that she was doing so by way of applause. One after another the windows of the square squeaked upwards and the watchers followed the example of my patroness. To me the sound resembled that of faraway pigeons leaving a wood at eventide. I was a warrior being rewarded for valour under stress.

I felt proud. I was also conscious of the slight additive of derision implicit in the accolade. To me it was acceptable - like vinegar in a salad. I acknowledged the applause in the spirit in which it was accorded. I bowed in turn to all the windows, half jocularly but wholly in earnest. Raising my hand I blessed my disciples as piously as Padraic MacAlprainn had blessed the western shore from the hill of Ardpatrick in the long ago. Several of the old ladies blew me kisses from lips pursed and lined with age. I returned the compliment. The elders were offering me a gift of commingled appreciation, glee and gentle mockery. And I was pleased with the tribute.

Suddenly the beagle got up and started to howl. The pair of American tourists, now out in the street, clutched one another as they looked around them.

As I drove off, I spun the wheels of my car sharply on the gravel of the road edge so that the tyres whined in protest. I sounded the car horn in the tonic sol-fa rhythm of tapetta tah tah this by way of appreciation and farewell. Off I spurted then out of the magic town and its lovely daft inhabitants.

There was a little golliwog hanging from the mirror over my head. I pulled it down and in its place hung the scrap of cardboard bearing the legend, "Apples for Sale."

Some miles west of the town, at a stretch of the road where the subsoil was of a boggy nature, the surface was marked with widely-spaced folds or corrugations. Here the vehicle, which I still drove at a lively speed, began to swing and bounce so that I had the sensation of being in a currach moving out to sea through choppy inshore waves. Responding to the movement of the vehicle, the cardboard scrap began to dance on its elastic band; when I glanced in the mirror I saw that some of the apples on the seat behind me were springing upward with every downward thrust of the car. It then seemed that everything about me was dancing with delight; when some of the fruit fell to the floor, the knocking noise they made as they rolled against the base of the seat reminded me of the round of applause I had received in the town I had just left.

To this day I have never visited Moneeshal again. When asked to explain why I have not done so I take refuge in what the poet once said - that he cherished "the uncracked eggs of mystery." For the legacy of that day bids fair to enrich me for the rest of my life, inasmuch as it has left me with a series of dramatic images each of which, given its individual stimulus replenishes me on a different level.

The mention of St Patrick's Day causes me momentarily to close my eyes and see Grand Marshall Honey Fitzgerald stepping it out in front of the Irish-American exiles with an apple-cheeked lassie at his side. Whenever I hear a piano being played - hey presto - Paderewski is before my mind at once, his hands idle by his side as he glances smilingly at a girl bearing a duster of brilliant feathers in her hand, while through the open French window the waters of Lake Geneva are seen shimmering in the sunlight.

There are times too when watching an ocean liner moving up the estuary I am greatly alarmed at finding myself on the sloping stateroom floor of the Lusitania, its orchestra playing "Nearer My God to Thee," as the huge vessel slides ponderously to its seabed grave.

But the clearest vision of all is this; whenever I hear the smoky clamour of a boxing match being broadcast on the radio, I conjure up a picture of John L. Sullivan, heavyweight champion of the world. Mark you, I never appear to see him sweated and bloodied in the boxing ring nor even kingly in the convivial company of the bar-room after victory. In my perception, he stands in a corner of an Irish field before the low mud walls of an Irish cabin. A most rueful expression is on his face as he gazes down in disgust at his elegant patent shoes, soiled and smeared with the honest cowdung of his ancestral sod.

❦ THE GENTRY BELL ❦

The old man in the shabby dressing-gown shuffled and tapped his way across the upstairs living-room to the head of the stairway that led down to the shop below.

Thumping the floor with his stick, "Nora May," he called out in a plaintive voice.

"All right, Father," came the reply. "I'll be up in a minute".

Muttering to himself in a querulous tone of voice, the old fellow tightened the grip of his long white fingers on the crook of his walking-stick and moved impatiently about the room.

He paused to look up at the all too noble attitude of Robert Emmet on a picture hanging on the wall, then moved to a framed picture of a small group of younger men wearing cloth caps, carrying short service rifles and wearing old style leather bandoliers. A web of spittle joining the thin lips of his open mouth, he suddenly seemed to lose patience and, moving unsteadily on flopping carpet slippers, he went to the stairhead and began again to thump the floor. "Nora May," came his cracked voice. "I want you."

"For God's sake have patience," came the voice below. "When I've put back the boxes I'll be up to you."

After a short pause the sturdy steps of the daughter were heard on the stairway. The woman was grumbling aloud. "Before God, I'd want the patience of Job to tend a shop and play with a contrary old man." A little out of breath, the middle-aged woman was in the room. "What in the name of God do you want?"

"Did you send him word?"

"How many times do I have to tell you that he's in town and that I sent him word."

"You said the same this day month and he never came."

"I told Jack Mahoney this morning. 'If you have to put a halter on Senator Mulholland', I said, 'get him here to see my father.'"

The old man's face seemed to become thinner and more contrite.

"He's not a Senator any more," he said limply.

"It doesn't matter a damn to me what you call him. Get him here, I said." In a more kindly tone of voice, "Will you go back to your room like a good man."

Stubbornly, "I'll stay here till he comes."

"Have it your own way. You didn't sleep last night. Nor the night before. Hadn't you the priest on Friday? Shouldn't that be enough for you?"

"I want to see Peter Mulholland - that's all."

"Your old nerves will be the death of you. Do you want to fall down the stairs and have me bullragged in every pub in town - that I couldn't look after my IRA warrior of a father in his old age?"

The father grew petulant, then walked away from his daughter.

"I'm nearin' the sea," he said in a low tone of voice. "I have to talk to Peter before I go. Six weeks ago I wrote him askin' to call. No answer." With a glance at the mantle clock, "Ten minutes to five, if it goes any later he'll be gone. And he won't be in town again for a month. 'Twill be too late then."

"Imagination!"

"I feel death in my bones. A few words about the ould times - that's all I want."

"I know. Guff about Spike Island, the Cat and Mouse Act, Bally-bloody-Kinlar and Frongoch. I could write a book about your ould times."

"We did our best."

"And who gives a damn about you today? "

"You're bold and wicked like your mother's people."

"Very few daughters would put up with this."

"We tried our best to give our country respect among the nations. Did we do wrong in that?"

"For God's sake, take yourself easy. He'll be here soon." Nora May walked towards the window. "Is that his car?" she blurts. "Begor it is. Compose yourself now and don't let on you're upset over things that are dead and gone."

The bell attached to the top of the glass door of the shop goes ping. The woman goes downstairs. Her voice rises in greeting.

"Welcome, Senator Mulholland. It's an honour to have you here. He's fine. We all have our good days and bad days. You seem younger than all of them, God bless you."

The daughter's head shows above the top of the stairs. "Father, I've a visitor for you," she says.

Peter Mulholland is a grey-haired well-groomed man to whom the years have been kind. He brings an air of being all things to all men into the room. His eyes have a tendency to bulge. He betrays the public speaker as he addresses old John McCarthy.

"It's your old comrade. Let me look at you man. By God, you're carrying your years ... fairly well." The bluff and hearty manner falters for a moment as Peter glances shrewdly at John. His tightened eyes indicate that he appreciates that his friend is seriously ill. Then, "Bravo, man. Bravo!"

Limply as he turns away, "You're welcome Peter," John McCarthy says.

"We old comrades should see one another more often," Peter says.

"You're taking life easy, Peter, I see. Fine for you."

"I've the name of being retired - I've a pair of women at home, the wife, and the son's wife who keep me goin'. 'Better wear out than rust out,' they say."

"That's the son the TD at home?"

"Bravo! Peter the Second. Have to show him the political ropes. To meet old friends who want ... concessions. I'm kept busy, I assure you."

"Your second boy, how's he doing?" Nora May asked.

"Chasin' women! Won't get married for us. A lively tongue. 'Why should I buy a cow when I get milk?' - that's all his cry."

"Sit down, Senator. I'll get you a drop of something," Nora May says.

"I'll sit for a minute. The daughter-in-law is under the drier at the hairdresser. Sit is it? I nearly got corns in my arse all those years up in Dáil Éireann."

"Take that, Senator," Nora May says as she hands him the glass and starts to pour the drink.

"Cut glass and Black Bush - hard to whack 'em. You're not drinkin', John?"

"I'll pour a small drop myself."

"In a lot of water," his daughter says.

John pours a little whiskey from the bottle into his glass. The lip of the bottle clatters against the glass as he does so.

"Long life to all of us!" John says weakly.

"To hell with poverty and tyranny as well," is Peter's toast. As he sips the whiskey he glances sidelong into John's bedroom. A smile creases his face. "Is that a canopy bed I see?"

Nora May says, "'Tisn't everyone has a canopy bed."

"A good bed is where we spend one third of our lives," Peter chuckles. "Many's the great voyage of adventure took place in a bed. Bravo for the bed!" He takes a full drink from his glass. "I'm in a class of a hurry today so I'll be off with myself."

"Sit for a minute," Nora May says with a glance at her father.

"Stay where you are, Peter," John adds in a slightly stern voice.

"It's the daughter-in-law..." he begins, then breaks off.

"Her own name is Tobin?" from Nora May.

"That's it. A long-tailed mountainy clan the Tobins. They control hundreds of votes up there."

The shop bell rings. "I'll leave ye at it for a while." Nora May goes down the stairs to tend a customer.

When the two men were alone, the atmosphere in the room changed. Peter's apprehensive eyes followed John who was restlessly moving about. After a long pause, John said quietly, "Not many of the old crowd left now."

"No!"

"Only me and you of the real ould crowd."

"Aye."

"Soon there'll be only yourself."

Peter drained his glass. "You'll do the hundred. We'll have to get a gun and shoot you." After an awkward pause. "That was the wrong thing to say."

"The way my mind is working it was the right thing to say," John McCarthy quavered.

Peter stood up abruptly. "I don't want that brought up," he said.

"For me it's now or never."

"Nonsense! You're as hardy as a hare ... "

"A matter of a month or two, Dr Joe says." John was looking at the picture of Robert Emmet. "Latterly it troubles me fearfully. Wide awake and looking up at the ceiling in the small hours it goes round in my skull. Sometimes I jump up thinking I hear the sound of the shot. It's hard, Peter."

"Aren't fellahs dyin' in wars every day of the week? What signifies the lousy little squabble we had in this country? You're making a mountain out of a molehill."

"For me it's as big as Carntuohill. I told the priest. That didn't give me peace."

"Shut it out, man. I could walk around the ruin of the great house in the middle of the night and it wouldn't cost me a thought. Wasn't I up there yesterday watching a girl hiker taking a photograph of the place. Do you think it bothered me?"

"I used to be like that too."

"Give him a long life and the bastard couldn't have lived thirty years more. And at that reckoning he'd have been buried twenty years ago. It took force to break the bone of Ireland and it took force to set it. There's no more to it than that."

"It's like a cancer in my mind."

"We promised never to discuss it. We swore to leave it in the world of dream."

"In the world of nightmare for me. I wasn't so bad until I heard about the bed."

"What bed?"

"The canopy bed was his. It was at Joiner McNulty's the night the Great House went up. Auctioned off later, Nora May bought it after three removes."

"Who told you this?"

"The Joiner's son. He was doing a job here three months ago."

Peter walked to the bedroom door and looked in. "That's a damn good one - his bed," he said with a laugh.

"The young Joiner laughed too. 'A better man couldn't die in Colonel Douglas's bed,' he said. I gave him the door."

There was a long silence. Peter looked sharply at the stairhead as if wondering when he could get away. John stood looking down at the cold ashes of a fire in the grate.

"The hiker campin' near the ruin - who's she?" John asked.

"No idea. A good lookin' filly. That chaser of a son of mine - Paul - female hikers come between him and his night's sleep. I'll hit the road."

"Wait! I must talk this out to the end." John looked up suddenly. "We were young and mad. No more than the killin' of a fox did it trouble me then. In all that happened on that night, the memory of one thing never left me."

"What was that?"

John smiled bitterly. Looking down at the fingertips of his left hand. "The monkey-puzzle tree outside the door. As I went to touch it in the dark I thought the leaves would be soft. But the hard prickles pierce my fingers yet." Then, "The other three are dead. For me and you, death cancels all."

"Where's death?"

"In my flesh, blood and bones."

"Face it like a man."

"I'll face that too. First I have to come to terms with my mind."
After a pause, "He did little harm."

"Only for we having the guts to do what we did then, we'd be
still slaves and peasants weedin' in the fields, our ears cocked to
hear the ringing of the Gentry Bell."

"He was a bold man. A brave one too."

"He had the land," Peter said in a loud voice.

"For all I got of it! No, I'm not begrudging you the 200 prime
acres you got. 'Tis not that at all."

"What is it, so?"

"'You may go and get a bayonet and stick a fellah through,
Government ain't to answer for it - God'll send the bill to you.' I feel
better already for having the few words with you." Then, "You're
givin' up the politics, Peter."

"It looked too much of a thing havin' a TD and a Senator under
the one roof. I asked you again and again if I could do you a turn,
didn't I? Although we were on opposite sides of the political fence,
didn't I? Wasn't I genuine?"

"You were." John looked out at the gathering twilight. "When
darkness falls my limbs start shivering."

"Keep up the ould heart! Good luck now, John."

As Peter turns to leave, footsteps are heard on the stairs. Nora May
appears.

"There's a girl hiker below. An English girl. I tried to put her off.
She wants a word with you, Dad."

Querulously, "What does she want me for?"

"Some class of folklore she's after."

"I'll leave ye to your folklore," Peter says. "Wait! Would she have
blond hair like this?" Peter's hand describes a shock of blond hair in
the air.

"That's her. She's camping somewhere out your direction."

Peter stops. "That's the lassie at the ruin. I'll wait and size her up.

That young son of mine is smellin' around there for the past few nights. I'd like to know what he's up to."

John marches determinedly towards his bedroom.

"Don't go, John," from Peter. "Don't spoil sport."

"You can't be hidin' away, Dad." Nora May says, "It might do you good. Some old legend of the banshee and the Earl of Desmond maybe she's after."

"I've enough to trouble me," John says as he enters the bedroom leaving the door a little ajar. Nora May moves to descend the stairs. "Steer her in here to me," Peter says, "I'll make up some yarn to keep her goin'. And if you hear a screech out of her, take no notice." He laughs heartily at his own joke.

After a few moments Nora May returns followed by the hiker. The Englishwoman is dressed unconventionally but with an element of accurate restraint. She carries a camera slung from her shoulder. Peter adjusts his tie as she enters, and draws himself up to his full height.

"I'm sorry, Miss, my father is resting. Not in the best of health. But here's a man who knows this area inside out - Senator Mulholland. He made most of the history of this locality with his exploits in the Troubled Times."

"You're very welcome, Miss," Peter says, doffing his hat.

"Thank you," from the young woman.

"Take a seat, Miss," Nora May says. To Peter, "Will you lose your drive?"

"Not at all. Bridgie won't be out from under the drier till six. Just after half past five now … "

"Would you like a drink, Miss?" Nora May asks the visitor.

"Yes, please."

"Whiskey is all I have here. I have minerals in the shop."

"Whiskey will be fine, thank you."

Nora May pours out whiskey for the hiker and Peter.

"Will I get you some water?" Nora May asks the young woman.

"I'll take it neat, if I may." "So will I," says Peter. "Who wants to die of dropsy?"

Nora May replaces the bottle on the sideboard. "Your health," Peter says, raising his glass. The young woman responds.

"I didn't catch your name," Peter says.

"Sandra."

"Sandra. Is that the name of a flower?"

"It's short for Alexandra."

"I see. And what part of England are you from?"

"A village in Hertfordshire."

"The country is nice. And if you don't mind my asking - do you have a profession?"

"Not yet. I'm in college."

"What college?"

"In Oxford."

Nora May says, "You must be a clever girl if you're in Oxford."

"Clever?"

"She means intelligent. Are you now?"

"I never asked myself the question."

"Bravo!" Peter says. "Will we call you Miss or Mrs?"

"Miss will be fine."

As the shop door bell pings Nora May with an exclamation of annoyance goes downstairs.

"Campin' you are, is it?" Peter probes. "In the demesne?"

"Yes."

"Right at the back of my place."

"Oh. Yours is the large house with the roses?"

"The very house. Folklore and legends you're after, I bet?"

"Something like that."

"Not much to see there, apart from the old ruin?"

"The house was designed by John Nash."

"Great contractors, the Nashes. Built several creameries around here. It must be lonely for you up there. Crows cawin' away!"

"I don't find it lonely."

"You've had visitors so?"

"One or two."

"Young men I'd wager."

"Yes. Did the alcove above the yard gate once hold a bell?"

"It did. An old bell green with the weather. We called it the Gentry Bell. To distinguish it from the chapel bell."

"Did a monkey-puzzle tree once grow beside the main doorway?"

"One of your visitors told you that?"

"He did."

"A sprawling spiky old tree. It's gone this many a year."

The girl looked up sharply as the ping of the shop bell indicated that a customer had left the shop below.

"Come to think of it," Peter began in a measured tone, "It *was* there."

"You got some of the land?" the girl probed.

"For generations we worked for the Douglases. I got my rights."

"Of course. Your rights."

"A few acres around the house were left to one of the Douglases. For sentimental reasons. None of them ever turned up to claim it. How do you intend using all the knowledge you have collected?"

"Largely for my Master's thesis in History." Addressing Nora May who has just returned, Peter said, "She's writin' a thesis and maybe 'twill turn out to be a book."

"What will you call it?" Nora May asked her visitor.

"The Decline and Fall of the Anglo-Irish Ascendancy."

"That should make a great book," Peter said with a shrewd glance at Nora May. "I didn't catch your second name, Miss."

"It's ... Douglas."

"Did you say Douglas?"

"Yes, Sandra Douglas."

There was a long pause. Nora May looked at Peter. Peter looked at the woman. "That's a coincidence, your being a Douglas," Peter said with a still sharper glance at Nora May.

"What is?"

"Your being a Douglas. The people who owned the Great House and the estate were Douglases too. Isn't it a small world?"

"It's not *quite* a coincidence."

"No."

"The last Douglas who lived there and indeed died there was my grandfather."

Nora May took a step forward. "Was old Colonel Douglas your grandfather?"

"Yes, indeed. I believe I am the owner of the ruin. And of the forty acres of rough woodland to the west of it."

"Well, well, well. What do you think of that, Senator?" asked Nora May.

"Did you tell all this to the young fellah that came visiting you?" Peter said.

"No. He did all the talking."

"I see," Peter said, his joviality set aside. "You'd be Master David's daughter?"

The girl nodded. "You remember him?"

"I saw him as a boy. The Colonel's only son."

"His only child too."

"Is your father still alive?"

"He escaped the entire war. Dunkirk, North Africa, Italy - not a scratch. Knocked down by a silly scooter near the Crystal Palace. Never recovered. Died. His wife, my mother is also dead."

"Life is strange."

"He was rather bitter about this place."

Sharply, "Why did you come here then?" Peter asked.

Sandra paused. "Because of something one of my professors said."

"What was that?"

"To know yourself, you must know your grandparents."

"What did that mean?"

"I hope to recognise myself as it were in an old mirror. I have come back to see Colonel Clement Coburg Douglas and his wife Jennifer, before they were … uprooted."

Nora May broke in and said tartly, "How can you hope to see them if they're dead and gone?"

"By speaking with those who knew them."

"Is that all you want to know?" Peter asked.

"Not quite all."

"No?" Peter said quietly.

"I know that my grandfather, the Colonel, was shot of course. I want to know more."

"More?" Peter said slowly, conscious that John was standing half-hidden in the bedroom doorway.

"More?" Peter said a second time.

"I want to know if he died bravely or howling for mercy beside his monkey-puzzle tree!" The young woman paused, turned and looked fearlessly into Peter's face. "Were you one of those who shot him?"

"What did you say?" from Peter.

"I don't have to repeat it," the girl said calmly. With a glance at the bedroom door Nora May blurted. "If you came here to stir up trouble, my girl, you'd better be going!"

"Perhaps I'd better ... " Sandra came to her feet.

Peter said in a loud voice. "Let her stay. The fellah who visited your camp told you some of this. Who was he?"

"A likeable chap. Inclined to boast. My fault really."

"How was it your fault?"

"I wagged my tail and he followed me. 'Did I sleep alone in my tent? Was there any need to light the lamp ... ' He stayed."

"You bitch! So this is where my son Paul spent last Sunday night."

"Oh." Coolly.

"That's what all before you did - slept with their tenants' wives," Nora May said.

"A pagan crowd with morals like dogs," Peter added.

"Tellin' an Irish father to his face," said Nora May. "On your road, my girl!"

All three turned. John entered from the bedroom. He shuffled to where Sandra stood and looked sharply into her face. Nora May moved forward. "Father, you're in no condition to be up," she said.

John was peering closely into the girl's eyes. "A Douglas, eh?" he said. The young woman nodded. "I knew that one of ye would come back." As if speaking to himself, "You're welcome, girl. You're flesh and blood whatever. I'm tired of cardboard giants walking through my brain." With spirit, "I'd rather it was a man of ye that came. So that maybe I could fight with him. You had a drink, had you?"

The girl nodded.

"You'll have another. Nora May."

"I'll pour no drink for her."

"You'll do so, if I say it."

"Pardon me," Sandra said. "It was wrong of me to come."

"You came at the right time, for me!" John said. "Ask what you want to ask. I'll give you a start. 'Twas I that took the Colonel's life. Under his monkey-puzzle tree. Peter! Add your word."

"Well met, a traitor and a bitch in heat. I'm damned if I'll darken your door again." Peter clamped on his hat and made for the stairhead.

"Peter, old comrade, wait." Peter stopped. "This girl has ghosts to banish. So have I. For both of us, it's now or never. Don't you see?"

"I see nothing," Peter said.

"I see less," said Nora May.

There was a moment or two of irresolution. In her level English voice Sandra asked, "What did the Douglases do to you? Or you? They made order and beauty in a wretched land."

"They made us beggars at our own table. They owned the land. They got it by force." Peter said.

"Me and Peter were born in slavery," John said in a weak voice that battled to sound strong.

"The land was crying out to be broken," Peter snarled.

"The land for the people and the road for the bullock," John said.

Sandra looked John up and down. "Some of you were probably better off even then than you are now."

"Maybe. But then we had no dignity," said John. "My father and mother couldn't marry without going cap in hand to your great-grandmother Amelia Douglas and beggin' her permission."

"My father and mother the same!" Peter said. "Tell her about the mowing, John."

Old John paused and repursed his lips several times before he spoke. "In his day, my father was a famous mower," he began. "After he married, Amelia Douglas said to him, 'Mower McCarthy, as payment for work done, you may have as much hay as you can mow in a day.' This amount was called a 'scythe.'"

"Bravo John!" said Peter.

John paused to recover his threadbare composure. "At the crack of dawn, my father took his scythe and began to mow a wide meadow below the lawn of the Great House. All day he mowed ... a blistering summer's day. My mother, throwing her light shawl over her shoulders, came across the fields to bring him tea and bread. He gulped it down and again commenced to mow as if he was a madman."

"Tell on, John," Peter shouted.

"Old Amelia watched him from a window. A twisted smile on her lips. About midday she told Benton, the butler, to bring her a jug of buttermilk. 'Take this to the mower with my compliments,' she said."

"A kindly gesture," Sandra's murmur was answered by Peter crying "Wait!"

"She had pickled the buttermilk with Glauber Salts," John said. "Well you may smile, my girl. My father couldn't hold his bowels in check. Soon he was runnin'. No sooner out of the wood than back again. She up at the window smilin' away!"

"Tell it to the end!" Peter interjected.

"And give this girl real cause to laugh," said Nora May.

"My father spotted the trick. He stripped off every screed he wore and mowed naked all that summer day. 'A bargain is a bargain,' he shouted at Benton the butler when he came down to tell him to behave himself. Sometimes he crouched where he stood so as not to lose mowing time. Rising from his grug, off with him mowin' again."

John paused. He had difficulty continuing his tale.

"Listen now, young woman. When I shot your grandfather all I could see was my own father in his pelt and he crouchin' like a dog.

And for deprivin' a man of his dignity, even if he was the lousiest tinker in the land, I still believe that the man who did it should be put to death."

"What have you done with your tinkers?" Sandra countered.

"Let 'em keep the laws or take the consequences," Peter broke in.

"Did you keep the laws in your day?"

"They were crooked laws," said Peter.

"The girl has a point," John said.

"What point has she?" Peter retorted.

Old John drew himself up. "I read in the paper that in the city of Limerick with its Confraternity to storm heaven, two tinkerwomen, one with six children and another to come, their horses sold, had to pull their wagons through hail and rain to find another resting place. Peter Mulholland, is that the Ireland we helped to create?"

"They smash the fences. Their horses trespass. They leave litter everywhere."

"Do you know who pulled those wagons through the Limerick streets?" John countered.

"Who?"

"Your mother and mine. I'm a sick man and soon to face my Maker, but I spit Shantalla and Rahoon out of my mouth. I see Ireland as the unjust Steward of the Gospel - forgiven a great debt, he choked another steward for a paltry sum."

"Wasn't there some peaceful way to get what you wanted?" Sandra had spoken in a controlled voice.

"Peaceful way?" said John scornfully. "The rabbit on your grandfather's lawn was thought more of than the people of the cabins."

"He called us by our second names," Peter said. "Donegan! Meehan! Mulholland! McCarthy! It cut us to the quick."

"And for that you shot him in cold blood?" from Sandra.

"That blood was boilin' for many a day. Your grandfather called in the Yorkshires to cow us," John said.

"We jumped a bicycle patrol below the wood. Milo Shanahan got shot," Peter broke in. "They bayoneted him to death. Tied a rope around his heels and dragged the body after a Crossley tender into town. And photographed his body squatting on a water butt. 'Twas then ... "

"'Twas then we said we'd need the guns," Peter said loudly.

"The land as well?" from Sandra, still cool and as if taunting the old pair.

"Yes. To have it at last in Irish hands," said John.

"Three centuries we were here. If we weren't Irish, what were we?" the girl countered.

"Bastards! Except for an odd good one here and there."

"What are you now?"

"You tell me. You know it all," said Peter.

"Usurers? Hucksters? Would these words fit the bill?"

"Not quite," Peter said. "Out of the estate came twenty farms."

"Including your own?" the girl shot.

"Exactly. But out of those other farms came priests, doctors, teachers, lawyers. Bravo for that!"

"We gave you peasants a culture," the young woman continued.

"We had an older culture than yours. Keating, Merriman, the Kerry poets. In our own language too!" from Peter.

"And fifty years after your so-called revolution you can't speak a word of it."

"Who kept Irish out of the schools?" John said, his voice breaking.

"Your young people - where are they now? Your Gaelic dream? Your country broken in two?" from Sandra.

"Who broke it?" John said with intensity.

"You'll soon be drowned in a European sea." Then in an altered voice, "Before I go ... "

"It's 'go' and nothing else," said Nora May.

"You know what's in my mind?" the Englishwoman asked.

"I won't stand for it!" from Nora May.

"I'll stand for it!" John said in a loud voice. "For I want it too." Turning to Peter, "She wants us to tell out the story of the Colonel's death."

"And why should I want to do that?" Sandra wore the thinnest of smiles.

"To test the mettle of those who went before you. Right?"

"Right!"

"And I want it too," from John.

Peter with a muttered exclamation made for the stairhead. Nora May came before him and put a hand on his forearm.

"Senator Peter, please! Do as my father says. Then let him go his road in peace." Peter turned in irresolution. Nora May drew the curtains. The rings moved with a screech to leave a small aperture of light. The noise of traffic on the roadway was muted.

John walked to mid-room. His hands were shaking. He appeared to battle down his terror. The others stood in silence waiting for him to speak.

"We met at midnight in Meehan's forge. Meehan the Smith was one of us. Five in all. Jack Donegan killed after by a car in the Isle of Wight. Tom his brother, died in Long Island, New York. Peter here and me. What light had we, Peter?"

"A candle on the hearth," Peter said after a pause.

John turned to Sandra. "A bunch of country boys calling ourselves volunteers. Preparing to attack a city."

"Bravo!" Peter said, unexpectedly. "The Great House was like a city. Grooms, chambermaids, butlers, gardeners, gamekeepers and under-strappers answerable to a steward."

Limply from John, "I had a single-barrelled shot gun. Two cartridges was all."

It was Peter's turn to speak. "Halfpast twelve at night. I carried the can of paraffin. Going through the woods we shook with dread. John, I went first?"

"Aye, you went first."

"You next, carrying the gun. The house was before us - big and white. Above us was the Gentry Bell. One man was for goin' back ... "

"No names!" John almost shouted.

"God rest him - no names!" Peter agreed. "We passed the harness room and stole round to the shade of the monkey-puzzle tree. All except me tied the rags about their faces. The caps down, shadin' our eyes. I threw a fist of gravel up at the Colonel's window," Peter went on. "After a while the window opened. 'Who is it?' the Colonel asked. I stepped out, a letter in my hand. 'Sir,' I said, 'Parson Wilkinson gave me an urgent message for you and no one else.' 'Who are you?' he wanted to know. 'Alfie Miller from Ballyvoureen,' I said. I heard a woman's voice. A boy began to speak, as if in his sleep."

"The boy was my father," Sandra said.

"We waited," Peter went on. "He closed the window. The front door was boldly opened. He was too proud to open it inch by inch. Of a rush we were into the polished hall. Under the paintings of ould Douglases."

"For a minute he stood glarin' at the five masked faces around him. 'Scum!' he said. Then 'Scum!' again. He was tryin' to coward us."

"But not for long," Peter broke in.

"Meehan spoke up, 'Colonel' he said. 'All we want is your guns.' 'I'll see you all in hell first,' was his answer. We heard footsteps on the landin' above. The boy, your father, was out in his little nightshirt. Your mother was stirrin' too."

"We dragged the Colonel out then," said Peter. "I pitched him head first into the monkey-puzzle tree. He bounced back up shouting 'Scum! Lice!'. He made a lunge for John. 'Fire if you're a man!' he shouted."

"I stood back," said John McCarthy, "and dodged him." He spoke in a calm tone beyond hysteria. "I lifted the gun. 'Don't defy me,' I warned. 'I defy!' he shouted as he came at me the second time. I fired! His sideface jerked, opened, and blackened. He fell like a paling post."

Sandra placed a restraining hand on Nora May who shook it off.

"I ran to the back of the house," Peter said. "I broke a window at the cellar step. I poured in the oil. I cracked a match. Up go the flames. Then I ran like a redshank past the bell to where we had made up to meet. The others were there before me - white as ghosts."

John gave a sudden snort that defied interpretation. "I had a prayer book - the Key of Heaven. We put our hands on it. I have it here!" He was fumbling in a drawer until he found it.

Peter gave an odd laugh. "Crackedness gave me a poet's mind. I made up a fancy oath of secrecy."

"Each of us in turn kissed the book," said John. "We went home." After a pause, "We two being the last alive, have the right to call back our oath."

For several moments there was silence. Nora May threw open the curtains. A sense of twilight seeped into the room. John stood apart from the others. He was limp and downcast. He raised his head. "Peter!" he called out.

"Yes, John?"

"Today they call us funny men."

"That's it, John, funny men."

"We weren't funny men at Headford Ambush. Nor at Tooreengarrive Glen!"

"By Christ, we were not!" Peter said.

Nora May moved to Sandra's side. "See how this has left me," she whispered. "Bitter and barren, havin' given my life to tendin' him."

Sandra placed her hand on the woman's forearm. "It's been a good day for me," she said. She unslung her camera and took it out of its case. "May I?" she asked.

"Take our pictures? Not bloody likely!" Peter said.

"Why not?"

"Because you'd show myself, and that man there, all over Oxford as a kind of rogues' gallery. 'Tuppence to see the wild Irishmen who shot my grandfather.'" Looking at John who had struck a pose. "You're not going to stand for that, are you?"

"Go ahead, girl, take your picture," John said.

"I want none of it," Nora May said. Seeing the girl fit a flashbulb and raise the camera she slipped in beside her resolute father. "Take me with him!" she said.

"Bravo!" says Peter. "Me too, begod. Peter Mulholland once MCC and Teachta Dála - now ex-Senator Mulholland - Photographer, get my credentials right."

As Sandra lowered the camera and started to replace it in its case, "You're not going to take it?" Nora May asked. "Why?"

"Because you were willing to stand for it". To the men, "Did I tell you I was a Socialist?"

Peter gave a loud chortle. "Hear that, John McCarthy? Now we're the bourg-eois-ie and she's the girl standin' barefooted at our castle gate. That's a turn in the world."

There was a tentative titter of laughter from all four.

"Bravo again!" Peter shouted. "There are Douglases rowlin' and roarin' in their tombs today. You John dyin' in one Douglas bed and my son Paul canoodlin' in another!"

There was general laughter and Sandra moved towards the door. At the stairhead and on the point of leaving, unexpectedly Peter gave a loud whoop of discovery. Turning, his eyes slitted in cunning and merriment he stage-whispered into Sandra's ear.

"You married, girl?"

"No."

"Are you a woman of means?"

"I'm not poor, if that's what you mean."

"Bravo! I've the brainwave of a lifetime. A fitting finale to a glitterin' career in public life. Listen to me, girl." To the others, "If I bring this off 'twill be a stroke that will be remembered." "Bravo!" he shouted, and waved his hat in the air.

His lips were again close to the English girl's ear. "Throw off that anorak till I get a proper look at you." With a look at the faces of the other, the girl did as he requested. Peter walked around her as if he was a buyer examining a beast at a fair. To John, tremulously watching, it was as if Peter Mulholland was back again in the early days of his first election. There were thousands cheering. There were torchlights and white horses. As he spoke, it seemed as if he were taking a host of people into his confidence and not addressing Sandra alone.

"Politics for me is the art of the impossible," he whispered. "I'll put a proposition to you, Miss Douglas. For your life don't say 'No.' Sssh! Not a word. You own the ruin and the rough land beside it. 'Twould be easy to slap a roof on the house for the walls are sound. I'd go halves with you in it and the Great House would rise again. One stipulation - you'd marry my son Paul."

Sandra laughed aloud. "You are an incorrigible rogue," she said.

"I'm that, and more. Think of it. The house rebuilt. The lawns laid out. The garden tended. A new gentry rising up. Hunt balls, beagle packs, lights in the window. You could even get the canopy bed. Paul is to fall in for what land I have - the other son has a career in politics."

Still laughing in spite of herself Sandra said, "He's an RC - I'm an agnostic."

"I don't care what religion you have - I'll box it all up. No registry office in this country! Get buckled abroad and I'll wangle a blessin' for both of ye in some chapel in the hills. Everything will go smack smooth. Sssh now - don't say the word 'No.' You have the hips and the creameries my girl. You can christen your children, Peter, David and Amelia Douglas-Mulholland. Bravo, begod, bravo!" As Peter again put his laughing lips close to the girl's ear. "Say, 'I'll think it over'. C'mon, say it!"

As if doing so to please him, Sandra said, "I'll think it over." Peter yelled in triumph.

"You can drive in here to Nora May of a Saturday to buy your groceries. I'll wangle her a branch of one of those new chain stores. The chance of a lifetime, Alexandra! Foolish men start wars: wise women end them - in bed!" As a car horn sounded in the roadway below. "That'll be Bridgie, her face all red. You'll go home in the car with me, sittin' beside me in the back seat! Tonight, you'll sleep in the house with the roses."

As if playing along and yet probing, Sandra asked, "What will the local people say?"

"They'll love it, girl. Country people are breeders first and last. I'll be the talk of the country. Ould Amelia Douglas born again. 'Twill collar the last half a hundred Protestant votes for the Mulhollands. The more I think of it the more I like it. Bravo! I never lost it. Did I John?"

John McCarthy responded with the thinnest of smiles. Nora May came forward. "Miss Douglas," she said, "will you have a cup of tea before you go?"

Peter yelled with delight.

"Give her a mug of buttermilk," he shouted. "And pickle it with Glauber Salts. With her camera I can take her stickyback and she havin' her bloomers down. Yehoo! This country isn't settled yet. We haven't made up our minds whether the shootin' of a landlord is a tragedy or a comedy. Good luck, John McCarthy." He roared as he gripped John by the shoulder. "Wait for me at the gates of Paradise, you havin' the Key of Heaven in one hand and a rusty shotgun in the other. You looking like a cross between Rip Van Winkle and St Lawrence O'Toole. Bravo man. What the hell about it? We'll take pot luck on the life to come."

Turning to Sandra, his eyes roguish, "Keep close beside me on the road home. But never forget that 'twas often an ould chimney caught fire."

The shop bell rang from below. "Bells!" Nora May said with some annoyance as she hurried down the stairs. Peter followed.

Sandra stood at the stairhead and looked back at John.

Then, "Are you all right, sir?" she asked quietly.

The old man had moved across the room and was turning on the radio. He looked at the girl and in a calm voice replied. "Yes, I'm all right." The sound of the Angelus bell being broadcast filled the room.

Sandra watched for a moment as the old man crossed himself and began to mumble the prayers. The girl's eyes glinted with an impish sense of adventure.

❧ THE CLOAK OF FIRE ❧

It was late afternoon, as, gripping my young nephew's hand, I toiled along the track that led upward from the dunes. In my other hand I carried a suitcase containing the boy's clothes. Before us a rabbit dragged a lazy rump into the furze that grew at the landward side of the track.

"Come Brendan," I said to my elder brother's son. "This place will be different from the city. But you will be happy here just the same."

The boy made no reply. He looked dismally upward to where a huddle of houses crouched under a peak, of which the northern flank had been sheared downward to form a cliff face above the sea. Following the boy's gaze, I found the white face of the house which had been pointed out to me by the postman in the village.

After walking for a while, I stopped and turned to look backward at the view spread below. The boy turned too. Together we saw the tents of the mountain range that all but ringed the bay. To the east, on a ridge above a village, was a red-roofed shed in which the Gaelic language was taught during the summer months. The western ocean was all silver: this same silver was splintering fiercely on the roof of my car, parked at the mouth of the strand. At the ends of the headlands the Atlantic swell recurrently bloomed into spray.

"Speak Irish only: here the language is still alive," I advised the boy. "That is why I have brought you here, to learn your own language." Brightly, I added: "Here, too, there will be sheep and a sheepdog. And, of course, cows and hens."

The boy looked sidelong away from me.

"If the people here keep you," I went on, "you'll be lonely when your time comes to leave. The people here are so ... so ... "

So what? I asked myself. I failed to find an answer.

Standing there the thought crossed my mind that what I was doing was, in essence, selfishness. Was I just imposing my personal vision on the boy? I had always raged against change in its many manifestations. The phrase "the very last" was one that continued to dominate my thinking. I was constantly firing salvoes against the uncertainty change engendered in me. Or had I another target? Was it myself I wished to renew when confronting the clash of new and old? Of archaic and futuristic? Of stagnation and dynamism? Perhaps too I would find at the moment of impact a still centre of experience where my imagination would find repose. In short, would I discover here, a place of "the very last", a rich provider of experience that would save me from falling into decay?

Brendan looked dolefully at the hills, the bay, the dunes. He then eyed the ragwort in bloom beside the track.

"When you have settled in," I said, "I'll go back to the village for a meal. Tonight I'll return to say goodbye. Early in the morning I'll drive back to the city."

The boy's lower lip began to tremble.

"No tears," I said, taking his hand and resuming our upward journey. "This place, remote as it is, represents an Ireland that has almost vanished. I want you to live in it, if only for these few months of summer. Before long the world will break in upon this way of life. Later, when you are a man, you will look back with pride and say: 'Yes, I saw it before it was no more!' You understand?"

The boy began to say something but, as if thinking the better of it, stopped short and fell silent.

"Up!" I said cheerfully. The boy's hand tightened in mine. We moved upward.

Presently we reached the cluster of houses. These faced in different direction; some had caps of old thatch held in place by nets weighted down with dangling stones. Cowdung was everywhere underfoot. I crossed over a stream by a crude bridge of flagstones and walked towards the gable of the house I sought.

As I did so, I was aware of faces half-seen in the dim interiors of the houses. Of twinkling half curtains, some mere rags of lace. I realised that the faces were those of the old. I realised, too, that the strange silence that hung above the place was due to the absence of children's cries.

Beside the gable, a break in a drywall gave us entrance to a shabby enclosure. Here nasturtiums grew in crude flower beds edged with old car tyres. The front of the cottage had been freshly whitewashed: there were three dormer windows half-in and half-out of the crudely flagged roof.

As we entered the enclosure, a sheepdog came bounding out and rushed past up to do puff-ball battle with hens scuffing in the clay by the gable. Brendan crouched against my side. I felt the sweat ooze through the boy's hand as the dog swept by.

The open doorway was a step above me. Peeping in I saw a wide airy kitchen. Directly opposite the doorway was a settle-seat. At first I thought that the place was empty: then I saw a girl seated near the far corner of the kitchen. She had her back turned to us and was leaning towards a low open fire. Her head was bent and her hair was down about her face. In the act of combing her hair she seemed stilled as in a dream.

The boy looked sharply up at me. I was conscious of the pounding of the sea.

As the sheepdog came bounding back, the boy, anticipating an attack on one of us, gave an exclamation of alarm. The girl looked up. Her face was flushed and wildly alive. Pegging her hair back over her ears, she sprang to her feet. Until she had betrayed herself by glancing downward, I had not noticed that her feet were bare. The girl - she was eighteen at most - blurted "*Cad é*' - "What is it?"

Releasing the boy's hand, I came up the step. As I did so I was conscious of an access of power.

"*Cad é?*" she asked again, as I walked forward.

Quietly, my mind not fully on my words, I began to explain in bookish Gaelic that I wanted to find a place where a child could stay. I had been directed to the house. Glancing at the suitcase the girl answered me in broken guttural sentences. The village, the cart, her grandmother who would be back later - I caught that much of her meaning. Her father at sea on the trawler - that too I understood. So there were difficulties.

Then the girl looked past me and saw the boy.

"*A Dhia na Glóire!*" she breathed. "God of Glory - a boy!"

She started to rush past me, then checked herself. She raced through the open doorway of a bedroom beside the foot of a ladder that led up to a loft. Almost at once she came out wearing a pair of once-fashionable slippers. She then hurried out into the enclosure.

With women who move past me in agitation, I go by smell. It is the bull and the stallion in me, for these male animals are in me and in every man. The smell of her fresh sweat - was wholesome - and exciting.

Outside the doorway, the girl, her face ashine with delight, had crouched before the boy. She held his hands in hers. Endearments tumbled from her lips. "Son of my heart inside," "My share of the world," "My only, only treasure" - these appellations I mentally translated from Irish into English. The boy seemed to be struggling with the pleasurable turmoil of his age.

Again I heard the insistent beat of the sea.

After a time the girl seemed to realise that the boy did not understand her fully, so she began to address him in hesitant English:

"White-child, I understand - yes. Here you will stay! A cock with a red comb we have. On the mountain you will see the turf-baskets slung across the ass's back. Together we will have sport and we milking the cows. When my grandmother will come home, she will put cartloads of welcome before you. At night, too, the old man will come in to tell stories."

"Stories?" I asked.

The girl came to her feet. She glanced at me coldly. As she returned to the kitchen, the boy followed her much as a calf follows a cow.

I was suddenly aware that I was superfluous. The child and the girl were engrossed in each other. "Would I have tea?" "No, if you don't mind." So having promised to return from the village at nightfall when the girl's grandmother would have come home - I made my excuses and went away. The boy did not seem to mind my leaving him in the cottage.

At dusk, I returned. Thoughtfully I drove through lanes lined with fuchsia blossoms brilliant in the headlights, swung off the narrow road, bumped along a rutted lane, switchbacked on the hummocks of the sandhills, by-passed the loud mouth of the strand, swished through a stream, accelerated on the rough incline, and at last pulled up at a point where, later, I could turn the vehicle without the risk of pitching into the ravine beside the track.

I locked the car and strode upward. The smell of sea flowers was powerful on the night air. The wind had freshened. There was no moon.

After a time my eyes sensed, rather than saw, the sliced-down peak; guided by its shape I moved upward. At a corner in the track I blundered into muck. Muttering to myself I drew my soiled shoes back and forth in the bent grass of the track edge. Wild iris blades slapped against my trouser-ends as I trudged on. I crossed the slab bridge and swung in by the house gable. Again and again I asked myself what I was up to. In an age of micro-this and micro-that, of pocket calculators too, was I trying to set the clock back a century or more?

I knocked at the door; the door was opened from within. I entered the kitchen.

Inside I saw a variety of people, late middle-aged and old, obviously neighbours. An erect old woman came forward. My eyes went over her shoulder to see the girl, now brilliant in a red dress. She was standing in the doorway of a room beneath the ladder stair. A yellow nasturtium was set naïvely in her hair.

The Tallystick

An old man was seated by the open hearth - obviously my entrance had made a break in his storytelling. Brendan sat beside the storyteller; on his face was an expression of impatience, directed, I saw, at me.

The grandmother, her hands held out in welcome, greeted me warmly. Under her thin grey hair her eyes were brown and her face was a criss-cross of age-lines that gave her complexion a dark cast. She addressed me in a Gaelic that had a faint nasal resonance to it.

"The boy - he will be all right with us," she said. "See! - already he feels at home. We have fallen in love with him. My sorrow that the young people have gone from us across the sea." Then: "Have you eaten?" she asked.

I told her that I had just finished a meal at the little inn in the village.

Brendan was eager. "*An scéal!*" he said. "The story!"

But the old storyteller had become encased in offended dignity. I murmured for leave to mingle with the people at the end of the kitchen; eventually I took a seat near the foot of the stair. The girl pleaded with the old man to resume his tale. After a time he relented. The girl smiled at me, and, raising Brendan from his seat, sat in his place and taking him on her lap, clasped her arms about him.

A gust of wind roared in the chimney. The storyteller, spreading his hands before the fire, began to speak.

"With the fall of the night," he said in Gaelic, "there came a storm that'd blow the horns off the cattle. The King's son journeyed on until he reached a cottage by the shore. He knocked at the door but no one opened it. He lifted the latch and went in. By the light of a pine knot aflame in a crack in the wall, he saw a girl seated by the fire. The girl was combing her hair. Seeing him enter, she stood up, pushed her hair back over her ears and looked at him without speaking ... "

(For me there were two fires in the kitchen; the fire of blazing turf to which the storyteller seemed to be addressing his tale, and the fire that was the girl in the red dress, her arms tightly laced about the boy.)

"As the prince looked at the girl," the old man went on, "he found his heart snared with love. Suddenly the girl snatched the cloak from her shoulders and flung it about the prince's head. Of its own accord the cloak took fire. The prince clawed at the blazing cloak. As he did so, his hand touched the girl. She tried to break away but he gripped her firmly and pressed her body close against his. The cloak fell to the floor and quenched. The prince felt the air grow cool about his face. The girl smiled up at him and nestled closer to his body ... "

Out of an eye-corner I noted the girl of reality - her cheek was on Brendan's cheek, her eyes were alight, and her lips were apart as she listened to the tale.

"Just then an old man came into the cottage. He had a sack slung across his shoulder. In the sack was something wet and heavy. 'A young bull seal,' the man said. 'I clubbed it on the head at the edge of the tide. It's as near death as makes no matter.' He set the sack down in a corner of the kitchen.

"Later the old man made a bed of rushes beside the fire. The prince lay down on it, drew his cloak over his head, and was soon fast asleep. In the dark morning hour he awoke. Again the cloak was about his head choking him almost. Above the sound of the wind he heard like-as-if-it-was a human voice crying in the distance. 'Ro-o-o-ona!' the voice said. As the prince threw off the cloak and came to his feet, the sack in the corner stirred. The seal in the sack began weakly to answer the voice calling in the faraway ... "

(The girl - for me, her dress a flame, her body a flame. I found myself jealous of the boy where he sat with the girl's arms clasped tightly about him.)

"The King's son heard a footstep behind him. He turned. The girl of the blazing cloak was standing there. 'What is it?' she whispered. 'Listen!' he said. Together they listened. 'The young cow seal is calling from the sea,' the girl said. 'Together we will take the sack to the tide.' She threw her cloak about her shoulders. The prince did likewise. He lifted the sack and accompanied the girl. They came to where the tide was a flock of white animals jostling in the dark. They saw a black shape in the broken inshore water. Its head was twisting this way and that. 'Ro-o-o-ona!' the shape cried. The prince and the girl caught the sack by its toes and spilled the young bull seal out on the sand. The bull seal hobbled towards the tide. The prince and the girl stood and watched while the seals' heads caressed and made off into the open water. As they turned to go back to the cottage, prince and girl looked deep into each others' eyes."

As the story went on I found passion like a stairway mounting before me. Inevitable? I asked myself, my head fixed in one position, my eyes straying to the red dress, is there no power strong enough to keep me away from this girl? Is it preordained that her fingers should falter up along my face, her fresh young sweat be perfume in my nostrils, her body come congruent to my body? Must I, of compulsion, answer her mating call?

I resolved to test what appeared to be the inevitability of my fate. I was determined to prove that I was stronger than a clubbed seal thrust into a sack and slung into a corner.

The storyteller ended his tale. The boy, loaded with sleep, almost fell forward out of the girl's arms. With a cry, the girl raised him up and helped him before her up the stairs. The storyteller and the neighbours stood up, bade their guttural goodbyes, and headed off into the night. The old woman and myself were left alone in the kitchen.

I sat on a rope chair looking down at the dying fire. Upstairs the girl's lullaby was a caress set to music. "Cow with a single horn," - that was the air she hummed and sang. Once, as the old woman moved to the fire to set a saucepan of milk on crushed embers, I tried to catch her gaze; it seemed as if her eyes were deliberately avoiding mine. I heard the sound of a door creaking slowly shut and the light footsteps came down the stairs. "He's asleep!" the girl said, her face alight with excitement.

Sitting at the table-head, I drank a mug of hot milk with pepper and a knob of butter in it; I ate a buttered sector of bread made from

Indian meal. Serving me, the girl moved swiftly about. As the old woman passed the delph on the dresser I sat that her dark wrinkled face seemed to grow darker still. She seemed fully on the alert.

The meal ended, I thanked them both, murmured something about paying for the boy's keep and prepared to go. The girl looked sharply at her grandmother.

The old woman said wanly: "*Ní fanfair?*" - "Will you not stay?"

I gestured vaguely in reply.

"Here we have an empty room," the girl broke in, indicating a doorway leading to a room at the back of the hearth.

"The bed is aired," she added. "Shivaun's father is on the sea. You need not trouble about your car - no one ever comes that road." After a glance at the girl: "If you have a case in the car, Shivaun will get it for you. Give her the key."

I stood in indecision.

The girl saw my pause. "Yes - yes!" she said. "In the morning the boy may be lonely for you. For tonight - you will stay with us?"

I found my lips murmuring acceptance: "The lock of the car is hard to manage," I said lamely, looking at the car keys in my hand.

"The girl will go with you, and show you the way." The old woman was standing in the doorway of a bedroom at the foot of the ladder stairs. There was something of resignation and sadness in her tone.

Together the girl and I went out into the night. The peak towered above us. Shivaun did not go by the track - she went by a series of crude gaps and low stiles across the fields. Entering a fuchsia-choked pathway we came to a gap in the low cliff where, below us, the waves were brawling in the dark. My car was a short distance along the torn road. After a pause the girl moved down to the beach. I followed. On the dry sand she took off her shoes and stood on tiptoe looking about her. She glanced at me where I stood, a little distance apart.

Night, sand, sea, stars, headlands, hills, dune smells mingling with the smell of fresh sweat of a body grown lately into womanhood, the memory of the cloak of fire and the caressing seals - all began to overcome me. I moved. The girl moved. The pretext of a gust of wind flung her against me. I caught her and swung her around to face me. As I had anticipated, her body was firm, warm and welcoming.

For a moment she was close to me, utterly womanly as I was manly; then she broke away. I followed her as she raced across the strand, making for the corner where the dark cliffs were. "Shivaun!" I called, my cry served only to make her increase her pace.

As I ran, I was taken with the feeling that I had touched a spring of ungovernable emotion in the girl and that she now intended throwing herself into the sea. This fear made me race the faster. I was at her heels, when, like a hare dodging from a hound, she swerved to the right and into a cave. I followed her, sensed her in the dark and, in a lull of wave thunder, pounced on her, gripped her, and swung her to face me. Using all my strength I bore her backward until I had pinned her against the cave wall.

"*Cad é?*" it was my turn to ask - "What is it?"

Of her tears, her broken phrases in Gaelic and English, her odd gesture, I could make no sense. She kept twisting her head this way and that, her hair a torrent about her face. Nothing that I could do or say would comfort her. Caress was out of the question. She was like a wild-born kitten brought into a house for the first time.

After a time I pushed her from me. I strolled to the comparative brightness of the cave mouth, lit a cigarette and, setting my shoulder against the rock, looked out on the powerful waters. Presently I sensed that she was behind my shoulder. Even when I found her hand faltering, first on my shoulder blade, then on my shoulder, I didn't turn.

Her voice was level, as she said in English: "Please! You do not understand!"

I drew deeply on my cigarette.

"How hard it is for you to see what life is like in places such as this," she said. "Here it is all dream and story. The gull with the broken wing, the rabbit wounded by the snare - these sorrows I can suffer. But the coming of the boy - that is so terrible because soon he will go away. The same it is with you - only deeper. So real you are, that I will be wounded. If you were always to stay, it would be different. Stay I must, to see to my father and grandmother. But like as it is now, knowing that I must lose you, it could not be suffered."

In the intervals of silence we had that sense of intimacy as if we had known one another since childhood.

After a time I set an arm around her shoulder and locked my cool hand in her warm armpit. Side by side we stood, looking at the sea. The waves came gathering, rearing, thinning, tattering, toppling, thudding, hissing up and in and away, until at last they sank into silence. A seabird flew above us: we could hear the rustle of its wings. I found my eyes searching the inshore water, as if I were seeking the questing head of a seal.

"Kiss me once," I heard her say.

I kissed her fully as she had asked. Then, laughing, she twisted away and flung me an invitation to follow her in a race across the sand. I took her at her word. This time I was rough with her. Tripping her, as if she were a boy, I caught her ankle as she fell and threw her down sideways. With a cry of joy she rolled over and, finding her feet like a cat, was off again to renew the game. I began to yell at the wind, at the waves, at the sea, at the girl dodging swiftly before me. At last, tiring of the sport, she took my arm and, tightening her nails into the back of my wrist, shuddered fully. Then she directed me to the point where she had left her shoes. There, shaking her shoes free of sand, she leaned calmly against me as she donned them. Together we moved upward to the car.

That night, hour after hour in the room behind the hearth, I tossed without sleep. I dropped off once but awoke with the feeling that a cloak of fire was about my body. It must have been three o'clock in the morning when I swung out of bed and told myself that what I needed was a drink of water. I recalled seeing a white enamelled pail of water on the ledge of the dresser, and having spent a short time looking out of the bedroom window at the ragged sky, I slipped on my showerproof coat over my pyjamas, opened the room door and quietly entered the kitchen. As I did so, I heard the sheepdog pad on the gravel outside the window.

Tiptoeing forward, I took a cup from a brass hook on the dresser, dipped it into the pail and, leaning against the dresser, began to sip the water.

My eyes kept straying to the doorway of the left hand room beneath the stairs. The door was ever so slightly ajar.

The kitchen was quiet and strange. The fire was soundless with only a few sparks in the grey ashes. As I continued to sip, the house seemed to draw a common breath of expectation. Once I glanced at the corner of the fire, as if half-expecting to find there a sack containing something wet, heavy and alive.

For a long time I stayed there, sipping slowly at the water. I kept asking myself if it had been pretence on the girl's part; if she had been playing a game designed to bring me to the climax of this hour. Again I glanced at the room door, then drained the cup and placed it on the dresser ledge. I had begun to retrace my steps to my own room, when, coming to a sudden decision, I turned and moved forward to the doorway of the girl's room.

I was almost there when I heard a door creak. I glanced at the doorway of the companion room at the front of the stairs. Behind the newel post I saw the face of the old woman. I stood still. As her eyes came out of the darkness to find mine, she came forward to meet me. She had a small shawl thrown about her shoulders.

"You are there?" she said softly.

"Yes!"

She padded forward until she was quite close to me. "Can you not sleep?"

"No!"

"Sit on the chair, son!"

After a pause, I sat on the rope chair beside the fireplace. The old woman took the tongs and raked out the fine seed of fire from the ashes. As she did so, her face was coloured by the glow from the embers. I saw the tongs drag to a halt on the flag of the hearth. She looked at me, then rose and closed the door of the girl's room.

"It is the strange bed that prevents you from sleeping," she said. "That - and the youth that's in your blood. You and me," she added, with a lilting sigh, as if what she was saying was part of an old song. She glanced at the store of fireseed she had heaped together, then set the tongs against the wall, and stood before me.

"Give me your hands, son," she said.

I gave her my hands. She kissed each of my palms in turn, then pressed the back of my hands against her face.

"She with her arms about the boy," the old woman said. "Me with your prime hands to my old lips."

I did not reply.

"What am I to say to you, son?" she went on. "Go now, and take her in your arms? And then, after the wrong, would there not be a taste of ashes in the mouth?" Again she kissed my hands. "I do not know," she said wearily. "Between man and woman God has made a long war, to which there are many truces but no peace."

With a deep sigh, the old woman released my hands. She moved a few paces away from me. As she did so, I noticed the shadow of coquetry to her carriage. She stopped. Her hands grew uneasy.

"The fire that's in you both is no stranger to me," she said in a strained voice. "When I was twenty-one, by my manner of walking alone, I could draw men to my side. Once, in Checkopee Falls in America, there was a young Greek with a head of curls and eyes of lightning who ... who ... "

"Your hands!" she cried in a broken voice.

Again the old woman pressed the backs of my hands fiercely against her face. There again, as in the granddaughter, was the shudder and the nails digging into my palms, only this time they were weakened by the span of years.

"Almighty Shining God!" the old woman said. "I, too, have known the cloak of fire about my face."

"I came home to marry an old fisherman," she went on, "and bear a daughter whose body was cast up by the sea and whose one daughter this is." Dropping my hands: "Everything in me bids me encourage you in what you are tempted to do. But, yet, she is too lovely to break. And again, after the rattle has stilled in my throat, will I not have to answer for my guardianship?" She sat on a chair before the fire. "Stay with me, son," she pleaded: "the stress on both of us will pass."

I stayed with her in the kitchen until morning was grey in the window.

"Now!" the old woman said, rising to her feet.

I went back to bed, slept soundly and rose later.

Breakfast was a prosaic meal of porridge, tea and eggs. The boy took little notice of my goodbyes. As I was going away, Shivaun set him on the donkey's back and led the animal up the boggy hillside. Walking down the track, I turned once. The old woman was just inside the doorway, watching me go. Shivaun and Brendan did not turn at all; they moved steadily upward to where the broken peak bulked big against the sky.

THE HOUSE OF SILENCE

Mishkill, the County Councillor, was up for re-election. This time he was more than eager to head the poll in his own electoral area. If he did so the likelihood was that he would be put forward as the official party candidate in the General Election to be held the following year.

To win a seat in the National Parliament was the summit of Mishkill's ambition. Victory would mean having people at his door whispering for favours. For his wife it would mean shopping in Dublin while he won a daily mention in the media for his statesmanship and oratory. Why, eventually he might even be offered a Ministry. The possibilities were delightfully unmeasurable.

But if Coughlin, the councillor standing for the opposite party, were to beat him by even a single vote it would be a black mark for Mishkill. His henchmen told him that it would be touch and go between him and his rival. There were other candidates, but they did not count. To each of the two main rivals every Number One vote was like a golden coin.

What galled Mishkill was this. At the top of his own village stood a convent with thirty-three holy women who never voted. Secluded with their vows of poverty, obedience - and silence! Locked up behind walls, praying away for themselves! Their votes with their outlandish names of votive saints were on the voters' list, but at each election these votes were going abegging.

How could these virgins be made to emerge on polling day to cast their votes for their fellow villager? The uncertainty almost robbed Mishkill of his night's rest.

If he engaged in a blunt attack he had to remind himself that they had formidable protectors. These were the parish priest, a most erudite man - and the awesome traditions of the Holy Roman Catholic and Apostolic Church. Mishkill warned himself to step warily.

Then one of his advisers, a spoiled priest who rarely spoke at party meetings, suggested a course of action which, amid vows of secrecy, was adopted. A letter appeared in the local newspaper. It went as follows:

Refusal to exercise the franchise in a democratic country is reprehensible by any standard of responsible behaviour. In recent years two referenda have been held on matters of the gravest public morality, the results of which could have been determined one way or the other by a handful of votes. Yet we have among us those who most laudably have devoted their lives to the passive service of Our Divine Lord and have consecrated their meed of days to chastity, poverty, humility, prayer - and silence. And these same pious persons seem reluctant or unwilling to emerge from their cloister to maintain the moral fabric of our people for generations to come. The tale is told of Nero, the Roman Emperor who fiddled while his capital city was consumed by flames.

The letter was signed *Pro Fide et Pro Patria.*

"Haha", the people of Ahafadda, and the voters of the countryside at large, said almost with one voice, "That's Maurice the spoiled priest and sidekick of Peter Paul Mishkill. And they're on to the holy nuns behind the great varnished doors of the Old Demesne." The parish priest, a scholarly and philosophical old man who had been ordained in Salamanca, on reading the same letter, nodded his head a few times: he refilled the bowl of his turned-down pipe, lit the tobacco, drew a few thoughtful puffs and then blew thin wisps of smoke towards the serried rows of leather-bound books that lined the walls of his study.

The sisters so surely identified were members of an enclosed and contemplative order of nuns - the Poor and Silent Sisters of Our Saviour. This was one of the strictest orders in the Church; so zealous and rigorous was their code that, over the centuries, its Rules had been modified by three Popes.

Even their relatives spoke to them only on the rarest occasions. And then the conversation had to be carried on through a grille. (There was a space at the base of this grille through which offerings could be made.) The members of this pious order addressed each other only on Easter Sunday, on Christmas Day and on the feast day of their foundress, a devotional lady from Sardinia.

Of course, certain named nuns like the porteress, the bursar, the laundress, the cook and, very occasionally, the Sacristan were partially exempt from the strict observance of the rule of silence but only on condition that oral communication was reduced to the barest minimum necessary to fulfil the duties of each particular office.

Peter Paul Mishkill kept the target of thirty-three votes firmly in his electoral sights. A nod to one of his aides during half-time at a hurling match saw the supporter sidle up to the Bishop's secretary. "A good deal of grumbling out our way, Father," was the tallyman's opening gambit. "Ye can't expect the layman to carry all the burden." Even the wise old parish priest was kept under the subtle bombardment: his housekeeper, the conduit of parochial gossip and a most emotional lady, was fed items designed to be conveyed to the pastor as she served him his meals.

Eventually there came a phone call to the presbytery from the Bishop's house. Since the village phones had not been automated the subsequent conversation was carried on in Latin. That afternoon the parish priest strolled up the village street on his way to the convent. By long tradition the villagers were equipped to deduce what message the pastor was to convey. Mishkill had won! The nuns were going to be flushed out to vote on polling day.

Odd though it may seem, the people of Ahafadda knew a great deal about the nuns. And vice versa. The washerwoman, the gardener, the postman, the grocer, even the occasional beggarman who asked for a meal and was given one - all were meagre yet fruitful sources of information. Though the local doctor was close-mouthed, the reasons for his visits to the convent in his white car could be interpreted fairly accurately.

On their part, the sisters, on those festive occasions when the rigid rules were temporarily relaxed, gleaned much information from visitors. This knowledge was avidly shared before the curtain of silence again descended. But most of all, the small printing press in the basement, which turned out mortuary cards and acknowledgements of sympathy tendered to the bereaved, was a rich source of information. Added to these were the semi-anonymous requests for prayers from all corners of the land. Prayers for fine weather, for success in examinations, for the avoidance of a family break-up, for health after an operation and for the return to sobriety of a confirmed drunkard. The offerings that accompanied these requests and the moneys earned by the printing press, together with the proceeds of the modest sale of flowers and vegetables at the back door, served to keep the convent going. But it was always something of a struggle to do so.

There was a high window in the roof of the little convent which looked down on the comings and goings of the village. Some of the younger nuns, with perhaps a few minutes to spare, often climbed the stairs to the attic and as it were playing pious truant, observed the comings and goings in the long street below.

The villagers in turn knew a great deal about the nuns: much of their knowledge was tinged with the imagination. One of the sisters, they claimed, had been a brilliant doctor who, blaming herself for the death of a mother in childbirth, had thrown up the prospect of a wonderful career to retire to a life of prayer and silence. Another sister - this story the local old gossips relished - had been engaged to be married on three separate occasions only to have her first two fiancés die unexpectedly, while the third, possibly fearing the fate of his predecessors in love, had taken to his heels on the pretence of having received God's call to become a Viator Christi in Somaliland. Yet another of the nuns had a glorious singing voice: rumour had it that she could have married a Papal Count but she too had set aside an operatic career. There were holy days when the villagers said, "Hush," and came to their doors to hear her voice raised in the "Ave Maria" as it floated down from the little chapel among the trees.

Polling Day arrived. The villagers waited. Would the rumour of the nuns' emergence prove true or false? The roadway was spanned by a banner which read "Mishkill is Your Man". The road itself was daubed with rival slogans. Posters bearing a picture of Mishkill were nailed to telephone poles - each poster carried the legend "The Voice of the Poor and Silent". A loudspeaker attached to the roof of a car shouted hoarsely at the villagers: it then moved up to the top of the street and directed a stream of exhortation at the house of silence. Rumours were whispered across railings. The party leader in Dublin, or so it was said, had visited the Papal Nuncio on the failure of members of enclosed religious orders to vote. The villagers twittered and chattered like a congregation of starlings.

Meanwhile all the sisters, except four who were old and bedridden, had gathered in their chapel for the noonday prayers. The prayers said and the psalms chanted, all bowed their heads in silent meditation.

Sister Calisanctus had left her seat. She had been the last Reverend Mother prior to the Vatican Council when consensus became the rule in the case of such communities. Old Sister Regina Coeli also staggered to her feet. The pair of nuns stood outside the low brass gate to the sanctuary with their backs to the altar. Sister Calisanctus cleared her throat. There was a rustle of rosaries as the nuns raised their heads. On a signal all were seated.

"My dear sisters in Christ," Sister Calisanctus began. "I have been in communication with our beloved Bishop and also with our pious and scholarly pastor on a matter of the gravest importance - one that has troubled my mind for the past week. I am to address you now on this matter.

"It concerns the relaxation of our age-old rules of silence and enclosure for a period of two hours this afternoon - this to enable us to cast our votes in the election that is taking place today in this area."

At this point the speaker paused to listen to the loudspeaker blaring outside. When the din had passed, she continued her address.

"The last occasion when our holy rule was suspended was, you will recall, on the wonderful occasion of the Papal visit to our native land. We then unanimously agreed to have a television set installed in the parlour. This, you will agree, was a joyous occasion." A cheerful murmur rose from the ranks of the sisters.

"Things are different today. I regret to say that we have received much adverse publicity recently in what is called the media for our failure to emerge and cast our votes, especially because nowadays matters concerning faith and morals are involved, directly or indirectly with elections."

The nun paused, then looked about her. All was silence and attention.

"Both our Bishop and our pastor have stressed one point. Nothing will be done except in accordance with our wishes. It all depends on us. The choice before us is clear: either we decide to ignore this election or we choose to emerge. If the latter is our choice, we go out this afternoon at four p.m. and return when the evening Angelus rings at six o'clock.

"I ask you now, dear sisters in Christ, to bow your heads in meditation. It is not an easy decision to make. The weight of the centuries of our beloved order is upon our shoulders. I shall turn my face to the altar and, like you, I shall ask the Holy Spirit for guidance. When again I ring this bell, do not raise your heads. Just wait for a moment. Then those of you who are in favour of emerging will raise the index finger of their right hands above their heads. The others need give no sign: I shall count those who offer no sign as being opposed to leaving. Now, dear sisters, think well on what you are about to do."

At this point Sister Regina Coeli returned to her place, knelt and bowed her head. The community of nuns also bent low. Mercedes and Hildebrand, Enda and Cyprian, Nicholas of Myra, Aquin and Columbanus, Kristin and St. John of God. They held this posture until the bell tinkled.

For a moment or two there was no movement. The eyes of the older nuns were observed swivelling to left and right. Then a single index finger poked up beside the veil of Infanta, the youngest nun of the community. Slowly then, finger after finger poked up here and there among the sisters. When it was clear that no other fingers would be upraised, Sister Calisanctus began to count. She found that the tally was fifteen.

"This places me in a quandary," she said. "There are obviously fifteen for and fourteen against. The three oldest nuns, now bedridden, must not be disturbed. Since my vote has not yet been cast it is up to me to do so now." She faced the altar and bowed low. Then she turned and raised her index finger above her temple. A discreet mingling of murmur and cheer rose from the little congregation.

Calisanctus signalled for silence. "There is a question of the road being widened to take in part of our well-loved garden. It is not for me to instruct you how to vote but the local man would understand matters better than ... "

The ex-opera singer's voice was raised in the hymn "How Great Thou Art." Those present joined in. The sound moved out through the small opened windows of the little chapel, sieved through the young summer foliage of the trees and floated serenely over the village.

That same afternoon of polling day, girls skipping on the village pavements were instructed to keep a sharp eye on the entrance to the convent and report any unusual activity in that area to their parents. There were two or three false alarms about half past three: at ten minutes to four o'clock the girls idled to halt in their hopping and, their fingertips to their open mouths, stared upwards at the house of silence. Suddenly all ran into their homes shouting, "The nuns are coming."

And so they were! As the villagers gathered to their doors and windows, they could clearly note a stir among the oaks and rhododendrons of the short convent avenue. The sounds of the drawing back of the bolts on the great twin-leafed outer doors resounded down the long street like so many rifle shots. Then, as the doors were drawn fully open by Infanta, the youngest nun, the file of nuns could be clearly seen forming up just inside: on the stroke of four o'clock the first visitants emerged from the convent enclosure.

They walked forward in pairs. The sun shone through the young foliage to haze above the embrasure and dapple the ranks of the sisters. The nuns continued to come forward - that was Infanta racing back to close the timber doors and emerge through the wicket-gate.

Calisanctus and old Regina Coeli came first; they set a slow pace for the others to follow. The little procession moved prayerfully and calmly forward, their eyes for the most part fixed on the roadway beneath their shoes. They kept to the centre of the road on the incline that led down to the village. Their cream-coloured habits and dark brown veils, their leather girdles and wooden rosaries that rattled ever so lowly, presented a picture both remarkable and commonplace when set against the background of the young leafage of May. The scene, if reduced to stillness, suggested a sampler rescued by chance from a long-vanished parlour. Added to this was the fact that the road edge was selvedged with fallen cherry blossom petals, reminding the villagers of the rose petals strewn before the golden monstrance containing the Host borne beneath its canopy on the occasion of the Quarante Ore procession.

After the initial surge of excitement, the villagers with an awed glance uproad, retreated to the recesses of their hallways leaving their front doors fully open. The lace curtains of their front parlours twitched. Eyes watching the sunlit procession glittered and were gone. A boy of five standing by the front railings of an estate cottage, his thumb and forefinger set awkwardly in his dribbling mouth, was snatched away by his squawking mother who dragged him indoors with yells of "Don't gawk, Edward." Before she disappeared indoors the woman bobbed a sketchy curtsey towards the approaching procession.

The scene was far too noble to endure. At the moment when solemnity was at its most intense and the crowd around the doorway of the school polling booth were watching in silence, an incident occurred which could have had serious consequences.

Out from a roadway leading down from the hills came a herd of rough looking Friesian heifers. They entered the village to the accompaniment of a confused clatter of hooves, a baffled lowing together with loud shouts from the drovers, and the rat-tat-tat of ashplants beating on the rump bones of the beasts. A black and white collie dog, its nose low to the roadway, raced and laced about the bunch snapping at houghs and barking ferociously at the more wilful of the beasts. The cattle were driven by a stocky, red-faced man and what was clearly his son, an equally stocky lad of ten years of so.

The boy stopped suddenly. He seemed rooted to the ground in terror as he saw two of the heifers break away from the herd and threaten to crash through the parade of nuns. His father, however, did not appear to be taken aback. A "What-the-hell-are-you-doin'-there?" response emanated from the way he glared. "Head 'em off, Butch", he roared at the collie; this could be interpreted as ordering the dog to round up either the beasts or the nuns.

The pair of heifers stood stock still on the edge of the parade. Fingers holding back the curtains of the cottages tightened their grip on the lace. The file of sisters had come to a halt: they resembled Christian martyrs facing lions in the Colosseum of old Rome.

Relief was at hand. At this moment of crisis, Infanta, the young nun, rushed forward to face the beasts. She seemed to be transformed into a female dervish in defence of her holy sisters. Showing an agility and fierceness at odds with her devotional garb, hissing through her teeth and flapping her habit wildly, she faced the pair of heifers. "Out!" she yelled in a most unconventual tone of voice. The leading heifer stood unmoved, its eyes baffled and its black and white nose glinting like a salmon's skin. As the mass of beasts behind, irked at the stoppage, pressed forward one of the herd mounted on the back of a paused beast. The moment of menace increased and Infanta herself seemed in real danger. But in matador fashion she stepped aside to avoid catastrophe. It was at this moment help came from the collie, who certainly knew its business, for it attacked the herd at nostril and heel so that the whole bunch as a unit lurched and began to trot down the roadway. The single indignity came from the last beast to move: it left an irregular stream of ordure in the pathway of the consecrated ladies. Infanta to the rescue again: she hurried out in front of the leading nuns and directed the course of their passage. She then resumed her place and poise and joined the procession on its stately way. The rat-tat-tat of sticks on bones was then resumed.

By this time, the men of the village were out in their small front lawns and gateways. They began to shout indignantly to one another. "That bastard is a first cousin of Coughlin's," one said and another added, "He did it on purpose" - these remarks in reference to the elder drover. Anger was replaced by admiration of the valour of Infanta. "A right spunky dame," one man shouted, to be answered by, "Isn't her father a cattle jobber from up the country?"

But the gauntlet to be run by the consecrated virgins was not yet at an end. Closely observed by the parish priest through the window of his study, and by the parish clerk from the darkness of the church porch, they reached the schoolhouse. The entrance to the building was flanked by large billboards bearing pictures of rival candidates whose main supporters stood in knots about the gateway.

Mishkill himself was there. He now stepped forward and shook hands with Sister Calisanctus whose handshake in return was limpness itself. The candidate wore a large muscular smile which was rewarded with a glance from the narrowed eyes of the good nun which was clearly meant to convey, "You're the cause of all this commotion." But the councillor ignored this; he had counted the file of sisters and then said indignantly, "Only thirty! Where are the other three?" "Bedridden," Calisanctus hissed. "Couldn't we lift 'em out to vote?" from Mishkill, who added, "Isn't that what Coughlin is doin' with the paupers in the County Home?" "Paupers!" the nun said with considerable venom. One of the tallymen of an also-ran candidate shouted, "Give O'Connell some ould scratch, sisters." The file of nuns treated this remark with disdain and walked into the school.

When later, having voted, they filed out of the building they found that the attitude of Mishkill and his cohorts had changed dramatically. To the supporters inside, the nuns seemed to be what spent fish are to the spring angler. With an absent-minded glance over his shoulder at the reformed file, Mishkill turned eagerly to greet a small skein of voters emerging from a car.

But if, as a source of interest, the sisters were now expendable in the eyes of those involved in the election, the reverse was true in the attitude of the villagers. It seemed that, in the interval of the nuns' voting, the importance of the emergence of the members of the enclosed community had been fully realised. The population of the little village had set aside their sense of awe and were eager to explore the mystery and wonder of the occasion to its full.

Men, women and children were out in their doorways. The children, who had abandoned their hopscotch, were looking up expectantly into the faces of their elders so as to find clues to what their own attitudes should be in such unusual circumstances. By now the reformed rows of the parade had left the schoolhouse, had passed the scrutiny of the parish clerk, and later the keen eyes of the pastor, and were already skirting the splotches of cowdung. The eyes of the children became somewhat agitated. Was this memorable day to end ingloriously?

Old Maggie Molly proved to be the catalyst. The old woman, who as a wild adolescent and later as a sturdy young matron, had for many years been washerwoman and kitchen maid in the convent, was now wheeled out in a broken-down wheelchair to the gate of her daughter's cottage. There, surrounded by her daughters and

grandchildren, she shaded her blepharitic eyes against the sunlight
and peered at the cream and brown ranks of the nuns as they
approached. When the head of the column had drawn level with her
gate she raised her voice.

"Are you there, Sister Borgia?" she said in the loudest croak her
years allowed her to muster.

The procession faltered. It stopped as the question was repeated.
Strangled sounds of utterance came from Sister Borgia, the oldest
nun present - a fistful of a woman who was being supported by
Sister Infanta. The old nun broke file and followed by the young nun
staggered towards the gateway where the knot of people stood
gathered about Maggie Molly Sweeney.

"Is that yourself?" the old nun quavered as she neared her
destination.

"Come hither, girl, I can't rise outa this yoke," Maggie Molly said.

The old pair slobbered kisses on one another. There followed a
chorus of "Ohs" and "Ahs". Relations and neighbours craned forward
to overhear the conversation that followed.

"Do you remember the duck?" the old woman in the chair asked
through a wheezing and spluttering of emotion.

"Can I ever forget it?" the nun said.

"Me with the cleaver. The place all blood."

"You chopped off its head, you rogue."

"With one blow. And then ... "

"It flew up in the air. God bless us, with no head. And you used
choice language, Maggie Molly!"

"You enjoyed me cursin'."

"Weren't the pair of us young then. Finish your story about the
duck."

"Didn't it hit the windowpane!"

"With no head?"

"Fell down then."

"Oh - oh. We were in a mess. Can I ever forget you, Maggie
Molly, over the steaming tub of clothes."

"And I holdin' up Sister Evangelist's red drawers."

"Ssh, you rogue! Do you remember the mouse racing down the long corridor?"

"With the terrier skatin' after him."

"Tell me, girl, how many times did you marry?"

"First for love. Second for fun. Third for money. Buried 'em all."

The relatives, mostly women and children crowed with laughter.

"How many children did you have altogether?"

"Three clutches. Eighteen all told."

"Grandchildren?"

"Thirty-nine. Is that right, Bibby?" This latter to a rosy-cheeked woman standing above her.

"And three more goin' to Mass," the woman chuckled, then added, "She has nine great-grandchildren. And one great great."

"Well, well," the old nun said in astonishment. To herself she murmured, "Go forth, increase and multiply."

"How about a cup of tay," Maggie Molly said stoutly. "Isn't it once in a lifetime? Come on in."

"Tck, tck. Well as you say ... but we have to be back on the stroke of six o'clock."

Once in a lifetime! The phrase swept through the irresolute ranks of the nuns. The majority of them broke ranks and accepted the hospitality of the village women. A few of the sisters tried to continue on their way but their hearts weren't in it so they too succumbed. Besides, all knew that they had almost an hour and a half to spare before the Angelus rang. Come to think of it, weren't they making local history and bearing witness in a most Christian-like sense to the process of verbal communication with their neighbours.

In twos and threes all were soon seated in the front parlours of the cottages. They were sipping tea from translucent teacups that had never before held tea. They were indicating delight on being shown family photographs taken at wedding receptions in places as far apart as "The Spotted Dog" in Willisden, London and the Ramada Inn in Beloxi, Florida, USA. They grew suitably doleful at deaths, elated at the success of children in examinations, and oohed at the manly bearing of young men in uniform in far-off lands. They properly lowered their voices, pursed their lips and blinked at each other at underbreath news of operations of an obstetric nature.

So it was sip, sip, gabble, gabble, smile, smile, listen, listen, hush, hush in a damburst of genteel gossip. What made a profound impression on the village women, when later they compared notes, was the way the sisters showed an adroitness in skirting village scandals even when prim-lipped lures were cast before them, possibly with the intention of testing the limits of their awareness. Indeed, when it came to using language beneath language in female coding, the Poor and Silent Sisters of Our Saviour proved equal on any subject which, if probed to the full, could result in embarrassment.

The quietly vigilant pastor was still at his post, his eyes enfilading the street through one or other of the panes of his three-in-one window. A group of children, peering through front windows from under cupped hands, kept him somewhat abreast of how matters stood between the sisters and their hostesses. He took down a large tome with dimmed gold leaf lettering on its spine and began to turn over the pages with great care. Glancing through the windowpane at his left hand, he looked first at his watch and then at the belfry of the church.

The crowd around the schoolhouse gate had thinned somewhat - probably some of those electioneering had gone home for their tea. Now was the time for the priest to cast his vote with few around the gate to importune him. He took his hat off the hallstand and went to the schoolhouse. At the gate he apportioned his quiet greetings to left and right but his demeanour was such that no one approached him. As he left the building it was exactly seven minutes to six o'clock. He glanced covertly to the church as he doffed his hat while passing; he hoped that the clerk, wherever he was, would have noted that his pastor was on the alert to ensure that the Angelus was rung accurately and on time.

In the various parlours it was now evident that a tide of weariness and disillusion had overtaken the sisters. One of the older nuns crinkled her nose in disdain: a baby's napkin was being changed in a bedroom on the opposite side of the hall. And was that a smell of stale cabbage? Yet another looked sidelong out the window and surveyed the road where it had been soiled by the cattle: the full realisation of what could have happened were it not for the intervention of Infanta seemed to be borne home to her for the first time.

By their standards it had been a day of excitement and adventure but now a sense of nostalgia was uppermost - they seemed to long for the clean smell of beeswaxed floors, the nostril tang of candlewick, the lingering smell of incense, the scent of sweetpeas on the dining-room table or the smell of their palms when they had gently crushed rosemary, eucalyptus or lavender leaves between them. Here was the din of shrieking children; in the convent there was peace. In each of their minds the beloved ingrained rhythm of their enclosed life began to reassert itself.

As the hands of the church clock crept closer to six o'clock the sisters took small silver watches from beneath their habits, made O's of their mouths as they read the time and then clicked the little timepieces shut as a sign of their impending departure. Finally they dusted their lips with lace-edged handkerchiefs. As they did so, the church bell sent the vibrations of the evening Angelus through the village.

At one and the same time in all the parlours the nuns stood up and recited the prayer aloud, the people chiming in with the responses. The prayer ended, there was a chorus of goodbyes as the visitors began to leave. Again Maggie Molly was wheeled out to offer her farewell embraces to Sister Borgia. "We'll meet in the next world," Maggie said as with brimming eyes she embraced the old nun. "With God's help," Sister Borgia replied, then, helped by Infanta, she went slowly to her place in the reformed ranks on the roadway.

But adventure was not yet at an end. The parade was about to move off when the unexpected happened. Out from a passageway between two of the cottages straggled an impromptu group of musicians and dancers. There was a melodeon player, a piper, three fiddlers, five or six boys clacking rib bones and a low-sized man who beat the goatskin of a tambourine with powerful knuckles. The band took its place at the head of the parade while a boy and a girl in Celtic costume - step-dancers both - stood a little apart, yet prepared to march with the others. The bodhrán player provided the strong beat which signalled the move off.

The retreat began, the band played a lively tune while the dancers began to improvise steps. Then burrum-burrum, whinny-whinny, drone-drone and the clack of dancing shoes drew the whole village out of doors. With swifts screaming above the procession the retreat proceeded.

To the watching priest the music was that of a bizarre recessional. At first he rejected it; then the thought occurred to him that in the liturgy of the Church the tambourine had an honoured place. Again, God had often been praised by the dance. The names of the paired nuns too evoked old reverberations in his mind. Calisanctus, holy one now walked with Hildebrand, bearer of the sword. Chrysostom of the Golden Mouth walked with Francis de Sales who seemed to bear a purse of gold, won for oratory. Sister Thomas vouched for the Dumb Ox Aquin, a most learned fellow who evoked further images of Monte Cassino in flames; Infanta still supported Sister Borgia. Well, well, if that wasn't Sister Anne, God's grandmother if you please, paired off with Macarius the Elder, a man falsely accused of having deflowered a virgin. And look, Sister Kristin, who carries the name of Christ, walks side by side with a thin six-foot-three nun who rejoiced in the name of Augustine, a saint so fat that a semicircle had to be carved out of his table to accommodate his ample belly.

The pastor asked himself how it was that the native Saints, even as portrayed by their female votaries, seemed always to huddle together. As indeed they now did! Hermits, martyrs and half-crazy culdees on crags all were represented. Finian the Leper walked serenely beside Gobnait of Ballyvourney about whose head a swarm of honeybees buzzed harmlessly. Colmcille of Iona seemed to be followed by the wraith of an old blind horse - he was paired with Finbar of Gougane. Brigid of the Oak Tree had as marching companion ex-soldier Enda of the Aran Islands. And which of the nine holy Colemans did the next sister evoke? Hopefully Coleman of Kilmacduagh who kept three pets, a cock to rouse him at dawn, a mouse to nibble at his ear if he dozed off in the scriptorium, and a fly to mark his place on the vellum page of the Gospels. And there goes Killian, wanderer for the sake of Christ, keeping erratic footstep with Able Seaman Brendan who presents himself as being about to celebrate the Eucharist on the back of Iasconius the friendly whale. And what a ducking Brendan and his monks are in for when they light the paschal fire on the whale's back!

The old philosopher, the parish priest, continued to probe for meanings and subtleties in the events of the day, offering himself scant mercy as he did so. Granted that the pageant, through its nomenclature, portrayed the story of the Christian Church throughout its existence, were these parishioner nuns of his, their lives devoted to thought-piercing the mysteries of faith through contemplation, silence and mental prayer, among the last to be so occupied? Did this emergence and suspension of rule indicate a significant hairline fracture in the great wall of monasticism - slight though this fracture appeared to be. Would modern psychology, following on post-conciliar freedom (or licence!), inevitably lead to the extinction of a practice that had notably served the church. Or - here a radiant thought occurred to the old priest - could it possibly lead, by a circuitous route, to a full flowering in the approaching century?

Musicians and dancers offered the final honour guard for the sisters as they passed through the wide-open doors of the convent. The musicians then struck a plaintive note by playing in slow time the Scottish Jacobite wail - "Will Ye No Come Back Again?" - Infanta began to shut the varnished door leaves with their spread of black mock hinges. With a wave of her hand the young nun bade a cheery but somehow sad farewell to the watching villagers who responded in like manner. With the door shut and bolted, and the last glimpse of the brown and cream ranks vanished among the trees of the avenue, the house was silent once more.

But the villagers did not remain silent. Neither on that day, nor on the days that followed. With the passage of time the adventure of the nuns' emergence assumed significant proportions in their minds. Some of the villagers possessed mythofacient qualities so that, with the passing years, The Day the Nuns Came Out grew to have the same status in local folklore as The Night of The Big Wind which had happened a century and a half before. Of a dark winter night, when the trees whined and groaned under the last of the wind, children and adults, drawing aside the lace curtains of the cottages, claimed to have seen a ghostly procession of nuns pass by.

Maggie Molly died soon after these happenings but one of her daughters later maintained that one midnight she had seen the ghost of her mother and Sister Borgia, their heads together in close conversation, while above them fluttered a headless duck which sprinkled the pair with blood.

Mishkill lost the top of the poll position by a mere two votes. He blamed the nuns for failing to bring out the bedridden. When later a proposal was made in Council to widen the public road and take in a chunk of the nuns' gardens he voted for it. Coughlin, his rival, voted against it and lost by three votes. That's the way matters are arranged in country places. All this is reckoned normal by village standards of public life.

❧ SEAMAN'S WAKE ❧

A tremor of anxiety ran through the village when it became known that the body of a black seaman had been washed up on the beach.

The one publican closed his door and drew his blinds. Not out of respect indeed: he had hosted an inquest on a stranger similarly washed up some years before. The body had then been laid out in his back lounge where the inquest was held. For days afterwards he had to burn sulphur candles in the sealed room so as to fumigate the place. As he put it himself, he wanted "no more of that caper."

The chemist, whose shop was on the road leading to the pier, grabbed his camera and drove up into the hills. Sickness could be treated but a several-weeks-old death was no use to him. The village baker mounted his bike, left his wife behind the counter, and drove off to visit his cousin; people were odd, he said, they would associate his ice-topped cakes with a corpse if he himself was involved in the jury. And especially when the corpse was that of a black seaman.

The result was that when the donkey cart bearing the body trundled up the village street the place was deserted. Leading the donkey was a simpleton of eighteen or so known locally as Bobbaw. Some laughing idlers at the pier-head had slung the body on to the boy's seaweed cart and told him to drive up to the village. The boy had done as he was told. Gradually, on his face, the broad grin of centrality was replaced by the dropping of a dribbling jaw at the slow realisation that no door in the village was open. Lace curtains twitched and eyes flashed but no one emerged. Even the presbytery, which now housed a brand new pastor, remained silent and still.

The cart trundled on. From under the paint-soiled canvas covering the body the feet of the dead seaman protruded. These still bore rope-soled sandals which swung in time with every movement of the cart.

The last thatched cabin of the village stood by itself at the landward end of the long street. Only the half-door of the crouched building was closed. In this cabin lived Molly Maag, a woman shunned by the village wives. Her buxom form now filled the upper space of the doorway.

"What have you there?" she called out to Bobbaw. The boy drew his donkey to a halt. The grin reappeared on his face.

"A black fella - washed up. No one will take him in," the boy chortled.

"Show me!" the woman said. Her half-door screeched as she dragged it open and went out. She lifted the cover from the head of the corpse where it lay on a tattered bed of seaweed. A stench rose on the May air. It seemed to war with the scent of hawthorn blossom on the hedges on the hill to the east of the village.

Molly Maag twisted her head this way and that as she examined the face of the dead sailor. Pensively she drew off the cover and examined the full body. A man in his prime, coal black with a head of close curls. He wore a short coloured pullover with oil smears on it and old corduroy trousers. The navel was bare. Fish had nibbled at one side of his head. Also at the toes. The gentle boy looked closely at the woman. "Wait!" Molly Maag said.

Entering her cabin she took the ware off the kitchen table and placed it on the ledge of the dresser. She dragged the table to mid-floor. The table was covered with a patterned oilcloth. She then rejoined the boy on the roadway.

Bobbaw was strong. So was the woman. Yet they staggered under the weight of the canvas bearing the corpse. It was all they could do to lift the body on to the table. Then, "Tie your ass to the bush outside and come back here," Molly Maag ordered. Bobbaw shuffled off.

When the boy returned he found the body naked. The strong stench of putrefying flesh was now warring with the smell of Jeyes fluid. The woman sent the boy out with a galvanised iron bucket to draw water from the street fountain. She had a good turf fire blazing on the hearth when he returned. She filled the large iron kettle with water and slung it onto the hook of the crane to hang amid the rising flames. Presently the kettle began to sing.

When the water was boiling the woman poured hot and cold water into an oval zinc basin. Dipping a piece of flannel into the lukewarm water, and then rubbing it on a bar of carbolic soap, she began to wash the corpse.

Dribbles of spittle hanging from his open mouth, Bobbaw looked on.

The woman washed every nook and cranny of the seaman's body. Removing the sandals she washed between what was left of the toes. Bobbaw then helped her turn the body over on its face. As they did so the head lolled this way and that. Right side up again and the curly washed hair combed till it gleamed, the woman covered the body with a white sheet taken from a drawer in her only bedroom.

"I'll want a white shirt, a trousers, and socks," Molly Maag said. "Three candles, blessed or not - his own sandals will do." Then, "Shirt, trousers, socks, candles," she made Bobbaw repeat the message.

After a pause, "Ask the schoolmaster first - he's about the right size." she went on. "Drive your donkey away and come back as soon as you can. I should have visitors soon."

Bobbaw shambled off, repeating his errand aloud. Presently, the doctor-coroner's head appeared over the half-door of the cabin. He entered, followed by the Garda sergeant and some men, obviously members of a jury. They glanced furtively at Molly Maag seated on a stool by the fire; she was drawing deeply on a cigarette. The doctor raised the cover on the corpse and thumped the flesh of the dead seaman. "Rigor mortis," he said. "About three weeks in the water. 'Found drowned' I suppose," he muttered, and those with him hummed agreement.

With a word thrown to the heedless woman the newcomers moved off to the now open public house. Molly Maag inhaled deeply on her cigarette end. After a while a shadow robbed the upper half of the cabin doorway of its light. It was the village carpenter, a quiet-spoken man who always kept his own counsel. "I'll rap a few boards together," he said in a voice just above a whisper. "No great shakes, but varnished they'll be passable. Is that all right with you?"

The woman said yes, that was all right with her.

Bobbaw returned, his errand well done. Later, when clothed, the fingers interlaced, and the candles lighting on a small table by its head, the corpse looked quite respectable. After wetting tea for Bobbaw and herself, Molly Maag gave further instructions.

"Go from house to house. Say this: 'Molly Maag is waking the black seaman tonight. If you come to the wake bring your own stuff to eat and drink.' That done, you're to go up to Jackie the Dead and tell him to open a grave in some odd corner of the graveyard. Last of all you're to call to the presbytery and tell the new parish priest that we're burying the seaman straight from this house at twelve o'clock tomorrow. Remind the clerk to ring the bell. Say nothing more. Let 'em both do as matches them. Have you all that?"

The boy shambled off muttering, "Wake, shtuff, grave, priest, clerk." Molly Maag smiled in affection as if to say "Bobbaw is clever in some things. And only I know it."

As dusk merged into darkness some neighbours, mostly men, stole into the cabin one by one. Each carried a little parcel. On entering, each person put his hand to his nostrils but lowered it quickly when Molly Maag looked up from her seat at the fire. The villagers did not know whether to bless themselves or not. They shook limp hands with Molly Maag. The village gossip came in about eleven o'clock. She stood by the corpse, her thin nostrils quivering; having pursed her lips she forced them to say patronisingly: "Weren't you the great Molly Maag to take him in." Molly Maag was equal to the occasion. "Any man," she said, "young or old, black or white, dead or alive was always welcome under my roof!" For once in her life the gossip was silenced. Seated at the other side of the fire Bobbaw guffawed at this response.

Molly Maag sat up until daybreak waking the corpse. Bobbaw sat opposite her, his head occasionally falling on his breast and loud snores issuing from his open mouth. Firelight and candlelight played on the ware in the dresser and from there were reflected on to the features of the dead seaman which, by this time, had changed a deep purple not unlike the colour of some varieties of convolvulus.

As daylight showed in the small windows of the cottage, Molly Maag washed and tidied herself. She combed her hair and fastened it at the poll with a foreign-looking comb studded with brilliants. From a drawer in the bedroom she took a finely woven black and green Paisley shawl. Before laying it aside for use later in the day, she opened and flapped it, holding it up against the wan light to check for moth holes. The smell of camphor then mingled with the already strong stench in the kitchen. The snap of the flapping woke Bobbaw where he dozed in the chair at the fireside.

Outside a sea mist began to burn off seascape and landscape. Details of the higher crags began to show. To the north and east of the cabin, hedgerows of hawthorn blossom revealed their presence.

After a breakfast of sorts Bobbaw, eager to be off on his errand, clumped down the village street shouting hoarsely, "The funeral! The funeral!". He yelled in the direction of any morning stir. He rapped at several windows. An elderly lady off to first Mass questioned Bobbaw, "Who told you to shout like that? Will Father Lavitt attend? Are we expected to sympathise with Molly Maag?" The boy bowed his head and without answering trudged back to the cottage.

At half past eleven the coffin was brought to the cabin doorway.

Without addressing Molly Maag, the carpenter took out two chairs
from the kitchen and laid the coffin upon them head and foot. When
he had gone away Molly Maag, having first ensured that there was
no one about, came out and examined the coffin. On the breastplate
in bold black letters the word SEAMAN appeared, together with the
date. The woman gave a nod of approval. The varnish had also done
its work well.

Close to noonday, Molly Maag drew aside an inch of her window
curtain and peeped out. She saw a few loiterers half hidden in
recessed doorways. The meek carpenter arrived and, after some
glancing around and gesturing, he succeeded in luring four
pallbearers from their recessed hiding places. The four were led by
Bitter Mick, a one-time farmer who had drunk out his land and was
now reduced to the state of a village nuisance at odds with everyone
- all of whom collectively he blamed for his downfall. He had also,
when short of a drink, served as a deck-hand on a trawler that sailed
as far away as Arklow.

The carpenter leading the way, all five entered the kitchen.
Bobbaw brought in the chairs. The men lifted the seaman's body off
the table and into the coffin. They did so very gingerly. By now, the
almost navy blue head of the corpse stood out against the cheap
white lining of the box. Molly Maag, her shawl across her shoulders,
stepped forward, leaned down and kissed the lips of the dead man.
The joiner then lifted the coffin lid which the others screwed into
place. The coffin bearers stepped back to where the meagre air from
the doorway moved across their faces. All waited for the midday
Angelus bell to ring.

As they waited, Bitter Mick was heard to mutter the name of the
parish clerk. He coupled an obscene adjective with it.

As, at last, the Angelus bell began to toll, three of the bearers
sketched the sign of the cross on forehead, breast and shoulder
points. Bitter Mick growled sidelong and the others ceased
murmuring the prayer. When the bell ceased to ring there was a
dead silence. Implicit in the silence was the question; would the bell
recalling the Annunciation be followed by a deadbell for the black

seaman? Bitter Mick growled. Molly Maag put up her hand in a gesture advising patience. Just as she was about to signal a removal of the coffin, the church bell began to toll. Same bell, same sound but now its message was different. "Come villagers" it seemed to say, "Mourn for a dead seaman. Help place him in his grave."

The bearers lifted the coffin out onto the roadway, then raised it to their shoulders. Here and there along the irregular length of the street people began to appear. As it moved, the cortège began to take shape. Bobbaw shuffled before the coffin chortling with an odd enjoyment and pride. Behind the coffin, its mountings taking the morning sunlight, came Molly Maag, walking alone. The shawl was drawn across her face leaving a small triangular aperture in which a single eye roved to assess the attitude of the newcomers joining the little procession. Once, a man walking behind the woman, moved forward a step or two and plucking at her shawl said, "I'm sorry for your trouble Molly Maag." "I know that, John," the woman said, her reply muffled by the fold of shawl across her lips.

At the crossroads in mid-village, beyond which lay the church, the cortège turned right and moved up the hill to where the tops of time-spotted crosses could be seen above the surrounding wall. The parish clerk, who had been drawing the rope on the little belfry stand which stood apart from the building, ceased to pull and looked after the unusual procession which was now joined by a group awaiting its arrival at the crossroads.

All the while an unspoken query seemed to hang on the air - would Father Lavitt, the new priest, emerge from his presbytery to perform the rites of the occasion?

Presently the coffin stood on crude trestles at the graveside. The grave itself, deep dug in the dry sandy ground had its heap of removed soil beside it. A pair of shovels, their handles crossed, lay upon the pile. On the breastplate the word SEAMAN stood out clearly as if deliberately illuminated by the spotlight of the sun. The countryside beyond the wall of the little cemetery was at its most memorable; furze gold blossom on the top of the scarp, fuchsia rods gleaming orange between it and the bay, while inland was the bridal glory of the thorn blossom. Added to all this was the blue and silver flicker of an almost dormant sea.

The mourners waited, glancing at each other from under their eyebrows. Molly Maag's eyes were fixed on the coffin. The people continued to wait, not without a sense of confidence. Bitter Mick was the only person present to glare around and to indicate contempt.

Molly Maag's hand made its appearance outside the folds of the shawl. It was clear she was about to give the signal for the coffin to be lowered into the grave. At that moment a murmur ran through the crowd. As a unit the people turned their heads, then bowed them. A tall figure reminding them of a heron stood at the graveyard gate. A whisper passed sidelong from bowed head to bowed head. "It's the new priest," the whisper went. Without raising their heads the people around the grave parted to make way for Father Lavitt. He stood among them with his half-rimmed spectacles, his cropped head and his small ascetic features. He looked around him - Bitter Mick alone responded with a defiant stare. The priest looked down at the coffin, cleared his throat, and began to speak in a high-pitched womanly voice.

"My dear people, this is my first service among you. It's an unusual one. I ask you to bear with me while I, as it were, think aloud." The priest paused.

"We are gathered to offer the last rites above the body of a seaman which the waves of the sea have cast upon our shore. We do not know what creed, if any, this man possessed. Neither do we know whether or not he believed in the immortality of the human soul. Thus I find myself at a loss as to what prayer to recite - one which will be in keeping with the occasion. However I venture to say this: a mother, a wife, a son or a daughter, even a sweetheart is waiting for him to return. I feel also that we should respect his body as a temple of the Holy Ghost."

The priest paused. This time he looked about him confidently. "It is possible that in his travels this man came into contact with some form of Christianity. If this is so, I will now offer a prayer the authorship of which is attributed to Christ himself. Please recite The

Lord's Prayer with me. Recite slowly and reverently, picturing each word and phrase as you do so. Our Father who art in heaven ... "

The people responded as the priest requested. Those who wore caps or hats removed them - all except Bitter Mick who kept his soiled hat clamped to his head.

As the prayer ended the priest made as if to move away. Then, as if he had been pondering some questions, he turned and coughed for attention. With a glance at the shawled figure at the other side of the grave he began. "It is fitting that I should call attention to the exemplary conduct of Mrs Mary Margaret Devine in this instance." At this the mourners seemed startled. It was twenty-five years since Canada had swallowed up Jack Devine never to be heard of thereafter. The people had initial difficulty in realising that the priest was referring to Molly Maag.

"On behalf of all of you here present, and on my own personal behalf, I offer Mrs Devine our communal gratitude for teaching us, by example, a lesson in Christian charity. Thank you Mrs Devine."

As the priest made to move away Bobbaw, who had been watching events through wide eyes and an open mouth, exploded with an outraged cry of rage. "Me too!" he yelled. "I brung him in my donkey's car when none o' ye bastards would take him in." The mourners shook with laughter. Molly Maag closed the aperture in her quivering shawl.

The priest extended a thin white hand as if to restore order at the graveside. Then he went on, "I was just about to mention you John McSweeney. You too will be thanked by everyone in the community." He spoke through thin lips as if rebuking the boy for doubting his intentions. Father Lavitt then walked away with an air of lofty sincerity. After this the coffin was lowered into the grave and the pit filled with clean sand. "Hiss" the shovels said as they were driven into the graveside heap of sandy soil.

Afterwards in the pub each item of the wake and funeral was parsed, spelled and analysed. Odd as it may seem, the focus of comment rested on the priest's behaviour at the graveside for this provided clues as to his attitude and character which was important in the parochial sense. His mention of the name Molly Maag and Devine came as a surprise, for this was news to the younger section of the mourners who never knew her other than Molly Maag (a Redemptorist missionary had once referred to her as Mary Magdalen.) The priest's use of the waiting son also struck a chord for the woman's son had long since wandered off to lands beyond the horizon. And see how he knew Bobbaw's full name. And wasn't it great the way he handled the boy's outburst. Pretending he was just going to mention Bobbaw was a bit of a cod of course. He had clean forgotten it but, credit where credit was due, he recovered fairly well. 'Twas clever too the way he brought in the Lord's Prayer. Between spitting and drinking the majority of the public house gossip came to the conclusion that at last they had a wise, kind and resourceful pastor - one equipped to heal parochial misunderstandings.

Not all however. There was a cynical minority led by Bitter Mick. When all had finished praising the priest Mick laughed scornfully. "Codology," he snorted. "No credit to him at all! I'll tell ye how he sounded like a know-all. That cute little hoor of a parish clerk went and marked his card."

THE END OF AN ERA

Micky Joe, a teenage joinery apprentice, picked up a curl of home-filled black pudding as he dawdled his way through the back roads of the town. It was early morning and the lad was on his way to the workshop.

The young man's impish cry of "Ah," indicated both discovery and decision. "Why call it a black pudding?" he asked himself. "There are flecks of brown and white in its filling of baked blood mixed with particles of suet and onion chips. Its long and thin too," he added inconsequentially. He whistled joyously as, holding the dangling pudding behind his back, he pushed open the door of the workshop. His nostrils widened as they experienced the dust smells of different woods. His elfin ears appeared more pointed as they responded to the whirr, hiss, thock and whine of the place.

Satisfied that no one was watching, he slipped the coiled pudding into the daubed trench coat hanging on the first peg behind the door. The boy ensured that the pudding reposed in the left-hand pocket of the garment: the right-hand pocket contained the foreman's pipe and plug tobacco, as well as a clotted red handkerchief.

The office door opened and the Boss came out. "Johnsie," he called to the old man. "That skylight in the roof of the Bank is still leaking. The manager wants it done immediately. Take laths and lead keepers." With a glance at Micky Joe, the Boss added, "Take this fella with you."

The old foreman scowled a little. He glanced slowly but narrowly at the apprentice. The boy moved forward and then stood over the foreman's bast and made as if to take it up. The old man made a noise in his throat and the boy spread the mouth of the bast so as to admit tools from the bench. Micky Joe's heart almost stopped for a second as the old man swung the trench coat across his shoulders.

The pair set off, the boy carrying the bag of tools. The pair plodded down the pavement of the long main street of the town. The old foreman, his grey head bare, moved a foot or two in front of the young man. As Old Johnsie's hand groped in the direction of the left-hand pocket of his showerproof, Micky shot him a sudden query about an old shop front. The old fellow's bushy eyebrows lifted. After a moment he replied.

The Church of Ireland building stood in the centre of the town square. It was surrounded by an oval of rusty railings. At one point, on its front wall, a rough blanket of ivy had swung away from the church to reveal a tangle of knotted roots. The tall spire and the six pinnacles about the building vouched for an ancient dignity; one unrepaired pinnacle indicated decayed authority.

On the pavement before the bank the old man paused and, as if he were seeing through his open mouth, looked across at the open door of the church with a few vintage cars clustered around it.

Standing perkily on the step of the bank hall door, his finger on the button of the polished bell ring, Micky piped up.

"A funny guy, this fella?"

"Who?" from the old joiner.

"The bank manager."

"How?"

"Cigarettes that explode. Plastic mice. Buck false teeth."

Johnsie stared at his apprentice. He did not comment.

"Sings at goodbye parties for his clerk. 'Mona, my own love' and 'Let's have a song about porter.'"

The old man's tongue tip emerged to savour this odd item of information.

"We'll have to keep our eyes peeled," the apprentice chirped.

A maid dressed in black and white opened the door. "The skylight," Micky said chirpily, at the same time eyeing the girl from head to heels.

"Wipe your boots," the girl said curtly. She closed the door behind the pair and, indicating the stairs, returned to the kitchen. Micky sent a low whistle through his teeth in appreciation of the movements of her hinged buttocks. He took the raincoat off the old man's shoulders and removed his own jacket. He plonked the two garments down on the single hook of the hallstand. He covered both garments with a lady's coat. Having run his fingertips along the velour collar of a greatcoat, he took up a bowler hat which lay upside down on the glove box of the hallstand. A long black crêpe was attached to the band of the hat. The apprentice slewed the bowler with its trailing crêpe on to the side of his head, tapped it pertly and admired himself in a slice of mirror inset in the hallstand. He began to sing in a low voice.

"The relics of ould dacency
The hat me father wore."

As he did so the bell of the Protestant church began to clang rustily. Replacing the hat on the box the young man turned to the old man who was eyeing the stairs as if it was a mountain.

"Who's dead?" he asked.

In a growl, "The ould dowager."

"Buryin' today?"

"Aye!"

"The last of the Fairleighs!"

"Yeh. Come on."

"Big shots long 'go?"

"Too bloody big. Come on."

Gripping the banisters, the old man grumbled up the brilliant carpet, held in place by brass rods on white treads and risers. With a backward glance at the hallstand, Micky Joe, bearing the heavy container of tools, followed his master.

The great attic spread the entire length and breadth of the building. Piled everywhere were greening frock coats, military uniforms of forgotten wars, a parrot's cage, sections of fishing rods, an old German helmet and some small shell cases, clear relics of World War I. There was an old camera with concertina sides and the cracked glass of a large picture depicting a boy facing some kind of a court martial with the title, "When did you last see your Father?"

Johnsie was standing under one of the two large skylights. This allowed the two to look down on the Square. On a growl from the old joiner, the boy set down his load and lifted some old clothes on the floor beneath the window to reveal the wet stain of a drop down on the floor. Then each of the pair began to grapple with the holed iron bands which locked the skylight into place. The bands were rusted so that the old man and the young one had to strain to get the skylight open. Gratingly, protesting harshly, the frame was pushed upwards to be held open by the notches on the inner frame being inserted in two of the holes. The pair leaned their elbows on the frame ledge to have a grandstand view of all that was happening in the Square below. Micky was standing on a pouffe.

The old joiner's jaw fell slowly open. The slightest of breezes turned over the lock of his silver hair. Below them the last of the mourners were trickling into the church. One of the women wore a wide black hat kept in place by a white scarf across its top such as was the fashion of lady motorists at the beginning of the century. One old stumbler - a man - wore knickerbockers; another wore plus-fours. These were exceptions: the others wore severe black or pepper and salt grey.

The wheezing of an organ, and a few reedy voices raised in a hymn, issued through the small swing windows set in the larger windows of the church. A sidelong glance by Micky at his old companion told him that Old Johnsie's eyes were smouldering. And that now his jaw was clamped shut. The old man muttered something about getting on with the job but his elbows never lifted from the frame.

"The last of 'em," the boy probed.

"Aye."

"You remember them up at the Hall?"

"Aye."

"Where did she live after the House was burned?"

"In an ould caravan at the back lodge. Pidge Martin looked after her."

"Were the Fairleighs good landlords or bad?"

The old man looked sideways at the boy. "That'd take tellin'", he said bitterly.

Micky craned forward to observe the arrival of the latest mourners, the men doffing their bowler hats, the women in museum finery. The church music ceased. There was a pause. This was followed by the sound of prayer with responses. A dirge began. An old Rolls Royce with a liveried chauffeur drew up opposite the church. From the back seat of the vehicle emerged an old woman wearing a mauve scarf. This was followed by an ancient equipage like something out of Tsarist Russia. The cab, with a steel grey nag between its shafts, trundled soberly to the back of the church. A motor hearse had already backed up, its rear close to the gate.

The undertaker and his assistant moved towards the church door. As he did so he looked over his shoulder at three or four countrymen who stood stolidly apart. Newly arrived was a small group of townspeople, mostly shopkeepers, who also stood reverently apart. From their perch on the bank roof the joiner and the boy watched the drama unfold.

Micky's face suddenly twitched. With a barely lifted forefinger he indicated the object of his gaze. It was the figure of the Catholic canon who was standing discreetly in the recessed doorway of his presbytery which stood in one of the main streets leading out of the town, a place where the steeple of the Catholic Church loomed up above it. The clergyman was obviously awaiting the correct moment, and the correct place to appear, when and where he would not be part of, or aloof from, the ceremony.

The apprentice turned his head to query Johnsie about the priest's dilemma. To his surprise he realised that the old joiner was no longer there. In a small measure of agitation the boy stepped down from the pouffe and began to look here and there. Had Johnsie fallen amid the attic debris? Since the attic door stood ajar, the apprentice realised that Old Johnsie had gone downstairs, probably to procure his pipe and tobacco. With a mingled sense of relief and concern he heard the footstep of the old man resounding on the bare stairs that led to the attic. The old fellow came in quite calmly. He had his old trench coat and the boy's jacket draped across his forearm. In one hand he held his pipe and tattered tobacco pouch with a box of matches in the heel of his other hand. The apprentice appeared to be examining the surrounds of the skylight as if to determine the source of the leak. Again to his surprise the old man seated himself on a basketwork armchair under the skylight and addressed himself to the task of milling the tobacco between the palms of his gnarled hands. The pipe lit and the smoke going up through the skylight, the old joiner said, "Shift a few slates!" The boy rocked a few slates close to the skylight frame.

"You're right about yer man," Old Johnsie said solemnly.

"Who?"

"The manager."

"How so?"

"D'yeh know what he put in my raincoat pocket?"

"Whah?"

"A black pudden."

Gulp. Pause. "What'je do about it?"

"Heh-heh-heh," Johnsie cackled. "I wrapped it ... (puff) around the band of ... (puff) his bowler hat. (Puff-puff-puff)."

"You didn't!"

"The crêpe hid it ... (puff). Left it ... (puff and cackle) crown down on the hallstand."

(Heh, puff. Heh, puff.)

"Sufferin' Saviour," the apprentice breathed. As the church bell began to clank he leaped on to the pouffe and looked down.

"Holy You, Divine God," he almost shouted, "We're scuttered."

In trying to rise from the wicker chair, Johnsie slewed sideways and fell into a heap of discarded clothes. Doing so he dislodged the helmet and the parrot's cage. The old man still held the pipe firmly between his ancient teeth as Micky Joe dragged him upright and later helped him to his feet. The pair resumed their observation of the scenes unfolding far below them.

The bell continued to clang. Preceded by the parson in surplice and soutane and wearing a long black stole the while he chanted from his book, the coffin was wheeled out towards the gateway of the church. The final members of the ascendancy stood reverently around. By some alchemy, the parish priest had moved a few steps toward the core of the action. He stood there, occasionally pursing his lips up under his nose - a tic which admitted to several interpretations. On the rooftop were the two heads; Micky now wore the German helmet which overwhelmed his head, ("For fear the skylight'd fall," he muttered sidelong to Johnsie), while the old man's fine hair fluttered like a flag in the light high breeze.

Suddenly the lad began to hop like a monkey. He swore loudly. "Banjaxed," he shouted, pointing downward. "Look!" Johnsie took the pipe out of his mouth and cupped and capped the bowl in the hollow of his hand. Through his slack mouth he gaped down.

The bank manager had emerged from the hall doorway of the bank beneath. He was dressed in a dark pinstriped suit. As he hurried forward he kept a grip on the rim of his bowler hat, which, unaccountably to him, seemed bent on teetering on his head. He conveyed the impression that he was vaguely aware that something was wrong but that he was in too much of a hurry to stop and identify what it was.

The coffin had now halted at the gateway to the church. It lay there inert on its bier. The undertaker glanced sidelong at the knot of countrymen who stood a little distance apart. These had obviously once been tenants or servitors on the Fairleigh estate. Four of them shuffled forward and took their places around the coffin. The priest moved forward and shook hands with the parson. The parson shook hands with the priest. Each smiled at the other. Muscularly. At the head of the coffin stood Pidge Martin, the old woman who looked after the dowager. A large rosary bead dangled from her hand.

At this moment Molly Devine drove up in the barony's ultimate ass and cart. At first her eyes were raised to observe the pair on the roof of the bank. They then swivelled to look down at the coffin which was now quite close to her. Molly was a huge haystack of a woman whose size ridiculed the donkey and vehicle.

"Whoa!" she yelled. As she looked down into the coffin she added in a loud voice. "The last o' the Fairleighs. Put my grandmother in the workhouse. Left the countryside full o' rushes, bushes and bastards." She seemed to direct her observations directly at the priest who blushed for the crudeness of one of his flock. "Gwan out!" she shouted at the donkey. The little animal struggled to obey.

The bank manager now came forward and stood at the foot of the coffin. He gripped the rim of his bowler hat and, with a military like movement, brought the hat down to his side. As he did so, the crêpe and pudding described an arc in the air and thumped down on the breastplate of the casket. The pudding, now free of the encumbrance of the crêpe, bounced off the metal and slithered sidelong to rest with half its curl dangling over the edge of the coffin lid. The manager looked down in disbelief from the hat to the swinging curl.

For a second or two everyone froze. The undertaker was quick to recover. Wearing a scowl he stepped forward and, using the crêpe as a protectant, disdainfully caught the pudding between forefinger and thumb, took it aside a few paces to the rear, and dropped it over the low wall around the church. Returning, he wiped his fingers carefully on a white handkerchief taken from his breast pocket.

On a signal, four of the countrymen came forward. They raised the coffin and slid it into the waiting hearse. By the insertion of silver pegs, the undertaker secured the coffin and closed the door at the rear of the vehicle.

The parson glared at the bank manager whose face was scarlet and who was now frowning down at the band of his bowler hat. The priest had begun to study the toecaps of his boots. The parson extended his arm with the palm of his hand turned outward towards the undertaker, ordering him to delay the departure: he then moved into the porch of the church and quickly reappeared with surplice, soutane and stole across his arm. Locking the church door with a ponderous key, he looked up at the pinnacles and steeple as if to imprint on his memory the image of this final ceremony for the last member of his once powerful flock. His face turned and his eyes enfiladed the open Square, the motley collection of vehicles and the waiting hearse. His raised eyes rested for an appreciable moment or two on the bank roof where white hair and metal helmet were over-busily hammering nails into laths of fresh timber into the open section of roof close to the skylight. The minister then entered his small car and drove off to head the cortège out of the town.

The priest stood solemnly until all the vehicles had left. He then walked slowly back to his presbytery. As the broad area seemed deserted, a tinker man, driving a flat cart with a piebald pony between the shafts and a lurcher dog tied to the axle, moved cautiously into the town. Leaping from the flat of the vehicle, the tinker tied the reins of his pony onto the railings around the church. Crouching, he freed the dog and ordered him not to stray far from the cart.

High in the attic of the bank Old Johnsie took out his heavy watch and looked at it. "Hannan's for tay," he said. Micky still wore his impish smile. Dragging on their jackets, the pair went warily down the stairs. As they reached the hallway the front door opened and the manager entered. Johnsie touched his forehead in deference. The manager eyed the two. There was a pause.

"Any of you at this hallstand?" he asked sharply.

"Hallstand?" Old Johnsie repeated, his open mouth faking extra senility. He looked about him at the floor. "We were in the attic, Sir. We're off now to get some lead flashings.

"Must be that blackguard Marshall," the manager muttered.

The old joiner and the apprentice strolled up the main street together in silence. As they approached the laneway leading off to the teashop they met an old lady walking piously along. She stopped. Her eyes grew spiteful.

"I suppose you were at the funeral, Johnsie," she said.

"No, but I hope to attend yours," Johnsie answered.

To reduce tension as they entered the laneway Micky asked: "Have you your pipe, Johnsie?"

"Have you your senses?" the old man shot back.

"What do you mean?"

"You planted that puddin' in my pocket."

"That I may be as dead as ... " The boy swallowed quickly. "Yeh, I did," he blurted.

"Your face gets pale when you tell lies. Remind me to teach you about that too."

Suddenly the old man began to heave with secret laughter.

"That debt stood for a hundred years," he said cryptically. "Settled today," he added.

The old man seemed locked in reverie. He looked down at the lane's end where hills and tilled fields constituted the horizon.

A teenage girl appeared at the door of the teashop. "Are you comin' in, Granda?" she said brightly. Old Johnsie led the way into the teashop. The pair seated at a table were silent for a while.

"What debt?" Micky asked sharply.

The granddaughter floated up with a large teapot. Johnsie shut his mouth. As she poured the tea into two large mugs she eyed the apprentice narrowly. She then looked at her grandfather.

"What were they up to?" her eyes asked.

When the girl had left the table: "What's settled today?" Micky pursued.

Johnsie took a mouthful of tea before replying.

"The hurt of history," he began. "Old Jonathan Fairleigh, the dowager's father, was a hoormaster," he went on. "If a tenant's daughter spread her knees before the fire her father would say, 'Shove back Mary an' don't burn the rent book.'"

The old man, oddly amused, went on.

"A sister of my mother, a strapping young girl, was called up to be kitchen maid in the Great Hall. Everyone knew what that meant.

Ould Jonathan put a bun in her oven. He did indeed. When she began to show he banged her off to Nova Scotia. Gev her a small purse of money. There she let on she was a widda. She called the child Jonathan. She married later - a well-off man in that country. My mother called the dowager's crowd the Unfairlies. The boy in Canada grew up and was well educated. He had a big business in Halifax - the place where the great explosion was. Lots of his descendants are now scattered over Canada and the States. Some of them used to visit me in summertime. I took one of them up to see the ruins of the Great Hall. I even showed him the Ould Dowager and she sittin' outside her battered wagon. He broke his heart laughin' at the final cut of his great step-aunt."

Back in his presbytery the parish priest stood looking at the gable window at the Square. "Well, well," he mused, "gigmanity is a thing of the past. Cromwellian and Williamite confiscations are cancelled. The ghostly screaming of the workhouse is silenced. Tenants, who once greeted their landlords on their knees, now have grandchildren with doctorates in this and that. Those same tenants once spread dung with their naked hands on the fields of estates. The rough and tumble of history! The blood and pus of it! The irony of it! Ha-ha, the Great O'Neill sprawled drunk at a table in the apartment given him by the Pope. St. Patrick's Day in Rome. The room is crowded with his exiled followers. Hugh strikes the table with his fist. The room falls silent as the chieftain staggers to his feet and shouts, 'Before Christ, we shall yet see a bright day in Ireland!' Foolish talk! Heard by the English spy in the room. Times have changed. The wheel has turned full circle. I've seen the end of an era. And it finished not with a bang, but with a whimper."

"More tea Granddad?" the girl asked Old Johnsie in the teashop.

"I'm fine," the old joiner said. Indicating Micky he added, "This fella might fancy a meringue." "No, no," Micky said, his eyes sidelong on the girl. "I'm fine too." The young couple looked at each other. There was the remote suggestion of a pact. The girl smiled and whisked away. The old man leaned across the table and whispered,

"The black pudden came in handy," he said. "I'll put that piece into the story if wan of the Nova Scotians turns up again!"

"Do," Micky said absent-mindedly, his eyes elsewhere in the room.

In the presbytery just off the Square, the priest was now spooning and licking sugar taken from the bottom of a teacup. Placing the empty cup and saucer on the mantelpiece, he resumed his post of observation at the window of the parlour.

"Was it all loss and starvation?" he asked himself. "Did not the clearing of the cabins provide areas to be used later as town parks? And what remained of rundown mansions - did not that provide asylums where poetry and music could be read and played by candlelight? And isn't the end of one phase of history the beginning of another - this in the ebb and flow of time. And what about our own gombeen men? Their chainsaws screaming as they fell the copper beeches? And the polluters of our rivers and streams?"

His eyes on the empty church building in mid-square the priest added, "What's to happen that place? Will it become a bingo hall? Now that the country is creeping with sects from abroad, could it become a rival to my own steeple?"

The curl of the black pudding dangling from the lid of the dowager's coffin suggested many questions. What are the ascendancy now but a scattering of White Russians no longer of consequence or power. No secret police to back them. The crowd who blackballed the pushy Irish who ventured to apply for membership of their tennis clubs are no more.

The priest's mood changed abruptly. He pursed his lips upwards as he continued.

"Sleep in peace, children of the Trá, lying huddled on the strand in famine days, the drool of grassy leakage staining your purple lips. 'Bread or blood,' you cried in outrage and anguish, your pleas falling on the deaf ears of the landlord. Our Church, once the Church of the outlawed, now holds the power! But should we not use that power wisely? And with humility and discretion. Should we not be on our guard lest we earn contumely as did the ascendancy of yesterday?"

The old joiner and his apprentice were on their way back to continue making a big job out of the skylight leak. And to ponder on the events of the day.

By the wall of the mid-square church, the lurcher, having reappeared from beneath the flat cart, began to nose around and sniff the air. Presently he found what the air had informed him was surely there. The loop of pudding hanging across his mouth, he tried to sneak under the cart to enjoy a long-delayed meal.

"Drop it, Prince!" his master roared. Mournfully the dog obeyed the command. Crouching down the tinker caught the pudding, surveyed it, smelt it, then having wiped it on the seat of his trousers, he began to eat and chew. The dog sat on his hunkers in front of him, saliva dripping from his jaws as he watched his master.

Near the end of the meal, the tinker looked down at the stub of pudding in his hand. Gathering the remnants of sausage skin from his mouth, he pressed them into a spitball about the pudding stub. "Catch, Prince!" he said, throwing the mass towards the dog. The lurcher leaped, caught it expertly with a hungry snap of his jaws. In one extension of his neck he gulped down the gift of his master.

High up on their grandstand of the roof of the bank, the joiner and his apprentice watched these antics. The tinker grinned up at the pair. The priest's face was remotely visible at the window of the presbytery. Despairing of receiving more food, the lurcher went off and found the crêpe. He nosed it fruitlessly. Then, raising his hind leg, he pissed freely on it.

Finally, as if to add insult to injury, the dog turned about and with a violent one-two of his hind legs, cast dirt and gravel on the already dishonoured mourning band.

✿ THE RICH FIELDS OF MEATH ✿

The day they were to leave was the most exciting day ever known by the people of the glen. For weeks before, young and old were in a fever of mingled eagerness and anxiety. If the truth were told, only a few had had a full night's sleep in anticipation of the great adventure and the immense change.

Think of it! In exchange for the surrender of their few rocky acres perched on a sloping lap of land above the sea cliffs of the south-west, each family was to be given thirty acres of golden loam in the County Meath. There the large estate of a landlord was to be divided among the native speakers of Irish from the congested areas of the western and southern coasts. Each family was to be endowed with a neat tiled cottage together with farm implements and seed, not to mention a quantity of artificial manures necessary to sow a garden of potatoes. It wasn't easy to come to terms with bounty of this magnitude.

Jack Sullivan had already made up his mind to use the English form of his name during the journey to the north-west. He advised his wife Síle to say she was Julia, and his children Peadar and Siobhán to change their names to Peter and Joan. "Start practising your English now," he said. "Once ye go out through that pass up there by the churchyard people will laugh at us if we speak to them in Irish. And when we settle down we might be scattered and the Irish of our new neighbours from the north-west might be as quare to us as English. Aren't there hundreds of years between our dialect and theirs? 'Twon't be smooth sailing on another account too. The locals are kicking up blue murder to have the land divided among themselves. I'm blamin' no one. All I'm sayin' is that we must play our cards properly until we understand our neighbours and make peace with the locals. Above all we must do as my mother, Éibhlín, always says: 'Walk aisy when your jug is full.'" But it was significant that he never gave advice like this in the presence of his mother.

Jack Sullivan knew what he was talking about. He was one of the heads of the families the Commission had taken up to view the lie of the land. With the other men he had returned with tidings of joy. "Wait till ye see," he told the women and children. "It is beyond our wildest expectations."

Time went by like a racing hare. Suddenly the day of departure had arrived. Hurry, hurry! Any minute now the fleet of old open lorries and vans would pull down from the pass: one by one each vehicle would peel off to take its place in front of its appointed thatched cottage and there it would splutter to a halt. Already the migrants had piled their meagre possessions outside their doors. This so as to lose no time loading up and leaving for the rich fields of Meath.

The Sullivan children were up at the crack of dawn. They raced in and out selecting the toys and trinkets they could not possibly leave behind. A kerchief of "Kerry diamonds" from the cliffside, a shabby golliwog called Dulamoo, a large sweet jar filled with glassy marbles, a fancy doll that had come all the way from Holyoke Massachusetts in the USA. The hens and chickens were in their coop which stood against the whitewashed wall outside. Chep, the sheepdog, was on his metal chain and studded collar. The kid goat, bound with a súgán rope, was tied to the bottom of a bush and was bleating for freedom. Sibby the cat was hiding in a sunny nest under a fuchsia bush - she could easily by caught at the moment of leaving. Beds taken asunder were on the low dry wall of the tiny front garden. Out came a feather tick together with a tongs, a griddle, and a pot-oven. The delph from the dresser was already packed in straw and placed in a tea-chest together with some of the smaller holy pictures. Special care was accorded to a large stitched willow-patterned dish with a recess on it to save the juice and gravy of a roasting goose. Finally, the kitchen clock was brought out, carefully wrapped in an old linen sheet. Yes, all was ready.

Jack had stated that the holy pictures had woodworm in the frames and that they could not possibly be taken into the new kitchen. Nor the table and chairs. As usual, his wife Julia tried to overrule his protest: there was stuff on sale, she said, for killing woodworm and she'd give the frames a good dose of it. She'd even fill the holes herself if it was necessary. Jack said she could take the pictures but she'd have to leave the table and the dresser behind.

During all the hubbub Jack's old mother, Éibhlín, sat by the fireside hunched up in her súgán chair. From where she was sitting the old woman could look out the small front window and see the sea below. She could tell the mood of the sea from the way the waves lapped, crashed or bloomed against the point of the headland. A backward glance over her shoulder through the back window and she could tell by the clarity or mist on the mountain top whether or not the day following would be wet or fine.

From time to time, as they came and went Jack and Julia would glance at the old woman. They would then look at each other. The fire flat on the hearth was almost out, yet from time to time Éibhlín, crumbling small pieces of turf between her fingers, would drop a piece on a point where a coal of fire glowed warmly in the ashes. At last Jack and Julia came in together. Their attitude indicated that they had come to a decision. Jack addressed his mother.

"Your clothes are across the chair in the room, Mother," he said quietly. "You'd better start to change. The lorry'll be here any minute."

The old lady sniffed loudly and dropped a piece of turf into the ashes. Jack went to the half-door and looked along the road rising to the pass. Outside every cottage door there was a pile of household goods. Moving from house to house was Séamus, an old neighbour left behind: he was to acquire several of the small holdings and so would have a decent patch of land on which he and his family could live in modest comfort.

Jack could hear Séamus's raised voice outside the house next door. "Fine for ye to be off to the rich fields of Meath! What are we here but cormorants drying our wings on a rock above the waves. Ye'll be always welcome back here under my roof in the summertime. I'll miss ye. Good luck go with ye now, good neighbours."

This was answered by, "If any of ye go up to Dublin to see a doctor or to attend a match it won't be much out of your way to come out and stay with us in the County Meath."

Séamus now stood outside the Sullivan cottage. Jack raised his voice. "*A Shéamuis,*" he said "*is leatsa na líonta agus an naomhóg,*" at the same time indicating the nets drying on crossed poles in the haggard, and vaguely indicating the little harbour under the cliff where his black currach, laid upside-down on its stand, glistened in the morning sunlight. Almost as an afterthought, he added, "I've signed over my share of the commonage." "*Níor theip sé riamh ort*" came the acknowledgement that Jack Sullivan never lacked generosity.

Séamus was about to push in the door to bid goodbye to old Éibhlín when a signal from Jack caused him to shake his head and turn away.

During the exchange of courtesies, old Éibhlín Uí Shúilleabháin kept looking down at the small rounded sea stones with which the hearth was paved. She was awakened from reverie by the voice of her son.

"Time is running out, Mother. We're going in convoy, so that none of us'll go astray. As it is, the lorry is overdue."

As he spoke voices were heard outside and the bulk of the lorry robbed the small window of light. "Make no delay. The road is long," the driver sang out.

"Hurry, put on your good clothes, Mother. Don't shame us in the

County Meath."

Éibhlín looked up. Her face was tight and stony. "I never shamed anyone in my life. I'm not going to start now," she said.

"We'll soon have everything loaded, Mother," her son said.

"Everything?"

"Yes, Mother."

"Will ye have the dead?"

"What dead, Mother?"

"Your father - my husband of sixty-one years. His father and mother. My own parents. Your brother too. Are ye goin' to load them up in yeer lorry?"

"Have sense: we can't dig 'em all up and take 'em with us."

"You can't. But you can leave them lone without a relative to pray over their graves."

Julia had come in. "God hears prayers in Meath too," she said.

The boy and girl had entered the kitchen. The girl carried Sibby the cat in her arms. She had her hair tied in a ponytail.

"They'll have a fire lightin' in the range, Mammo," the boy Peter said, his freckled face aglow.

"And a white Persian tomcat. Daddy seen him when he was up," said Joan.

"Seven lovely fields," Peter added. "Level as a table for kickin' football."

"An in-calf heifer in the spring," the girl said. "And we'll grow lovely flowers."

"Electricity, Mammo," from Peter.

The old woman looked hard at the children. "Will ye have the sea?" she asked sharply, "- and the gannets?"

"No sea, Mammo. No gannets. But fields of rich grass."

"No bog? No rocks? No mountain?"

"No, Mammo."

"I see." Her lips working furiously the old woman came to her feet. She walked in silence to the bedroom. With the exception of Joan, the others went out. Cradling and caressing the black, brown and white body of Sibby, the girl stood in mid-kitchen her eyes on the room door. At last the grandmother came out. She wore her Sunday shoulder shawl. There was a white brooch on her black blouse. Her face was small and stern. She looked at the girl.

"Look around you, child," she said in a level voice. "And don't forget what you see. I came in here as a girl of nineteen. A made match! 'Twas under these rafters I was mated to your grandfather. 'Twas in that room I gave birth to your father, my first-born child. 'Twas on that table my son Peadar was waked after his body was washed up on the Trá. The whole history of me is here. Think of that when your time of womanhood comes." Then briskly, "We'd best be goin'."

The two children and their mother had made a nest in the piled lorry. The mother sat on a low soft chair with the feather tick behind the three as a buttress against sharp edges. Joan still held Sibby while Peter kept a firm grip of Chep's chain. The young goat's head peeped out from behind a roll of linoleum. Mother and children too had peepholes to look through backward and sidelong. Jack helped his mother up into the cab where she was to be seated between him and the driver. A black cushion with a representation of a moonlit sea was placed behind her back. At the last moment she craned forward to see if she had inserted the wooden peg into the outside hasp of the cottage door as was her custom when leaving for a fair-day in town. Yes, the peg was in its place. The cottage stood, as it always had stood, with nets spread on its thatch to foil the sparrows and with dangling stones to keep it from being blown away in the winter storm.

A signal sound from the horn of the lorry which was to lead the way and the Sullivan lorry pulled out and into second place in the now forming file of departure. The vehicles began to blow their horns in farewell. The small group of neighbours remaining behind raised their twinkling hands as each laden van or lorry passed by. A few women on the roadside thrust the tails of handkerchiefs into their wet mouths. Sea, headlands and islands were touched with a morning haze already rising to reveal the prospect of a beautiful day.

Crouched up in the cab between the two men, old Éibhlín

appeared shrunken and tiny. Her eyes darted this way and that as the vehicles strained against the rising ground. "Stop at the graveyard!" She shot the words at the driver. The driver looked over her head at Jack and received a nod of approval of the old woman's request.

The Sullivan lorry came to a halt at the recess of the graveyard gate. The other vehicles also stopped. Jack helped his mother down from the cab. The old woman briskly drew the shawl down off her head and tottered down road along the low churchyard wall.

She stopped and began peering over the wall at an old and spotted graveslab on which the grass had encroached on all sides. The occupants of the line of lorries could hear her voice as she raised it to address the grave.

"I'm goin' now, Tom Sullivan, and I kem to say goodbye. I'm off to what they call the Rich Fields of Meath. The young people today don't understand that you can't transplant an ould cabbage, but I have to do what I'm told an' not be upsettin' and shamin' them. But Tom, are you listenin'? Here's my promise to you, my loyal comrade of over sixty years! Strict instructions I'll leave that when my time comes I won't be buried in their new churchyard. I'm to be brought back here to lie down beside you as I always did - here where we can look down together on the sea that was our friend an' our enemy. That's all for now, my companion of times fed and times fastin', times cold and times snug, times arguin' an' times makin' up, times of sorra and times of happiness, times of storm an' times of calm. Goodbye now Tom Sullivan, and God rest you. You and our son Peadar there beside you."

The people in the cabs of the vehicles watched as the old woman turned away from the wall. After a few tottering steps she turned back and with a thin smile on her face she shouted over the wall. "*Ná corraigh as an áit sin go dtiocfad ar ais chughat!*" At this she laughed aloud and shouted up at one of the drivers. "What he used say to me, on a market day in town when he'd go off for a quick pint with one of his cronies. 'Don't stir out of that till I come back to you.'" Old Éibhlín Sullivan then went stumbling back along the wall to the cab of the waiting lorry. A muted chuckle of appreciation rose from the people in the vehicles.

Unexpectedly an upheaval occurred in the Sullivan lorry. Sibby the cat had escaped from the piled belongings. Chep the collie was barking and struggling to follow her example. Hens and chickens cackled loudly and beat their wings against the bars of the coop. The kid goat added its bleat of outrage. Leaping to the ground, the lithe cat then sprang onto the churchyard wall and began to mew a leave-taking to her known world. Joan managed to free herself from the clutter of the vehicle; flustered and anxious she ran forward to take up the cat, which surprisingly allowed herself to be caught without protest. The cat's four legs dangling to their full extent from her hands, Joan clambered back to her place in the vehicle.

The driver glanced through the back window of the cab. Assured that all was in order, he drove his lorry after the leader and over the top of the pass into the wider countryside from which the sea was no longer visible. The convoy followed on behind.

In the nest, in mid-pile, Joan hugged the cat to her bosom. She kissed her head and whispered in her ear. "You're a bold lassie, Sibby. Running off like that! And I thinkin' of making a match for you with a big white Persian tomcat in the Rich Fields of Meath."

Also by Poolbeg

The Master

by

Bryan MacMahon

Bryan MacMahon is one of Ireland's great writers. He is a teacher who, to use his own inimitable phrase, has left "the track of his teeth on a parish for three generations."

This account of his life's work, a bestseller in hardback, has all the magic, the drama, the love of language and the love of Ireland (the love of Kerry too!) that has made him famous as a talker, a ballad-maker, a playwriter, a novelist and a short story writer of international stature.

This intensely personal account of his life shows Bryan MacMahon's great wit and skill. His work in the fields of literature and education has touched the lives of very many thousands of people.

The Master is a book to relish and to keep.

"...a touch of genuine magic." *Irish Press*

"...a smashing story." Gay Byrne

Also by Poolbeg

The Honey Spike

by

Bryan MacMahon

Martin Claffey had a burning ambition to be the first southern member of the travelling people to look down at Rathlin Island from the Giant's Causeway. Now a year after his marriage he has succeeded. But Breda, his young wife, is near her time and she wants her baby to be born in the Honey Spike, the lucky hospital near Kenmare in County Kerry.

The Honey Spike describes the epic journey the young couple make, literally the whole length of Ireland.

Bryan MacMahon, who knows travelling people intimately and speaks their secret language, has written a rich and stirring tale full of adventure, humour and sadness set in an Ireland unchanged and unchanging.

"A novel of outstanding quality." *Irish Press*